The Soprano

A Supernatural Thriller

S. E. England

Copyright © 2017 Sarah England
Editor: Jeff Gardiner
Artwork: RoseWolf Design
All rights reserved.

No part of this book may be used or reproduced in any manner whatsoever without written permission of the author, except for brief quotations used for promotion or in reviews. This is a work of fiction. Names, characters, places and incidents are used fictitiously. Any resemblance to actual persons living or dead, business establishments, events, or locales, is entirely coincidental.

Note from the author: The inspiration for this story came from a true event, reported in local newspapers at the time. However, the characters, location, history and details included in this novel – other than the nature of the crime itself – are totally fictitious. Likewise, the fictional village of Ludsmoor is based on the village my parents grew up in, the dialect quite unique and totally authentic, but the characters are a figment of the author's imagination.

ISBN 978-1-5220-1096-8

www.sarahenglandauthor.co.uk

Tales of The Occult by Sarah E. England

About the author

Sarah England is a UK author with a background in nursing and psychiatry, a theme which creeps into many of her stories. At the fore of Sarah's body of work is the bestselling occult horror trilogy, *Father of Lies, Tanners Dell,* and *Magda*, followed by a spin-off from the series, *The Owlmen*. Other novels include *The Soprano, Hidden Company, Monkspike, Baba Lenka, Masquerade, Caduceus, Groom Lake* and *The Droll Teller. The Witching Hour* is a collection of short stories; and *Creech Cross* is her latest book.

If you would like to be informed about future releases, there is a newsletter sign-up on Sarah's website. Please feel free to get in touch – it would be great to hear from you!

www.sarahenglandauthor.co.uk

Acknowledgements

1. Dr John Beech – Thank you for answering all my questions about growing up in North Staffordshire during the 1940s; providing my grandad's scrapbook along with lots of local books and leaflets; and adding in your own inimitable way, a variety of humorous anecdotes.
2. Raven Wood, a traditional witch of Germanic and Celtic roots. Thank you for your invaluable contribution on pagan witchcraft – from the astronomy to the incantations, the herbs to the spells, and of course, the wicked hexes – it's a fascinating subject and I am most grateful for your help.
ravenwood369@yahoo.com

Ludsmoor

Wish Lane Cottage
Annie Bailey

Moody Street
Vivien and Harry Whistler
Louise, Arthur and Iddy

Lake View Villa
Ellen Danby
Marion, Rosa, and Lana

Alders Farm
Agnes and Grace Holland

Spite Hall
Vic and Nell Holland

Danby
Hazel and Max Quinn

Prologue
1887

"He is lying in his bed,
He is lying sick and sore,
Let him lie intill his bed,
Two months and three days more."

The boy jumped back from the doorframe, spine flat to the cool, damp staircase wall, adrenalin flooding into his heart and lungs. She knew he was there…her back had stiffened.

For several long seconds the only sound was that of dead leaves scratching around the front door. He held his breath. Perhaps she hadn't seen the flicker of movement, and maybe…maybe there was an outside chance he could still creep away? He looked towards the front porch, at the prism of light streaming through the stained glass square onto the hall rug; then to the dark, back kitchen where she'd been chopping, crushing and boiling.

The new baby snuffled and the cradle creaked on its hinges by the old range. A fresh gust of wind buffeted the walls.

Cowering into the hallway he made himself as small as possible, sliding onto his haunches and praying…praying so damned hard she hadn't seen him.

Her voice cut through the air. "Come here, Billy!"

The cold, hard blade of fear plunged into his stomach. Instantly his bladder relaxed and tears burned his eyes with shame as urine trickled down his thigh. Standing up, his good leg – the normal one – shook violently; the other – the one withered to bone – a lead weight that dragged behind the rest of his body as slowly, reluctantly, he forced himself to rise from the shadows and shuffle into the kitchen.

Not meant to be here today he'd caught her out, and they both knew it.

"Well now," said Annie.

He focused intently on the chopping board spread with herbs, nettles and thorns; at the pestle and mortar filled with insect wings and dirt; at the dead mouse…at anything except her. *Don't look into her eyes…*

Candles spluttered and oozed with wax, the flames now flicking higher, more strongly…

The force of her stare was magnetic. In desperation he concentrated on the open book spread out on the table. *Must not look into her eyes…must not…Do not…* Soon she will just tell him off and then he can go. He pictured escaping into the garden and hobbling down the lane. Still she did not speak. The ancient text blurred and the desire to look at her intensified. *Must not… must not…*Then to his horror his head started to creak around of its own volition, jerking with tiny movements on its stem, until finally their eyes locked. And a slither of ice slipped beneath his skin.

The air crackled with static and everything stilled. There was not the slightest movement or sound from anywhere inside the house or out, as silently her lips began to move and she raised her right arm to point directly at him with two fingers outstretched.

Paralysed to the spot, he stood helplessly as dark shapes slithered from the corners of the kitchen and began to crawl across the floor towards him. The table, the dresser loaded with plates, the cooking pots – all vanished into a vacuum of blackness. He gripped the nearest chair and tried to close his eyes but found he could not.

The day had chilled to ice, and wind screamed in a vortex of trapped, angry voices ripping through his head. Terror shot through him in fire-cracks. This was death. His heart would burst. Collapsing to the floor, he scrambled onto all-fours and skittered like a whipped dog for the door.

His next conscious moment was to find the hall skirting board in front of his nose. For a moment he lay there trying to recall where he was and what had happened. Leaves blew against the door and the sound of coughing came from upstairs. The light through the square in the porch door streamed onto the hall rug in precisely the same place as it had before; and in the kitchen she was still chopping and crushing, stirring and muttering as if nothing had happened.

However, life would not be the same for him again – not ever. And he would have to leave. Just as soon as his father had finished dying – retching and writhing in the room upstairs.

***

Chapter One
Sunday night, January 1951
Louise

Our breath misted on the freezing air as inside the chapel the temperature plummeted below zero. Positioned at various intervals along the stone walls candles flickered and faltered, failing to lift the gloom. And from time to time violent whips of wind lashed the building, buffeting the stained glass windows with an almighty force. The rafters creaked and groaned. Snow was coming – you could feel it.

High on the moors our small village would soon be cut off. We didn't have any streetlights back then and the nights were tunnel black. Later, we'd walk home blinded and gasping in the howling blizzard, holding onto each other's damp-gloved hands, chilblains stinging as we slipped and stumbled along the street. But that was yet to come, because right there and then, in that moment, the congregation stood swaying, mesmerised, with not a sound between us despite the bone-aching cold.

On a small wooden platform to the right of the altar, with the choir on the left, Grace Holland was singing. And while sleet spattered across the glass panes, the day darkened and thunder rumbled over the moors, the power of her voice eclipsed all else, transporting us from the damp tomb of Sunday Chapel to a higher place. She could do that, you see – with a soprano that carried away its listeners on wings. It made your skin prickle and your eyes fill up. I think, looking back, that Chapel made us feel part of something more important than life itself, dwarfing earthly needs, transcending the grit and grime of everyday routine. It's the only way I can describe it. The hymns did that to us, and we knew them all note for note, word for word. Chapel defined us. But when Grace sang it was more than that – it was heavenly. Well, she had a special gift, maybe divinely given - that's all I can say.

On that particular night – the one each and every one of us would later recall so vividly – Grace's voice soared over the top of a biting North Easterly that whined around the building like a gang of lost souls. That wind – it came from out of nowhere. It whistled under the heavy oak door and jiggled the lift bar as if demanding entry. It shook the very fabric of the building and juddered the foundations. But every Methodist in the village had turned out that evening and we weren't leaving until the show was over. The pews were packed with children huddled onto parents' knees; and men stood shoulder to shoulder along the back wall, caps in hand.

I was six years old, wedged in between my mother on one side and my older brother, Arthur, on the other. My two brothers had grey, woollen shorts on – their legs mottled with cold. And in front,

Auntie Flo's hat obscured the view almost entirely with a large, brown feather, but I could just see Auntie Grace and her wide-open mouth painted as red as a phone box. Uncle Handel, a small round man with a few strands of hair combed over to one side, was waving a short stick around in front of the choir. I thought he looked silly – jabbing and pointing it - dipping and darting like a bird on a rock.

I tugged at my mother's coat sleeve. "Mum, why's he waving that stick? Mum? Mum?"

She didn't answer. She never did. And besides, like everyone else she had her eyes fixed on Grace.

How Great Thou Art, sung with crystal purity, had every thumb-sucking babe, rheumy-eyed old man and washing-weary wife completely entranced. And when the choir, resonant with the rich bass and tenor voices of miners, mill-workers and farmers joined in with the refrain, *Then sings my soul, My Saviour God, to Thee…* it swelled many to tears, their faces quite wet. Even at that young age I too felt my heart surge and my senses stir. It never left me either, that feeling. To this day I hear a gospel or Welsh male voice choir and it chokes me a little – there's something about all that heartfelt passion and the soul in those voices. And I swear the more the wind screamed and the door rattled on its hinges, the stronger and more fervent the singing.

The chorus faded away as softly as velvet, and Grace's ice-fine soprano cut into the void once more. *That on the cross, my burden gladly bearing...He bled and died to take away my sin...*

A deep intake of collective breath and then the choir opened their collective voice and exalted the performance with a deeply rousing finale: *My God, How Great Thou Art...*

When it was over we stood as one, dazed and chilled; the silence sobering and the wooden pews suddenly hard and uncomfortable. It was time to go. A fresh squall of sleet battered the old chapel walls, scattering at the windows like grain. The roof creaked alarmingly, and something slipped and fell with a thud to the ground outside. You couldn't see out of the windows at all by then, washed as they were in a grey blur.

We turned to face each other in the flickering half-light. I remember my legs were trembling, whether from trepidation or cold I couldn't say, and I felt for my mother's hand. She was picking up her handbag, taking out a scarf, turning to speak to someone behind us, clicking it shut. My God, everyone knew everyone back then. It was such a remote, dark kind of place. I never thought of it when I was growing up, but it really hit me when I came back years later and saw it through adult eyes – all those battened-down, blackened stone terraces coated in moss and lichen, tufts of hardy grass blown flat to the ground, and bare-branched trees blasted into permanent submission. It seemed as though all the energy had been sapped simply from staving off the weather. It got me thinking though, that maybe the isolation was to blame in some ways for what happened? Certainly it played a part.

The villagers said their good-byes quickly that evening. Normally people lingered outside for the weekly gossip, but the minute the latch was lifted the great wooden doors slammed back against the walls with the force of the storm. A fierce wind flew inside, scattering dead leaves as far as the pews, causing grown men to stagger backwards and the candles to snuff out. Women pulled on their gloves and tightened their headscarves, shuffling into the porch to peer outside. Lightning flashed over the moors.

"Best get going."
"By 'eck it's a wild night."
"Ooh, I'm not looking forward to this."
"Will you be alright, duck?"
"Hold on to us…"

Staunch Methodists, there would be no tipping into The Quarryman for a tot of blood-warming liquor on the way back though, just huddled groups tramping home with torches bobbing in the blue-white expanse of an icy blizzard.

Yes, it's funny the things we remember. Maybe there are only a few truly pivotal moments in our lives – that point where we step out from the relative safety of everyday comfort and hover on the brink of uncertainty – but that was one of them: standing there in that wind-blasted chapel porch. The night before everything changed. I was only a small child but I remember it with total clarity – every snapshot of detail. I think we all can.

***

Chapter Two
Louise - continued

Having Grace Holland in the family was a bit like being related to a film star. My mother's cousin, Grace, was a tiny wren of a woman. She wore long, off-the-shoulder evening gowns on stage, usually dark green to highlight what everyone said were her striking, emerald eyes; although Dad said no one noticed her eyes with dresses cut as low as that! I do remember she had Cupid's bow, red lips and a coil of black hair like Liz Taylor's piled on top of her head. Oh, and she wore very high heels, which made her totter everywhere in baby steps – quite a contrast to the other women in the village. They'd stand there in sensible lace-up boots, thick tights and flowery pinafores, shaking their heads whenever she wiggled down the main street.

Mind you, they all dressed up for Chapel.

Everyone had a weekly bath and put on their Sunday best for that. For the women it usually meant a tweed suit, hat, gloves and pearls; maybe a brooch. I used to lie on the bed and watch my mother getting ready. Once dressed, she'd untie the headscarf she wore every day, then one-by-one pull out the little, pink rollers. This was the only time those rollers ever came out. Her hair was quite short and each roll of hair had to be loosened before being brushed and sprayed into a 'do'. Then she'd plonk a hat on top, which seemed a waste. Her only make-up was bright red lipstick, blotted on a folded tissue, re-applied and then blotted again. After that she'd pop her glasses back on and dab Nina Ricci scent onto her wrists and behind her ears. I never liked the smell of it and still don't, but she had it every year at Christmas from Grandma Ellen and made it last. I think my mother only had that one brown suit and hat, too. I never saw her in anything else anyway, apart from the clothes she wore every day to do the chores in. When she went to work she just threw a coat over the top of her house clothes. They all did.

It was only Grace who was different is what I'm saying: a Hollywood cut-out, living and breathing in our rain-sodden, grime-coated, post-war mining village. Arthur would stand there with his mouth open, gawping when he saw her teetering down the street in a pencil dress. Once, when we'd gone to choose from the penny tray at Auntie Flo's, we saw her get out of a car and walk past the shop. It was a warm, summer's day and she was wearing this tightly fitted, cream suit that nipped into the tiniest waist imaginable; and she had her hair wound up on top of her head – honestly, it looked like a sated, black python basking in the sun.

"Louise," he shouted. "It's a Jag. 'Er got out of a ruddy, great big Jag!'

"Language, Arthur!" Auntie Flo said without turning round from stacking the shelves, a cigarette dangling from the corner of her mouth.

Grace must have sensed us peeping out between the Co-op's lettering in the frosted glass, because her head turned and we got a flash of those famous emerald eyes from beneath a fringe of black lashes. Her complexion was the colour of fresh milk, her face a small, pointed shape with arched eyebrows and finely sculpted features.

"Blimey."

She really did take my breath away and even as a child I knew I'd seen true, knockout, trouble-inspiring beauty. We'd never seen anything like it – not on Ludsmoor, although Grandma Ellen took The Tatler and you'd see women dressed like that in there - you know, in ball gowns with fur stoles round their shoulders, or in the new full-skirted petticoats. Mostly though, they had no chins and big noses or frizzy hair and flat chests. Money couldn't buy what Grace had.

"She looks like an angel," I said.

"More like a sex bomb," said Arthur.

"We'll not have talk like that in 'ere thank you very much, Arthur Whistler," Auntie Flo said, now onto slicing ham, and still with a cigarette in her mouth. "Who's been teaching you that kind of talk, any road?"

Arthur grinned. "No one."

She toured, my mother told us. Grace 'toured' the whole county and beyond, and it was only because she was from Ludsmoor that she sang in our tiny chapel at all. We were honoured, my mother said, always taking care to pronounce the 'h.' Yet she'd been brought up here in wind-swept, grimy, dirt-poor Ludsmoor just like the rest of us. I tried to imagine Grace Holland ever being a child in a place like this – sitting cross-legged on the assembly room floor reciting times-tables in her bottle-green school uniform; queueing for the outside toilet in the school yard, or running to 'Spinks Chippie' for a fish supper.

To me, in my home-knitted cardigans (often with unravelled wool from someone else's cardigan), altered hand-me downs, and with a ribbon pinned to the side of my head, Grace Holland was everything I wanted to be when I grew up. I watched her. Yearned to be her. Tried to work out what she did to make herself look that way; imagined what it would feel like to be a star with everyone staring at me slack-jawed and goggle-eyed. Would I be beautiful like that when I grew up? Would I? I'd search the mirror in our front parlour every day just to see if there had been a miraculous transformation during the night, but no – it seemed as though, like my mother, auntie and grandmother before me, I was destined for currant-bun eyes, a long, thin nose and a slightly lop-sided mouth. My lips would not pout with luscious fullness, nor would my hair bounce into glossy curls, despite sleeping with rags tied into it. And after Grace sang in Chapel that Sunday evening my daydreams were once again full of her.

She'd worn bottle green – a long, velvet dress that looked as if she'd been sewn into it - plump, white pillows of flesh rising and falling over the neckline with every vocal exertion.

"Tut! Cut far too low," I heard my mother say to Auntie Rosa, who was sitting next to us in the pew.

Auntie Rosa nodded, her lips pursed together like she didn't trust herself to speak. She often did that with her mouth, did Auntie Rosa. Dad said she looked like she was chewing a wasp. I was thinking though, how did Grace not feel the cold? And how would she get home on those high heels? I wanted to ask Mum but there was never a chance; and even though I kept looking round when we were all in the porch at the end, I couldn't see her. I never saw her leave, is what I'm saying, and as soon as we stepped into the night the view of the chapel was quickly swallowed by the storm.

We trudged home against the full onslaught of the wind, blinking furiously against stinging pellets of icy snow. Half running and constantly tripping to stay in the darting light of Dad's torch, my toes sang painfully inside leaky Wellington boots and wet hair trickled down the back of my school gabardine.

"Beats me why she's still not married. It's not like she doesn't put herself about enough," Mum was shouting over the roaring wind.

I tried hard to hear what was being said – anything to do with Grace and I wanted to know about it. I so badly wanted to be like her; to be her...

Dad was marching ahead, saying nothing.

"I mean, it can't be much of a life living out there with her mother, can it? Our Agnes isn't much fun at the best of times."

Agnes was my grandma Ellen's sister, mum's auntie. We hardly ever saw her, though.

Dad speeded up, the boys disappearing ahead of him. Night was closing in, chasing us with a black cape.

"Wait, Daddy. Wait."

He stopped and swung the torch round. I could see his mouth etched in a hard line. "Hurry up, Louise. Come on."

Then from somewhere beyond our small pool of light we all heard it and whirled around – a long, low whistle that sounded like an oncoming steam train. In a second Dad reached down and caught my hand just as a fresh belt of snow screamed off the moors. We reeled and staggered with the ferocity of it.

"Hold on to me, Pigeon," he said. "Not far now. Keep walking."

We lived in a terrace at the bottom end of the village, and one or two house lights twinkled in the distance. They seemed miles away.

Still Mum kept up the commentary like she just couldn't stop. "Back of beyond out there at that farm. I mean, why she doesn't move into town beats me. And what our Agnes does stuck out there on her own all day, I don't know. We all said why not move in with Annie, what with Grace away so much. Especially now she's got herself a fancy man. Honestly—"

"Mum, what's a fancy man?"

"I mean, you don't carry on like that and call yourself a Christian, do you?"

"Mum, what's a fancy man?"

"She ought to be married at her age, any road. I really can't imagine that one tending to her elderly mother for the rest of her life, can you? Hauling in coal, chopping wood, cooking and cleaning and then—"

"Viv," said Dad. "Give it a rest, would you, love?"

The house that night was colder than a crypt. Beads of water bubbled under the wallpaper, the window frames shook so hard we thought the glass would shatter; and the fire in the grate hissed and spat, never properly warming the room. Although we huddled over the flames until our faces burned, our spines still crawled with icy shivers and soot blew down the chimney in dirty great plumes.

In the end there was nothing for it but to go to bed early and wait for the worst to pass. At the side of the open fire were two cast-iron compartments. One was used to keep food hot and the other was for laundry. During winter months my mother put bricks in there too, which once hot would be wrapped in cloth and placed between the freezing, cotton sheets upstairs before we got into bed. But despite those, and keeping dressing gowns on under layers of blankets topped with overcoats, it was still way too cold to sleep. Snow flew at the windows all night long, and funnelled through the cracks of north-facing walls that took the full brunt of the storm.

The trick was to bury deep down under the covers and curl up your whole body in a tight ball, clenching and unclenching throbbing fingers and toes until the blood came up. My two brothers and I slept in one double bed like hibernating dormice, bunkering down in the dark. But even under all those layers there was still that spectral blue light shining through the curtains; and the moaning, Arctic wind bringing what was to be one of the worst winters in living memory – one that would cut off power, bring down phone lines and isolate us in freezing poverty for three weeks more.

I think, though, that as a family we could have endured that. We were not unused to hardship.

***

Chapter Three
Lakeside View, Grytton
Ellen Danby, Louise's grandmother

Ellen Danby sat on the window seat in the parlour at the back of the house, staring blindly into a dizzy blur of snowflakes. A two to three inch white mantle now covered the lawns, ending starkly with the forest's blackened edge and a line of grim sentinels. *The Guardians* Snow called them.

Snow!

Suddenly remembering her granddaughter, she tilted her head towards the door, listening for any sound of the girl. Pray to God she hadn't gone outside in this. An image came to her, of a white-haired child playing alone in the woods, early dawn rays streaming through the canopy as softly she hummed to herself, totally unaware of the world around her – or the fact the entire household had been searching for her all night.

She shook her head. No, Snow was much older than that now… Wasn't she?

Ellen's joints were rigid with cold, and her knees creaked as she stood up. Goodness, how long had she been here? What time must it be? How thoroughly disorientating to have absolutely no idea! Panic seized her as desperately her mind floundered around for the day of the week, the year... What was she doing here? Who was she waiting for? But no answers came. Nothing. In the quiet, chilly darkness.

She needed to control her breathing, to calm down. This had happened before. It was just that everything seemed so still, so empty...and no one was here... She gripped the back of an armchair and took herself through the situation point by point as she had taught herself to do. The unlit parlour was cold and damp. A pile of ash lay in the blackened grate. And looking down from the walls, portraits of people long-dead, immortalised in oil paint, stared unseeingly from dark canvases. She shivered in her flimsy, floral dress, rubbing the goose pimples of her upper arms, pulling her cardigan closer to her chest. The Danbys. The Danby ancestors. Yes, of course, this was Lake View. Her chest relaxed and her breath smoked on the air. *Of course, of course...*

On the north side of the house there was little light or warmth. Most of the living quarters faced south or west with the specific objective of enjoying a view of the lake; no one ever anticipating having to live in these backrooms, overshadowed as they were by the sombre forest and towering moors.

Oh, this would never have happened if Aaron was still alive – none of it – the way they had to live, the house in permanent semi-darkness... How many years now? She stopped and thought. Well, there was a thing. She couldn't remember that, either. In fact, the harder she tried to think the more the outer reaches of her memory stretched into an endless abyss of emptiness. One minute she was walking down the aisle under the malevolent glare of her mother and sister...both dressed that day, in black...and the next here she was, gazing hypnotically at a darkening winter's day from this mausoleum of a house, wondering who she was and how she got here.

Increasingly it was an effort, a huge hauling of mind and body, to live in the present tense at all; to endure the relentless, hollow cruelty of it. Nothing had turned out the way it should have done - almost as if an unseen presence had meddled with every desire, every humble dream, and every relationship she'd ever had. But no, that was patently ridiculous, especially the notion that her own family could have had anything to do with it. There was no proof – it was totally inconclusive – with every situation rationally explained away. And yet the intuition twisting in her gut informed her otherwise. Time and time again. Perhaps that was why her own mind had finally shut her out? *Stop visiting the past, Ellen, because you won't like it there...*

She wrapped her cardigan around herself tighter as she walked into the hallway. Marion and Rosa had left for Chapel hours ago. Yes, that was it. So it must be a Sunday, then? Why then, had she not gone with them? And had she been asked to do something? Yes, she'd promised...they'd called out as they were leaving...but what was it?

As if in answer to her question, like an errant echo of a distant death knell, the Grandfather clock methodically chimed nine o'clock.

Nine o'clock.

She paused half way to the stairway, her expelled breath hovering in the freezing air. No wonder her body was rigid – she must have been sitting on that window ledge for five hours. And Marion and Rosa still not back!

What had happened to all that time?

A flicker of alarm caught and rushed through her veins, thumping into her chest, her ears, her head. Had something happened to them? *Oh dear Lord, please no…*

Wind whistled underneath the front door and squalls of snow lashed the hall window. It would be a treacherous walk home from Ludsmoor on a night like this – across those moors in total darkness and slippery underfoot. A good three miles. What if one of them had fallen? She pictured the two women holding onto each other, heads bowed against the prevailing storm, the torch lighting only one or two feet in front at most. Once on the lane down to Grytton the force of it should abate, with the forest to shield the most ferocious gusts. But then the forest brought hazards of its own…

Just as if it was herself walking through the trees and her own feet crunching on the fresh snowfall beneath its towering silence, she shuddered, iciness brushing her cheeks…*A warning…something was badly wrong…*

Immediately she quashed the thought. Her oldest daughters were sensible, grown women; perhaps too sensible at times – a little frightening with their no-nonsense good sense, in fact. Were you not, with advancing years, supposed to become wise and all-knowing? Instead, it seemed the brain softened and the body turned into a brittle-stick hunchback. All she had to do – one job, Rosa would say – was make sure Snow didn't go wandering off in weather like this.

Well, maybe the girl hadn't? Perhaps she was still in her bedroom and all would be well? Oh dear, though - neither she nor Snow had eaten a thing. She'd completely forgotten to cook an evening meal. With fluttering bird hands she stood undecided for a moment, wavering. What should she do? Look for the girl or make supper? Yes. Look for the girl. Perhaps put the kettle on first? No. If she did that she might forget to find Snow. The house though…it seemed so black in here, so unearthly quiet…so utterly still.

She held onto the newel post and looked up at the landing. The whole of the upper floor lay in darkness, save for a flickering oil lamp on the ledge half way up the stairs. The power must have been cut off again. Yes, that would be it. Rosa must have lit the lamp before she left? Funny, she didn't remember her doing it – not a thing - not when they left or what they were wearing or any instructions Rosa was sure to have left.

Outside, the wind soughed and moaned around the eaves, the storm gaining in strength, noticeably noisier as she climbed. Midway, she paused to pick up the lamp, her arthritic fingers closing around the brass stem with painful difficulty. Lining the walls, Marion's paintings seemed, as they often did, to have acquired ghostly figures in the background – dark-skinned, sombre faces with startling eyes, demanding an existence all of their own. Apart from the Danby portraits in the parlour, every other wall of the house was dominated by Marion's oil and water colours: mostly landscapes or trees, clouds massing over brooding moorlands or reflected in pools of water. She never painted people and yet it seemed they were there somehow, lurking just inside the tip of vision - lost souls forever roaming the landscapes of her daughter's paintings. No one ever spoke about those faces though, heaven forbid! If she mentioned it to Marion she refused to discuss it and became upset. Rosa would want to fetch Dr Fergusson because her mother must be 'seeing things', and God help her if she mentioned anything to Vivien, her youngest. 'The Funny Farm', was one of Vivien's favourite phrases: 'We'll have to send you to the funny farm.' She'd heard her say that to little Louise once or twice, too.

The top step creaked loudly and she stood for a moment to draw breath. Up here the storm was pounding the house in a drum of angry fists, windows rattled in the wooden frames, and inside the roof, the timber groaned alarmingly as the onslaught intensified. The thought crossed her mind that this was in the relative shelter of the forest. What must it be like up on the moors? Roofs could come off!

She hurried along the corridor to the west-facing bedroom at the far end and pushed open the door. The air hung stale and damp, the single bed neatly-made, the grate cold. A row of dolls on the bookshelf looked back at her with dead eyes. Dolls… how she hated the darn things. Well, Snow was not in her room and clearly hadn't been for some time. Her heart picked up a beat. Please God don't let her have slipped outside in this. Please let her be here…in one of these rooms… any of them…

Her heels chopped into the bare floorboards, a harsh and lonely sound in the big house. Wind whined around the corners, lamplight flickering on the wooden panelling, her shadow lengthening behind its oily, yellow glow as she creaked open each door along the corridor. Every room was empty. It was only as she reached the last one, however, that she suddenly became aware of sounds other than the storm outside – those from within the house itself – and stopped to listen.

Maybe her mind had tricked her into assuming it had been mice or some such creatures scratching in the walls. But no, there it was again –voices - and muffled footfalls…distant chatter. Something, now she came to think of it, that had been barely perceptible all day but now seemed more insistent, more frequent. Was it in her mind or was it real? Her spine stiffened. *You know what it is…Ellen, you know*! Surely it couldn't be happening again after all these years? *No, no and no! It could not be. Not that…*

Determinedly, she closed her ears to the ghosts and hurried across the gallery landing to Marion's bedroom door. This was the one room still in use that had a southerly aspect; Marion being the only one who didn't seem to mind as much as the others that her long, Georgian sash window no longer overlooked Grytton Mere, but instead now faced the light-sapping solidity of gritstone: the rear end of Spite Hall. Odd for a woman who liked to paint, but then again Marion's paintings were not of daylight.

Snow was sitting on an armchair by her mother's window, rocking to and fro as was her wont, repeatedly hitting a rubber ball with a piece of string. In the dark, with the light from the oil lamp too feeble to reach the four corners, the girl's appearance was unnerving, looking as she did from the back like a very old woman, humming to herself, swaying back and forth.

"Snow?"

She stopped.

"You must come downstairs now. It's freezing in here, child. Aren't you hungry?"

Ellen held the lamp higher in order to decipher Snow's expression; to gauge, as the bulky shape lumped out of her chair – dressed in zip-up ankle boots, thick tan stockings and a flower-patterned pinafore – what mood she might be in; trying not to flinch at the leery, brainless grin on the young woman's face as she lurched towards her.

"Come on now, there's a good girl. No–"

Snow had more power in one hand than most grown men; had been known to bang people's heads against the wall in a pique of rage, and Ellen, secretly because she would never confess as much to Marion much less Rosa, was terrified of her. The girl could snap bones between her forefingers if she felt that way inclined.

"Don't do that, Snow…don't."

As was often the case, Snow was in a temper and it seemed she'd been brewing this one for some time. Pushing her grandmother roughly in the chest with both hands, the shove sent Ellen stumbling backwards.

"I know you're hungry and cold and it's my fault, you're quite right. I'm so sorry, dear, I forgot the time. Come on, now."

Snow loomed over her as she cowered against the wall, so close she could almost taste the girl's stale breath. Pale, watery pink eyes stared directly into her own and she felt the chill of madness as it peered into her mind. Snow's breathing was escalating, her chin folding up over her lower teeth – an expression she adopted when concentrating or working up to something.

In the background the ball bounced and rolled along the wooden floor, bumping against the skirting board, and for several heartbeats it seemed the blackness of the moment would swallow them both. She knew Snow sensed her fear. She tried to swallow it down but still it kept coming, rising hotly in her throat, a sickening lump as she stared into the small pink eyes, searching for the humanity there, for a connection.

What would happen next no one could predict. This monster-child with her suet-pudding face and deadpan stare – born to her eldest daughter, Marion, and christened 'Lana' after a beautiful film star – was the family secret. As long as she didn't hurt anyone, said Marion, she's fine. She doesn't need special care and no one official needs to know. The Danbys could not have a mentally handicapped child. Did not have one, in fact. There was nothing wrong with Lana, who could be home-schooled, could she not?

Only there was. And she did hurt people. Snow's temper could explode without warning and for no better reason than not liking the meal put in front of her even though she'd wolfed it down the day before. Sometimes she could not even be touched. She'd sit in the corner of the kitchen rocking to and fro, hitting the ball with the string, flying into a fury if anyone interrupted her, even if she hadn't eaten all day or had soiled clothing.

A smattering of sleet blew across the window.

"Snow? Come on, now," Ellen said softly. "Let's go and get supper, shall we? Would that be nice?"

From somewhere deep inside the house there came a heavy sigh, a door creaking, and shuffling whispers in the corridor.

"I can hear them," said Snow, her stare finally tearing away from Ellen's.

"It's just the wind—"

"No!"

It was rare for her to speak and rarer still for what she said to be coherent.

"What do you mean, 'hear them?' Who?"

She knew, though, knew all too well, as Snow's cumbersome frame heaved away and ambled over to where the ball had stopped. Ellen let go of her breath, watching her, never taking her eyes from her, as picking up the ball Snow now began to scout around in an agitated manner for the string.

Ellen scrabbled for the lamp. "There, look, it's over there," she said, pointing to underneath the chair.

Snow lunged for it, then slumped back into the armchair and resumed hitting the ball with the piece of string, over and over, rocking and murmuring to herself, working herself up again; the rocking more violent than before and more determined.

Slowly and steadily, Ellen backed out of the room. The girl's mood would last for days now. Oh, she could hear them alright. Just like herself, except Snow didn't hide the fact. So it was real then, wasn't it? They were back again. But why after all this time? And who would it be for? Oh dear God, who? And why, why, why? Why any of it?

Terror stole across her mind so quietly, so stealthily, so imperceptibly, that absently stepping back into the corridor and closing the door behind her, she was quite taken unaware.

***

Chapter Four
Danby, 1951
Hazel Quinn

Earlier that same evening, Hazel Quinn switched off the wireless, poked the fire and for at least the tenth time in less than an hour, walked over to the window and peered into the street. Every house on the cul-de-sac was a 1930s semi, curtains drawn against the dusk - red, green and blue Christmas tree lights twinkling between the gaps, reflected on white lawns. Fresh snowfall topped the shrubs and car roofs alike, muffling everything. There wasn't a sound out there. In the glow of the street lamps flakes of it fizzed around like desiccated coconut – a wonder it ever settled, Hazel thought. The trains were still running, though. And Max should have been home hours ago.

Hazel was not a happy woman. At thirty-three, she'd been married to Max Quinn for seven years and it had taken her every one of those to realise why he'd picked her out of all the beautiful girls, as his late mother had so memorably sniped, he could have had!

She looked over at the Jaguar parked on the driveway, willed to her just last year by her father, along with the velvet mills, now sold off to Vic

Holland of all people. Max had wanted to invest in a nylons business in Leek – something that would make them far more money, he explained, than what would soon become the dying velvet trade. Everything was changing, he said, the fire of ambition in his eyes, and now that post-war austerity was over they must look to the future and be a part of it.

Yet as far as she could see, Vic Holland was the only one who appeared to be prospering, buying up chunks of land in Ludsmoor and Grytton as fast as they became available. She frowned. He must be greasing palms – had to be. She knew how business was done. Oh, he'd been seen right enough, enjoying drinking sessions with councillors, farmers, solicitors and the like in The Quarryman or The Feathers in Danby. He was one of those men she never felt comfortable with, the way he let his eyes roam all over a woman and then smirked. She shuddered at the recollection. Yes, quite a mystery when you came to think of it – the son of a dirt-poor miner in Ludsmoor now a rich and successful property developer with acres of land. And all without putting in a day's work.

'Shrewd' was the word Max, who seemed overly keen to join Vic's inner circle, used. 'Crooked' was the one she'd opt for. As crooked as the long, hooked nose on his face. And within months of buying her late father's mills, which dominated the Ludsmoor landscape and employed most of the local women, he'd also built Spite Hall. And no one was ever going to persuade her, not even Max, that wasn't just plain nasty.

Spite Hall overlooked the lake at Grytton. An odd name to call a house! But then it was an odd place to put it – slap bang in front of Ellen Danby's Lake View Villa. Where once the woman and her daughters had looked out over verdant lawns and the rippling expanse of Grytton Mere – Aaron Danby's legacy - the only view they now had was of drainpipes and guttering, their previously sunny rooms cast into permanent gloom by the audacious proximity of a solid stone wall. Quite a scandal that had been.

Oh, where the hell was Max?

She hurried upstairs to the front bedroom, convinced he'd be walking down the street any moment now. Handsome bastard, he was. Still made her heart flip – that first second when their eyes locked; the shock and confusion at his male beauty catching her off guard every single time. The trouble was he made every other woman feel like that too, with those big, sad eyes of his. What a combination – a strong, angular body and puppy-dog fragility. How easy he found the game.

She sat at the window, hunched on the dressing-table stool, picking chipped varnish off her finger nails. The air in the front bedroom was as cold as a morgue, the chill of it sinking into her bones. *Let it.* Somehow it felt better to be cold with her agitation. Who wanted to be warm and comfortable when they felt like this? She stood up and paced. Sat down again. Paced. Then sat down again. Who could settle to a play on the wireless or concentrate on a book when every few minutes their mind skittered back to what they really wanted to know?

Where was he? Where? Where?

But she knew. Knew the inevitable was coming. The screw had begun to turn a while ago – reality cruelly twisting into knot after knot with every more minute that passed. And the clock on the bedside table ticked on and on and on…from six to seven to eight. Until finally, finally, her heart plunged with hollow acceptance: he wasn't coming home tonight. And there was nothing she could do about it. *Nothing, nothing, nothing.*

God, it hurt… Every single time it just hurt so bloody much.

'Yes she did have brains in her head,' she'd snapped at her father. 'And yes she did know–'

"So why, then?" he'd demanded. "Why marry a bloke like him?"

It sounded lame even to her own ears, but so help her God it was the truth. "I love him, Dad. I just love him."

That had been eight years ago. Eight years since they'd announced their engagement into the echoing silence of family hostility. In her naivety she'd thought her parents might be pleased: there were precious few men of marriageable age around in the aftermath of the Second World War, and Max had been her father's protégé – successfully selling their velvet into major outlets all over the country. He was good-looking, had survived the war, made them money…She hadn't been able to take her eyes off him ever since he'd been invited to dinner at the house. In some ways, the small, fox-like face with a slight bump to the nose and a jutting chin, should not have worked – but boy they did, they really did – combined as they were with olive skin and a silvering of the hair. He had a slight stoop because of his height, and an easy laugh, gentlemanly manners and the softest of touches with long, sorcerer's fingers.

She shivered inwardly, aching with a long, distant memory of him nuzzling the nape of her neck, running one hand oh-so-gently down the curve of her waist; his breath soft against her hair - breathing her in as if he could never get enough.

So how long until she saw what everyone else saw? That he had the same effect on almost every woman he met? Christ, how it ripped into the soul when you knew you weren't special – not unique at all – and that your beautiful moment turned out to be exactly the same as someone else's. Yes, it tore you down and, yes, it left you on the floor, worthless and expendable. But that was as nothing compared to the thought of a future without ever seeing his face again or feeling his arms around her… not ever…

Tears dripped down her face and she swiped them away.

And at what point had the sharp wit he'd used to make her laugh, turned into ill-concealed, frustrated boredom? It was all so obvious now - the pique of irritation in his voice, the set of his mouth. God, when had that started? And at what point did he stop even trying to pretend - flipping full volte-face into cruel barbs?

"How long?" she said out loud to the empty room. "How long have I been like this?"

It was almost as if she had become the enemy, the way he spoke to her, treated her... The thing was, he hadn't been like this before meeting up with Vic Holland, had he? Was that the tipping point, then? Because there was something about that family - an undercurrent - impossible to pinpoint, though. Maybe she was missing a bigger picture? But what?

Perhaps it was simply that Max was driven and ambitious and wanted to be part of an upcoming group of men paving the way for the future? And like her late mother had said, 'All men stray...' So maybe there was nothing wrong at all? Oh God, this was just going round in circles. Maybe it was simply her own insanity talking – being alone again - always so very much alone?

Her stare burned into the spiralling, snowy haze – gardens and rooftops now white over. Must be what, maybe two or three inches fallen in the last hour? The air was dense with fat, fluffy snowflakes, as solidly and steadily they stuck and settled, spreading winter in a ghostly hush. Trapping her here. How could she sleep? How could she rest?

Oh, damn him! Damn him to high hell! He could at least have rung.

Her fingers were waxen-white. Dead. Flexing them to get the blood back, she forced her mind to tack onto something – anything - if only to stave off the madness, the impotence, the rage. *Think, think…* Yes, it was around the time he did that deal with Vic Holland that it all started. And why had Max sold off the factories so cheaply to him? Why do a fast deal with Vic Holland? Why ingratiate himself with the Hollands at all? This was the key – the key to understanding it all, she was sure…

Grace Holland!

She felt sick.

Of course…

It had been just before Christmas when she'd had the flu, Max had insisted they go to see Grace perform, *Pie Jesu* from Faure's Requiem. They should support local talent, he said. It had been over in Derbyshire somewhere – Bakewell, was it? Miles away, anyway; a trans-Pennine journey with her nose streaming and not an ounce of energy in her shivering limbs. When she caught sight of herself in the Powder Room during the interval she'd almost screamed in fright at the ghastly apparition in the mirror with its red-rimmed eyes and sickly pallor. Nauseous and exhausted, far from being a treat it had been an endurance to sit through the evening in a draughty church hall; especially since Max had not once held her hand or spoken one word of kindness.

Instead he'd been entranced by the vision on stage. Grace Holland was dressed in a long, white evening gown with a plunging neckline that exposed a pair of heaving, pillow-breasts. Diamante had been woven into a coil of gleaming black hair on top of her head; and scarlet painted lips with smoky, dark eyes upwardly inflected like those of a feline, completed the hypnotic effect.

"Absolutely magnificent," he kept saying. "Don't you find it moving? Can you not appreciate the beauty?"

She nodded. The music was heart-rending and the woman's voice could certainly shatter glass.

"Come on," said Max, jolting her sharply when the choir finished and people started to file out. "We've an invitation to go for dinner with the star of the show."

"What? No, no, I can't. I'm not well enough. You go and have a drink with them. I'll wait in the car."

"Don't be ridiculous, Hazel. Vic and Grace are expecting us, and the rest of the family are here too – Vivien and the kids. You remember them, don't you?"

Oh yes, she remembered the visit to Wish Lane Cottage and Grace's cousin, Vivien, arriving with her three children. Nice family, but Vivien's dark eyes hadn't missed a trick, eventually coming to rest on her own with an arched, raised eyebrow.

Her frown deepened. That night watching her husband flirt with Grace had probably been the most painful and humiliating experience she'd ever been forced to suffer; and after they got home he'd slept in the spare room until she 'stopped sulking,' and anyway, he 'didn't want to catch the flu, did he?'

Jesus Christ, where was her self-respect?

Silently, she nodded to herself.

Oh, why the hell had she married him when he made her feel like this? More to the point, why had he married her? There wasn't exactly a dearth of eager women around at the time, and he'd been a young man of talent and promise, with, as his mother had repeatedly pointed out, his pick of beauties. Her family weren't particularly rich back then either – the business had only taken off once the war was over and people had a bit of money again.

Max always said he'd liked that she was quiet, a thinker, didn't gossip or shout in the street, which in retrospect made her wonder at the kind of life he'd led, at the female company he kept. But he did love her, he said, loved that she enjoyed reading, music, sewing. Not that she could put her mind to anything of late. When had she last picked up a book or listened to any kind of music, for fear it might elicit a flare of emotion she couldn't cope with? And when had the anxiety, the need for pills and doctor appointments crept in? Weeks ago? Months? It had taken its toll anyway, leaving her weepy and exhausted.

Maybe she really was a barren, frigid old nag with a pancake chest, just like he said? But surely he could see how being childless had left her isolated among women? It was a rare event for her to be invited to any of the many social events around here; a polite nod or a pitying glance bestowed at best. Clearly it hadn't occurred to him she might need his support. He had never been cruel before, but now – now, he sure as hell was. Well, perhaps in a way it made the coming task easier.

The dull ache inside her opened up into a chasm. She hung her head. Her shoulders sagged. And volcanic misery suddenly erupted, tearing out of her body in a great riptide of sobbing and choking as the agony burst out.

It was time to let him go. Let him go… just let him go…

After a while, she sat dabbing her swollen eyes. That would be the last time. The very last time she ever cried over Max. She had mourned for long enough already. This man, when all was said and done, was making her intolerably miserable; but unlike many poor souls she was lucky enough not to rely on him financially. The money, thanks to her wily old father, was hers. Max could do nothing without her signature, and her parents were not around to witness the disgrace of a divorce. She could go anywhere – to the other side of the country if she wished – and start again. Maybe buy a small business: a café by the sea? And the wound he'd gouged into her heart? Well, in time that might heal over, mightn't it? As long as she never saw his face in her dreams and remembered how he had once looked at her.

She put her hands to her cheeks, letting the iciness of her fingers cool the burn. God only knew where he was tonight. Not with Grace Holland, though, because according to the local paper she was singing at Ludsmoor chapel this evening. So maybe it wasn't her, after all? Maybe he had another one? Maybe he had a string of women? What did she know, now she came to think of it? He was supposed to have been in Manchester talking to potential investors today, but in reality... well, in reality he could be bloody anywhere.

The point was that someone had to do something. No doubt Max was content to play the wealthy businessman and carry on as he pleased with scant regard for her happiness? So then, it would be up to her. If she didn't save herself now while she was young enough she would die. Of misery, of neglect, of pills... So when he came home, and please God don't let her sob all the way through telling him this, she would ask for a divorce.

Her handkerchief was soaked and she screwed it up to throw in the laundry basket, just as the phone in the hall downstairs began to ring.

Motionless, she waited in the darkness for the insistent trill to stop.

On and on it went. Echoing around the house.

In the dressing table mirror a pale, make-up smeared face beneath a cropped peroxide mop of hair, stared back at her. What if that was Max? She'd been thinking all of these terrible thoughts about him when maybe the truth was as he said – her own paranoia? Her own mental instability because she could not have children? Her own...

The phone stopped ringing.

And then into the static that sang in her ears like a tuning fork, it began to ring once more.

She stood up, swaying on legs stiff with cold. And then hurried downstairs to answer it.

***

Chapter Five
Grytton Forest
Rosa and Marion Danby

The moment sisters Marion and Rosa stepped into the frozen silence of Grytton Forest, the wind dropped. They stopped to rest for a minute. The long walk across Hilltop Road from Ludsmoor had left them exhausted.

"I feel like I've been put through the wringer," Marion said. "My face has frozen, and I can't feel my fingers anymore."

"I know, and my ears are killing me." Rosa jammed her hat down by the brim, making it look like a cloche. "Ooh, the pain – it's excruciating."

"I've never known anything like it."

"It seemed to come out of nowhere, didn't it - half way through the Service? I don't remember this being forecast, either." She pushed back her coat sleeve to look at her watch. Half past eight. It had taken more than two hours to walk across the moor – a trip that would normally take forty minutes or less. They hadn't dressed nearly warmly enough, in just ordinary overcoats with woollen mittens and neck scarves. "Still, never mind, we'll soon be home."

"My hat's ruined," said Marion. "Do you know, I can't talk properly - I think my jaw's seized up."

Blinking away a flurry of snowflakes, Rosa linked arms again with her sister. Soaked and frozen, fatigue weighed heavily. "Same here. Come on, we're nearly there. Do you think Mother will have had the wherewithal to light a fire and get Lana something to eat?"

"I just hope she hasn't fallen asleep and let her go wandering off again. Can you imagine? In this?"

"Hmmm..." They quickened the pace.

The path through the forest to the house was normally well defined and despite the covering of snow making it less so, they hurried along with confidence. They knew it well, having had the woods as a personal playground all their lives and using it as a shortcut to the village school. The forest was their backyard, their friend and protector. Where many would have hesitated to vanish into its black depths on a winter's night, they did not. But tonight the overhead canopy was a dripping cobweb of blackened spikes – an ineffective roof against a heavy sky awash with snow. Flakes dropped from bare branches and plopped onto the path, and even in the thick of the woods it was quickly beginning to layer.

Behind them the roar of the storm rolling over the moors became more muted with every step and they were grateful the sharp-toothed wind no longer cut into their faces. For a while the two women walked in companionable silence, each lost in their own thoughts, looking forward to a warm fire and mulling over the Service that evening; the only sound that of freshly fallen snow crunching beneath boots, and their breath expelled on the air.

Suddenly Marion ground to a halt. "Stop!" She turned to face Rosa. "Listen! Did you hear that?"

Rosa, with little choice, stood perfectly still.

Drip-drip-drip from the trees.

She shook her head. "No, nothing."

Marion frowned.

"Come on, Sis, we have to keep moving."

Marion stood fast. "Are you sure this is the right way?"

"What? Yes, I think so. We're trekking downhill, so—"

"It's just that I don't recognise the path anymore."

"That's because it's covered in snow. And it's dark. Come on."

Marion wouldn't budge. "No, it's not that. This just isn't right. It doesn't feel right."

Rosa sighed audibly. "As long as we're going downhill it doesn't really matter where we come out, does it? We can find our way home from anywhere along the lake, and we sure as hell won't miss the ruddy, great big thing built in front of it."

Marion nodded. "Okay, yes, I expect you're right." Seemingly reassured, she resumed walking; but after a few more yards slowed down yet again, dragging back. "No, I'm sorry – this definitely isn't right, Rosa. Doesn't it feel odd to you? Really odd?"

Rosa gripped her sister's arm. "Come on, Marion, dear. Now really isn't the time for a funny turn. Let's just get home."

Grytton Forest was not a place to linger, even for those who knew it well. And if she was honest with herself she had to admit to a feeling of increasing unease too. Actually it was the strangest thing, but it looked as though the beam from the torch was being consumed by a blackness that was getting denser by the minute. In fact, it was hardly shedding any light at all now. When they had first entered the woods, the torch had easily picked out individual tree trunks, darkly wet against the brilliant whiteness of the snow. But now the whole of their surroundings were totally, suffocatingly black. And maybe it was her imagination but weren't the trees packed closer together? And the canopy overhead seemed to be thicker too, closing off any loopholes to the sky. No longer the *drip-drip-drip* of icy water tipping off branches – there was a total absence of either light or sound.

Switching off the torch made little difference.

"Focus on the path, on the white of the snow, Sis," she said. "We're still tipping downhill."

"Not as steeply as we should."

The anxiety in Marion's voice resonated in her gut, tugging at her instincts. She had to keep her head, though. One of them had to. "Marion, it's okay. Hold on to me and just keep walking. We'll be out the other side in no time."

Although they both walked through the forest regularly and had both played here as children, her sister in particular knew it in intimate detail: Marion spent a good deal of time in the woods painting, collecting wild flowers and meditating. And if Marion said they were on the wrong path, then they probably were. Certainly the going underfoot was becoming more prominently veined with tree roots; twigs sprang back in their faces as the path narrowed further; and the boundaries now appeared to be hedged with holly bushes.

This was some kind of labyrinth or tunnel...

She stopped dead. "Actually, I think you're right. We're going to have to backtrack."

Marion's grip tightened on her arm. "Rosa, I'm scared."

"There's no need to be scared. We're just a bit lost, a bit off track—"

"No. You don't understand. Rosa, I don't recognise this part of the woods at all. There's something creepy about it – I've got a really bad feeling. Seriously."

"It's just dark," she replied, already turning round. "Come on, we've taken a wrong turn somewhere. We'll have to retrace our steps. It was easily done."

She'd spoken with gusto but as the two women hurried back the way they'd come, a sense of dark oppression fell upon them both – as if something or someone was behind them.

"We have to get home urgently," Marion said, panting now as she speeded up. "I've got this awful, awful feeling."

Rosa did not reply, but the blood vessels in her throat constricted and something close to panic bolted into her stomach as they tripped over bulging tree roots camouflaged by the snow, and pushed away wet, snappy branches. Marion's fear was contagious. It was the family curse – a kind of heightened awareness or 'knowing' that they all seemed to possess except for herself, and she knew not to question it – the gift or curse of second sight, that was. If Marion was feeling fear that meant there was a good reason; although she'd never confess to believing in any of that nonsense herself.

What was truly alarming in this instance, however, was that none of them except Ellen had ever been afraid of the forest before, despite the rumours of dark rituals and witchcraft. They were nothing more than muttered tales told over too much ale in The Quarryman, said Marion - old women's gossip to keep them all from going insane with boredom. The forest itself, she had always insisted, was a beautiful, magical place alive with a powerful energy that culminated in a holy well. They called it the magic pool as children – a swirling pond fed by sparkling, fresh water gushing off the moors. And Lana clearly felt the magic too, spending hours here, worrying them all half to death until they realised it was probably where she felt safest. She was watched over by the angels and guardians of the forest, she told them. And for some reason they all believed her. Who knew what went on in that girl's head? Or Marion's.

"Grace was in fine form tonight?" Rosa said, in an effort to relieve the tension.

"Yes, she's got the most beautiful voice. I have to say it was really very moving."

"I did think her dress was a little bit too low-cut, though. I mean, for Chapel."

"Well, that's just the way she is."

"I know, but I mean, for Chapel."

"Maybe," said Marion, almost breaking into a run. "Hurry, Rosa. We really do have to hurry."

"Or what, for goodness' sake? Slow down or you'll have us fall."

"There's this buzzing in my head - we have to get out."

They were racing along now, out of breath.

"I did expect to see Agnes there. I think it's a disgrace she doesn't go to Chapel."

"She won't go and you shouldn't expect her to."

"I'd expect her to go and see her daughter perform. That's the only reason Grace bothers."

"Grace puts on a front for the rest of them."

"You're too charitable."

"No such thing." Marion swung out an arm to bar Rosa from walking on any further. "Look, Rosa, where the bloody hell are we now? This isn't even leading back to where we came in."

They stood panting for breath, confused. The night was blacker than ever.

Rosa flicked on the torch but the beam was so weak as to be almost useless. A shiver of cold fear chased up her back, "You're right. I've never seen this place before either. But how on earth…?"

Unable to see her face, Rosa reached for Marion's hand. This must be the very core of the forest, where it was at its most oppressive and silent. The ground beneath was running wet, dipping into puddles, the trees choked with brambles and creepers, the path densely guarded with holly. Repeatedly she flicked on the torch until a faintly discernible shaft of light as thin as that of a spider's thread, created a shadow more menacing than any natural darkness.

"I'm getting a horrible, bad feeling here," said Marion. "I don't feel well. I don't feel at all well."

"Don't say that. We're just lost. There'll be an explanation."

"Can't you hear it, though?" Marion hissed. "It's so much louder now. I thought we were moving away from it. But–"

"What?"

"There's a baby crying."

"No, no I can't hear anything." She whirled around, the light from the torch misting into an ineffective, foggy halo. "Honestly, I can't hear a thing."

They stood as statues, each straining to see, to hear.

"Marion, we have to think rationally. From here on the ground slopes down again so that's all we have to do – keep walking downhill. Come on."

Her sister's face bobbed in an eerie orb above the torch. As motionless as a hunted wild animal she was listening intently to something Rosa couldn't hear, her gaze focused on something far away.

"No listen, there's a baby crying somewhere... No, it's stopped again... and there's whispering. Can't you hear it? People whispering? It's getting louder. Rosa, there's something terribly wrong here. I don't think this is real. I don't think any of this is real. Maybe it happened before or..." She shook her head, confused. "Like some kind of imprint. But we're trapped in it."

"What do you mean? You're spooking me now. Is someone here or not?"

Marion shook her head in that vague, disconcerting way Snow did when she tapped into things other people couldn't see or understand. "No, there's no one actually here. Quite the opposite, in fact. There is nothing here... absolutely nothing. It's more like a void, a total absence of life. Oh God, all the energy's draining out of me."

She began to crumple to her knees like a rag doll, eyelids closing. "We're trapped in the middle of it."

Rosa struggled to hold onto her sister. "What do you mean we're trapped in it? Trapped in what?"

Marion collapsed against her, slumping to the ground. "Rosa, hold me up. I think I'm going to pass out..."

***

Chapter Six
Louise. The same night.

On the night of the blizzard I woke up suddenly and with a bump to the heart, breathing heavily in the bluish hush of an early dawn. For several moments I lay there completely disorientated, the remains of a dream rapidly dissolving; although I don't think and never did, that it was a dream. The same one that often came, it invariably left its mark – an indelible imprint on my mind for days after. And as always, I had been convinced beyond any doubt that the shouts and cries outside my window were real, and were I to open the curtains there would be men on horseback charging at each other with swords and muskets; the surrounding fields a bloody battleground booming with cannon fire; the sickening stench of charred flesh and gun powder choking the air.

With my pulse still galloping wildly, I lay under the covers next to Arthur's pyjama-clad back, waiting for it to steady, afraid to make a sound, when a remnant of the dream flashed back without warning. I'd been picking through the mud in drizzly rain, kneeling amongst dismembered bodies to remove rings and valuables, when a decapitated head rolled towards me and lodged in a puddle. *No,*

I don't want to see this, stop it, stop it… I squeezed my eyes shut, forcing the image away because it was not real, it was definitely not real. *Make it go… make it go… Stop it. Go away!*

Miraculously, when I opened my eyes again the dream had dissipated completely and all that remained was a memory of the fear itself. It was just the old battle dream, and that was all. Thank goodness I hadn't screamed or cried out this time – at least I'd learned not to do that; had taught myself how to deal with it and think of other things.

As my heart rate steadied I became aware of the silky silence in the room, and remembered the storm from the night before – the power of it battering the windows as we drifted to sleep, whining down the chimney, clattering the roof tiles. Now though, all was quiet… apart from a low murmur of voices coming from the room next door. The parents were talking…oh, and my bladder was full. You never wet the bed in our house or you'd be tanned good and proper.

Slipping out of bed onto the freezing linoleum, I dragged the chamber pot from under the bed. It was a hateful thing to have to use, and impossible not to think about all the mice scuttling around at night with their waxy, rubbery pink tails. What if they slithered over your toes while you were sitting on it? But it was better than going downstairs in the dark to the outhouse. Our stairs were perilously steep, the stairwell black as a coalhouse, and every single step creaked loudly. My God, if you woke my mother up! And then you had to put on wellies, take a torch and let yourself out into the yard no matter what the weather. At the bottom of the yard stood the outside lav – a damp, unlit shed with cobwebs spanning the windows, the doorway, the corners - everywhere. Spiders could drop into your hair at any moment while you peed fast as a jet spray. Anyway, like I said - the chamber pot was better.

After I used it, I pushed it back under the bed and padded over to the window. I wanted to check the soldiers really weren't there – just to be sure – and then I could go back to sleep. The flowery cotton curtains did little to shield us from either the light or the cold, but when I put my head between the gap there was a marked increase in iciness. And what I saw made me gasp. Far from the blood-spattered fields I'd imagined, what faced me was a total white-out such as I had never seen.

Our house was in the middle of a row of terraces with a cobbled street between us and those facing. If you didn't have nets you could see straight into the house opposite we were that close (we all had nets). But that night the street was totally transformed. Snow had been whisked into huge meringues that blocked doors, cut off roads and banked high up against the houses. There were no kerbs visible on Moody Street that night, and no front doorsteps – the snow had piled half way up people's front windows. Overhead, a galaxy of stars glittered in an inky sky – the contrast startling against the blinding white of the scene below. Not a breath of air disturbed the fresh snowfall, but something amazing had happened and my young eyes widened with the brilliance of it: millions and millions of sparkles caught and glittered in the moonlight everywhere you looked, as if a fairy godmother had sprinkled it with her magic wand.

I must have been at the window for ages because I froze to stone standing there – the kind of mortuary-chill you never quite forget. The freeze first gripped my ankles, rising swiftly in a series of ice-cold clamps that quickly riveted me to the spot. My breath plumed on the air like dragon steam as the iciness incrementally tightened around my chest in a vice until I couldn't breathe. I really couldn't. The breath just wouldn't come. My lungs were set hard and I was going to die. It seemed to have happened so quickly, too. One minute the realisation of what was happening, the next I could neither breathe in nor out. I stood there swaying and holding onto the curtain, still trying not to make a sound lest I wake anyone up.

Finally, just at the point where my mind turned black and terror clutched at my heart, I started to breathe again. And that's when I became aware of something other than the mumbling from next door and my brothers' snoring. Looking back I realise now that it always started that way – a kind of otherworldly feeling, a sensation of being about to pass out and not being able to breathe properly. But yes, here it was again – an acute and growing awareness of whispering… as if there were people in the same room… and they were right behind me.

I let the curtain fall back and swung around.

Starlight flickered in the mirror on the front of the wardrobe – nothing more than a glint in the pre-dawn gloom - the tiniest of movements. And in that fraction of a second my young mind fancied it saw a woman's face – glacial and gaunt with feverish eyes, willing me to notice her… No, not one but more…several women now emerging from behind her and gaining in definition, moving towards me in quick succession. And the strongest feeling I had to acknowledge their presence. *Say yes, Louise… Louise…*

There was an almighty thump in the centre of my chest. I stared in horror. I couldn't stop myself from staring. I just couldn't look away. And then the one I had first seen suddenly lunged closer as if rushing out of the mirror and I clamped a hand over my mouth to stop myself from screaming. I fell to the floor, shuffled backwards against the bed and put my hands over my ears, my eyes. *No, no, no… not the ghosts again…*

If I screamed everyone would shout and my mother would demand to know what I was doing out of bed, so I lay there, still, quiet, trying to shut it all out. Soon it would pass. They were just ghosts. They would go. You see, this was not the first time. It was one of the worst but not the first.

The first time it happened I'd woken up in the early hours to see an unnaturally pale woman in an old-fashioned, long dress sitting on the bedspread. Everything about her was old-fashioned, her skin so pallid as to be that of one deathly ill. Only her eyes burned with a ferocious malevolence that defied even death. And the second I looked into them I knew she'd come for me and me alone. The air was smoky and there was a smell of bitterness, rotting flowers, decay and dirt. Fear shot right through me and I sat straight up and screamed from the depths of my lungs.

What happened next was a good telling-off and slapped legs. My mother did this thing of holding your ankles and your wrists with one hand and smacking the backs of your thighs with the other. Didn't I know she had to be up at five? 'Three in the bloody morning, Louise…'

So this time I sat with my hands over my face and whimpered for goodness knows how long. This was just a dream, I told myself, like the soldier dream. It was not real. How could it be real? I had dreamt the battleground and in exactly the same way I'd imagined the faces in the mirror too. *Just a dream… not real… not real…* And Mum and Dad were just next door… *not… real…*

But the whispers came louder and louder that time, almost impossible to ignore. *Louise… Louise… you are one of us… Look at us…* The same words over and over again, becoming more and more insistent and they just wouldn't go.

I tried to tell Mum about it once but she said it was in my imagination. Did I want people to think I was a lunatic? Did I want to be taken away and put into a special home for mad girls? I was bawling my eyes out by then, so she said in that case I'd better stop wittering on about hearing whispers and seeing ghosts or they'd pack me off to the funny farm. The thing was, though, that I heard them more often than ever now. It seemed to be escalating ever since the horrible night at Grandma Ellen's house when Mum was poorly. My mother said I couldn't stay the night there again ever, no matter if she was 'dying of the bloody flu'. Did it start then? I don't know. I only wished it would stop.

Eventually, after I really don't know how long, I dared look up from between my fingers. I had a feeling the ghosts had finally gone: the atmosphere had changed – was somehow clearer – and the whispering had stopped. Arthur moaned in his sleep, a huddled shape muttering under the blankets; and when I glanced into the mirror the only reflection was my own murky silhouette. The whole episode had probably taken less than a few minutes but it seemed like hours.

It was then I realised mum and dad were not just talking but arguing; snapping at each other in hisses. Occasionally one voice would rise and the other would say, "Shush!"

Slowly, taking care not to make the floorboards creak, I crawled over to the wall connecting the two rooms, shivering, teeth chattering, but propelled by curiosity. My mother often went on at my dad but it was normally when they first went up to bed, and soon after that his snoring started. My mother was one of those hyper-energetic women and the undisputed queen bee around here – always first to know things and the first to decide what to do about it. She didn't look or act like Auntie Rosa and Auntie Marion. My mother was the youngest of the three and didn't resemble either her sisters or Grandma Ellen, who were all tall and fair. Instead she had the same blackcurrant eyes my great grandma Annie had – glittering beads that darted and sparked behind horn-rimmed specs. If I had to describe my mother in one word I'd choose 'forthright.' Dad said you could slice a knife between Annie's daughter, Agnes, on the one side of the family, and her other daughter, Ellen, on the other. The only physical characteristic that bound all of the women in my family together (apart from Snow who was different to everyone) was a distinctive streak of copper in our hair. Even Grace, Agnes' daughter – amid that cascade of glossy dark curls there were filaments of copper; although where ours were at the front or to the side in a badger stripe, hers, I noticed, was virtually undetectable.

I should perhaps mention that my mother was an exceptionally busy woman too. During the week she worked up at the velvet factory and at weekends she helped Dad in the funeral parlour, and still she had time for a succession of visitors. We always had visitors. They were here before breakfast. She'd be frying bacon, talking ten to the dozen while they sat at the kitchen table smoking and knocking fag ash into a saucer. She talked over the top of her washing as she put it through the mangle, non-stop while she shopped in the Co-op, and was constantly at the back door of the kitchen nattering to some old biddy or other, arms folded; yacking, Dad said, to 'the coven.'

The key word that indicated something important was coming, I quickly realised, was 'apparently.' After the word, 'apparently,' the conversation would become subdued and more difficult to hear. But it would be by far the most important bit, you could bet your life on it. I think her true skill, however – and you had to be impressed – was to acquire far more information than she ever actually gave out; yet still leave her audience feeling privileged and part of her inner circle.

This time though, Dad's voice could be heard too, which always meant it was even more salacious and I should definitely know what was going on – partly because although my mother was a dyed-in-the-wool gossip, she didn't discuss family stuff with the other women. But she did with Dad and that was where the secrets were. Oh, the darkest, deepest secrets a family could keep. I had no idea, of course, despite instincts that were switched on like radar, just how truly dark and hideous our family secrets were; let alone what they would lead to. How could I? But I did know there were secrets.

I can't be sure of the time by then but guess it must have been around four in the morning because of the tinkling, quick-fire Grandmother clock in the hall downstairs ... *ching-ching-ching-ching*. Far too fast to be sure you heard the hour correctly. But I think it was four. Arthur sighed heavily again and turned over into my space in the bed, the mattress sagging visibly. Swallowing down my irritation I pressed my ear to the wall.

"Apparently–"

My father mumbled something.

"Well, we ought to check on 'er."

"I'm not bloody going now, Viv! Have you seen it?"

"I'm worried…first light, then."

"Aye, get some sleep, for Christ's sake."

"Well…not like mother… and in weather like this… out of her wits. And now the lines are down—"

"Viv! I get it."

"Shush! Keep your voice down."

"Well, be sensible…can't do anything right this minute…be holed up somewhere—"

"…five hours?"

"…home by now…go in the morning."

"What if…?"

The voices became too muffled, as if they were continuing the conversation from the bottom of a well and my eyelids were getting heavy.

But after a few more hissed exchanges I heard Mum say, "And Agnes—"

Dad said something rude like, 'bugger'. He didn't like either Annie or Agnes, and my ears strained as hard as they could now 'the witches', as Dad called them, had been mentioned. Great Grandma Annie lived miles out on the edge of the moor, in a tiny cottage without running water or heating. She had one main room for cooking in, with a big fire and a range. In the corner she had a table set with an oil cloth and always left the salt and pepper out, alongside bottles of pickles. I don't know what she pickled but there'd be dozens of bottles of them in the larder too. I used to like visiting her because she had cats and kittens that were allowed to run wherever they wanted, and she always gave us a sixpence each out of the top drawer of an old dresser; but my dad wouldn't go anymore for some reason, and knowing what I know now, I shouldn't have been within a mile of the place either. She'd smile at me, hold my chin up and say, 'She looks like one of us'. Never bothered with either of my brothers, but me – she kept saying I had 'the gift'.

Mum's face… it could've stopped a clock when she said that, but Great Grandma Annie… she'd be smiling.

I pictured that old cottage with snow up to its roof and the occupants frozen dead inside, but I couldn't hear what Dad said and had to admit defeat. And anyway, by then my bones felt like icicles and my teeth weren't just chattering they were gnashing. Suddenly bed seemed like a good place to be. I rushed over and dived in, giving Arthur a good shove over before rolling into the warm dip he'd just vacated. Squeezing my fingers and clenching my toes over and over I knew I had to sleep but I just couldn't. My mind was playing tricks. Images flashing… I had this awful feeling of impending doom, you see, and I'll not forget it, especially after what happened. But at the time I didn't know why. Maybe it was something in my mother's voice, I don't know. I was just convinced something terrible was going to happen and it was going to happen very soon. Turned out I was right, as well.

***

Chapter Seven
1908
Castle Draus, Ludsmoor
Annie Bailey, mother to Ellen and Agnes

Standing on top of the castle ruin walls with his arms flung wide, the man's voice lifted into the fresh March breeze, "All need to be saved!"

"All need to be saved!"

Echoing his words, the crowd worshipped him with their eyes, faces freshly scrubbed and wind-whipped pink. Maids holding onto their hats lest they were blown across the moors, had raced from duties, jumping onto passing carts to get here on time. Miners and factory workers who had hurried from their cottages after Sunday lunch, now all stood as one, breathless and expectant. Every square yard of the field was crammed with people, elbow-to elbow, squinting into the sun, straining to hear the most important sermon of their lives.

Castle Draus stood high on the top of Kite Ridge, which overlooked Ludsmoor and from where, on a clear day it was said you could see four counties – even as far as the coast if you were lucky. Originally a medieval fortress, it was now a crumbling but still imposing silhouette against a blinding sky; a beacon for miles around.

"All may be saved!" cried their preacher.

"All may be saved!" the crowd roared back.

The preacher's voice broke with emotion, "All may know themselves saved!"

"All may know themselves saved!"

Spring sunshine chased bundles of clouds over hotchpotch squares of land marked out with drystone walls, and a kestrel hovered overhead, riding the air currents – occasionally disappearing from view as it nose-dived for prey; the only sound apart from the speaker, that of a few bleating sheep from adjoining fields

A contagious feeling of anticipatory excitement now rippled through the crowd, mostly local workers standing in their Sunday best, a throng of avid listeners craning to see this man and intent on hearing every word, because this was for them and them alone. Aaron Danby was bringing the light of Methodism to the heart of their community – this lonely outback of a place where little had changed for working people like them in centuries. They still continued to labour six days a week up to their elbows in grime, and nothing much brought relief from that. Still worn down with poverty. Still second class.

Over a hundred and fifty year ago, John Wesley had stood in this exact same spot and preached the exact same words, but where once Ludsmoor had been little more than a string of wind-blasted sheep farms, it now housed hundreds of those who worked in its mines and mills: the working poor who felt excluded from the restraints of the Church of England, particularly a parochial church with separate pews for wealthy families.

The message here, though, was one of inclusion, morality and, above all, charity to the poor. And song played a huge part, with John's brother, Charles Wesley having composed over six thousand hymns – something which appealed greatly to those who had toiled hard all week and could now open up their lungs and vigorously praise the Lord who would save them. All of them. Not just those who presided over them and dished out the rules. This church was for them, about them, and would be run by them. And they couldn't get enough. The movement grew rapidly in the north of Staffordshire as it did in Wales and other parts of Great Britain, uniting working people in song and belief. No longer dry doctrine, this was exhilarating stuff and their hearts soared.

"All may be saved to the uttermost!"

"All may be saved to the uttermost!"

'Immortal, Invisible, God Only Wise,' now resounded across the bleak landscape in full glorious voice, a valiant and powerful chorus. Poor they may be but their faith, renewed and invigorated, was fast becoming invincible. And with Aaron Danby's help they would soon have a chapel of their own too. Certainly it was needed…by God was it needed…

Aaron was thirty-five, the only son of Edward and Clara Danby of Danby Grange – landed gentry who owned thousands of acres, including forests, rivers, moorland, farms and cottages. The family tree could be traced back to medieval times and the knights who fought in the Christian Crusades – their ancient tombs in Danby Church testament to this. However, fact had mixed with fiction somewhere along the line and become blurred. The story went that these same knights had returned with slaves – dark skinned folk who settled on the moors and would later farm their own patches of land. It was also said these people were heathens and had brought with them strange Eastern customs, notably black witchcraft; but there was little to back this up apart from certain members of the farming community possessing swarthier complexions and notably coarser features than others.

The family also owned several shirt mills, together with rows of terraced houses in Leek, Ludsmoor and Danby. And although Aaron had an older sister, she had died in childbirth many years previously, which left him, with the exception of his young nephew, Thomas, main heir to a vast estate including Blackwater Colliery, potteries in nearby Stoke-on-Trent, and all three of the velvet or 'fustian' mills as they were colloquially known, on the slopes overlooking the village. The family's enterprises had rapidly transformed the bleak landscape. Row after row of back-to-back stone terraces now lined the main streets of the village in order to house the ever increasing population, which arrived to work in these thriving industries. And directly opposite the mills on Tower Hill leading up to the mines, the Danbys had constructed several dozen more grim-faced but sturdy Victorian terraces complete with backyards and outhouses.

Mostly the mines were for coal, but the quarries, which had been passed down through successive generations of Danbys, were for gritstone, a substance later milled into a fine, white powder before being transported to the potteries and added to the clay. As a result, the whole area was constantly coated in grime - from coal dust, horses and carts churning up the lanes, and muddy fields swilling with rainwater running off the moors. Consequently Tower Hill Road became a dirt track with carts racing down it full of miners desperate for a pint at The Quarryman on the corner, which was precisely where and how those hard won wages clinked back into the Danby purse. The Danbys, naturally enough, also owning the public house.

After drinking their wages dry, many of the miners slept where they slumped until the next shift started at first light. Meanwhile, their children ran around without shoes; and wives shouted at their husbands from the pub doorway, but it made no odds. The men still drank. And thus their poverty rolled into another week. Women scrubbed floors and pounded sheets with a mangle, hung out the washing in winds that blew it horizontal, and all before labouring in the mills for the day – often shoving the children underneath the long tables used for cutting cloth, hissing at them to keep quiet down there in the dark. And to keep back from the knives as they swished up and down, up and down, dozens and dozens of times a day, in the barely lit rooms flickering with candlelight and cloyed with dust.

Prospective, Providence and Coronation Mills – the velvet factories on Tower Hill –employed, among many others, both Ellen and Agnes Bailey, two young sisters living with their widowed mother, Annie, at Wish Lane cottage in Ludsmoor. The work was arduous and the hours long. Annie, testament to this, had developed painful rheumatoid arthritis, which had grotesquely twisted and swollen the knuckles on her hands, and she now lived on the charity of her two daughters, who also had to cook, clean, and do the laundry in the two-up-two-down tiny, stone cottage. There was no bathroom. Like most people they used the cold water tap in the kitchen for a strip wash, and once a week there would be a tin bath in front of the fire, which they took it in turns to use. The toilet was outside in a lean-to with a corrugated iron roof; and there was no heating of any kind apart from the coal fire with great cast iron ovens either side, used for both cooking and drying clothes.

Widowed at an early age, it was now to her fury and distress that both girls appeared to be succumbing to a similar fate as her own. Working in the fustian mill was a dismal, draining and physically demanding job. The walk up and down the long tables cutting velvet pile demanded total concentration paired with considerable skill, on a noisy, sweltering, dark factory floor. They walked miles and miles a day. And they were paid per length of cloth. If a mistake was made cutting the pile the worker would not receive a penny. Some of the men carried two knives and made twice as much, but for girls already developing swollen knuckles and painful wrists, the future was worrying.

Amongst the congregation that day, Annie stood with her daughters watching the young man just back from Cambridge. After several years touring Europe on what was known as a 'Grand Tour' he had opted for religion as his raison d'étre. Her eyes narrowed to flint. Who the hell was he to tell these people not to drink and not to gamble? And now, 'Jump to it People! Build me a chapel to lecture and pontificate in'? Was there no end to his pomposity?

And worse, oh, so much worse, and when she thought about this she could barely breathe. He wanted it built on Pagan ground, as he called it, to stamp out the heathen culture of drunken immorality and reputed witchcraft. This was their chance for salvation, for a new life, and with it to oust all that had gone before. The chapel would therefore be built at the site of Odin's Tree – a piece of land 'generously donated by the Danby family' – a place used by those who had practised the dark arts and who had mired the whole area with their devilish practices and superstition. A place he most vociferously promised would be trounced into the ground back to the bowels of the earth where it belonged.

"So let us arise and build at once!"

The congregation broke into near hysteria.

He held up his hands for calm.

Laughing. The loathsome bastard was laughing...

"Concrete plans are at last being put into action", he told them. "This is no pipe dream." The Church of England was in full agreement and the Methodist Chapel could be constructed at Odin's Tree and work could start straight away. Christianity in the form of primitive Methodism would be brought to the working people of Ludsmoor and it was here now! Like most of the other towns and villages in this area they would finally have their very own chapel. In fact, with all hands on board, they could have it before Whitsun.

"Hitherto the Lord has helped us!" he cried.

People flocked, running towards him, shaking his hand as he leapt triumphantly down from the castle walls. Men slapped him on the back and bombarded him with questions. There would be a meeting in the village hall that very evening, he informed them. Yes, yes – it would then be decided who would do what. Oh yes, he would provide the materials needed... stone from the mines, mortar, timber, machinery. Indeed, it was on its way. Out of his own family pocket – the generosity of his father...

And tomorrow the tree would come out.

Annie remained standing where she was, a lone figure on the edge of the crowd, the black cloth of her dress flapping in the breeze, his words as resonate in her head as a funeral toll. *Tomorrow the tree will come out.*

"We must make haste at once!" He was shouting over the tops of heads, mounting his horse, kicking the fine, thoroughbred stallion to a trot.

She watched him leave, trailed by the masses as if he was the Messiah himself. "Then you will repent at leisure, Sir," she muttered. "You will repent at leisure."

***

Chapter Eight
1951, Grytton Forest
Marion and Rosa Danby

"Marion, you mustn't close your eyes." Rosa tried to support her sister's dead weight, grasping at the wet rags of her coat as she slumped to the ground. "No, come on. Stand up. We have to get home or we'll freeze to death."

In despair, she looked about them. Wind rustled through the barren treetops – an urgent rushing, which increased the sense of isolation – lifting snowflakes from the blackened boughs and whirling them into the air. An overwhelming, oppressive fatigue threatened to drag her down and she fought against it, pulling up her scarf to protect her face from the cold. This place, this sense of being trapped in a vortex, had an unnatural, otherworldly atmosphere to it. She tamped down a feeling of rising claustrophobia, a fear they would not be able to escape, and forced herself to think rationally.

"Marion, you have to stand up. We must keep walking. Listen to me!"

"I'm too tired. We've been walking all night… Need a rest."

It was true. Many hours had passed since they first entered the woods and they'd been walking in circles ever since. Disorientated from hypothermia, perhaps? Rosa struggled to concentrate on logical thought. A teacher at Danby Grammar School for Girls, she took Physical Education and knew a thing or two about motivation – keeping tetchy, tired adolescents running cross-country in driving sleet and rain when they hated every minute…Ah, but she kept them on course; and she could do it now. She had to.

"Marion, I think what's happened is we've become confused and disorientated. Do you hear me?"

Marion nodded.

"Okay, good, now listen. We're suffering from hypothermia and if we stay here much longer we're going to die from the cold. We have to keep moving. Do you understand?"

Marion's voice was slurred as if she'd been drugged. "No, it's more than that–"

"What? What do you say?" Crouching next to her, she took hold of Marion's hands and shook her. "Look at me. Look at me, Marion. Stay awake." A layer of ice was sinking into her back as surely as if she was drowning in a freezing pond. By now her jaw could barely move enough to speak, and the dark was so absolute not a single thing could be identified within it. Terror lurched inside her and with renewed effort she hurled her best teacher's voice into the void, the words sounding syrupy and muffled as if the blackness was a living, swirling thing that swallowed them whole. "Hold onto me and stand up. You must stand up. You can and will do it. Think about Lana. Mother can't look after her – she needs you. Stand up, Marion!"

The whites of her sister's eyes were no longer visible, her voice barely above a whisper, and she strained to hear. "They brought us here...on the hare path."

"What? No, I don't understand."

"The forest is built on ley lines. Beautiful, powerful... a thinning of the veil... but it's been—"

"No, Marion dear – you have to explain later. Come on now, stand up."

"Dark arts... and someone knows we're here... look! Rosa, you must look."

"For God's sake, stand up, Marion. You must..." Her words tailed off as unable to help herself, she glanced over her shoulder to whatever had her sister so transfixed. And her heart slammed into her ribs.

A white mist had appeared, revealing a stagnant pond and the long, spindly fingers of a weeping willow trailing in its shallows. Rosa blinked and blinked again, unable to comprehend the unfolding scene. Around the water's edges and now clearly visible were screaming faces of horror – great hollows resembling ugly gargoyles with wide open mouths, which it took a moment to realise were carved into the bark of every tree. And hanging from the branches, silhouetted against the hazy light, were bundles of sticks fashioned into human figures.

Comprehension sank in with a dead thud as the two women began to fully register what they were seeing. And the more they looked the more they saw: limp-limbed poppets made of twigs, rags and string, were swinging by the neck from branches arching over the swamp. Dozens of them. Larger dolls had been nailed to the trunks, many just charred and twisted remains, silver pins piercing heads, eyes and hearts, glinting against the blackened bark.

Rosa stood up and reached towards one.

"Don't!" Marion cried. "Don't touch it. Don't touch anything."

"What the hell is this place?"

A waxen image of a distorted, partially melted face dangled inches away from her, a rodent's tail poking out of its chest. A sodden bandage had begun to unravel and Rosa quickly shoved it into her pocket before Marion could stop her. There had been an inscription on it, no doubt smudged now, but it could be something…Her sister's voice seemed to come from far, far away, and everything viewed from the wrong end of a telescope. She'd only ever been drunk once and the dizzy, sick, lurching feeling of staggering home on a bridge made of rope revisited her now. She grabbed for the nearest branch to stop herself from keeling over. The air of thick oppression was almost palpable: laughter echoing from within the trees; wood smoke choking in her nostrils; the canopy whizzing around like a kaleidoscope.

Swinging around too quickly, she almost fell. The ground pitched and bucked beneath her and she snatched at twigs, leaves, branches… anything to stop herself from falling.

"Oh God, no, no…Rosa…we have to–" Marion's voice was tinny and disembodied. Then all of a sudden she was flying through the air towards her.

Rosa reeled back. And then there was silence.

"Where are you?"

Marion was nowhere.

"Marion? Sis?"

Like wading through water, her limbs heavy and her movements slow, it was with a delayed reaction she realised that Marion had fallen and was lying flat on her back.

"Oh, no! Marion, Marion!"

Down on the ground, on her hands and knees, the air was slightly clearer, the aroma of damp earth real - enough to fractionally sharpen up her senses.

"Are you alright?"

"I hurt my leg."

"You tripped on something."

And it was then they both noticed what it was. "Oh, dear God. This is some kind of graveyard. Look at this: four boulders…*one-two-three-four*…in a kind of circle. And there are names etched on them."

Marion sat up and helped Rosa brush the snow away. Roughly hewn from local gritstone were four crudely etched gravestones. Rosa flicked on the torch to try and decipher what had been scored into them, but the light was too weak. Using her finger she traced the names.

Meg. Agnus. Lizzie. Anne.

"Marion, these are un-consecrated graves. All these years we've lived here and yet never in my life..." She looked up in astonishment. "Did you...?"

Marion was shuffling away as fast as she could, wincing with a painful ankle. "God help us! Rosa, I know every inch of these woods, I swear, but this is... I don't know where we are but this is not Grytton Forest."

"Of course it is."

Staggering to her feet, Marion immediately hunched over as if to retch, her hands clamping both ears, groaning loudly.

"What is it? Is it the pain? Are you going to be sick?" Rosa rushed over. "Lean on me."

But Marion wouldn't move her hands from her ears. "No, I can't. There's screaming in my head – screeching - oh God, the pain!"

In desperation, Rosa looked around – at the macabre site of effigies and dolls dangling from the trees, at the four graves - and again the sting of fear burned into her stomach. She tugged at Marion's arm, pulling her away from the scene. "I don't know which way to go. I can't see a way out. It's as if we're in the centre of a maze—"

"It's a trick, Rosa. They're messing with the order of things again - using this special place—" She clutched at her ears and the agony was clear on her ashen face as silently she screamed, then began to pant rapidly. "It's been done recently and if we don't go now this second–"

"What have they done here? Who?"

"Blood. The dolls have blood on them. There's blood on the ground, under the snow – I can smell it. We need to go this second. Help me – pull me away."

"Where to?" Away from the mist everything was thickly black, visibility nil. "We've tried every path."

"Up to Green Man's Cave."

"Are you mad? Up to the moors in this weather? In the opposite direction to home?"

"I'm going to be sick. Uphill or I swear to God…"

Marion's body was crumpling to the floor again.

There was little choice. Rosa grabbed her elbow and yanked her towards what she hoped was an uphill direction. Her sister had better be right because there was precious little strength left between them now. Neither said another word. Until, with huge relief to them both the path began to steepen. From time to time low moans, like the cries of lost and despairing wanderers came from the misty swamp below; but neither looked back.

The cave Marion was talking about was on the opposite side of Hilltop Road but they should at least find some shelter there - maybe light a small fire and smoke cigarettes while they figured out what to do next.

After a few minutes of climbing, Marion said, "We're coming out of it."

Rosa didn't answer. She knew what her sister meant and that she wasn't referring to the forest; but the many questions she had would keep for now. The trek was tough going enough. Although both women were skinny and robust, the incline was precipitous and slippery and Marion had undoubtedly strained her ankle. Tired and weakened, they frequently fell, tripping over hidden roots; grabbing at the spiky undergrowth with fingers bleeding from scratches to prevent themselves from sliding down again.

After steadily ascending for a good twenty minutes more, a fresh current of air began to swirl around their faces and they gasped at it. Almost there. With one final push up the bank, they scrabbled over a dry stone wall and finally through the barrier of trees onto Hilltop Road. Immediately an Arctic blast almost knocked them both sideways, but they held onto each other tightly, panting, knee-deep in snow; surveying the scene.

"Oh Lord, Rosa, look at it!"

The road had merged with the horizon in a total white-out. At least a foot of snow now lay silently glittering under a midnight sky studded with stars; and the wind, although less ferocious, was lifting freshly fallen flakes from the surface and scattering them in swirls of fairy dust.

"We could take the main road and try heading home that way?" Rosa suggested.

Marion shook her head. "Two hours wading through that when we're exhausted - maybe more? What time is it now? My watch has stopped."

"How funny, so has mine. I'd guess midnight. How long to the cave, would you say?"

"Ten minutes tops, even in this. I can see it. See that rise of stone?"

"Okay, let's go."

The cave's opening was a narrow, vertical oblong. Small and slight as they were, the two women still had to squeeze through it before stooping almost double for a sharp descent into the cavern below. With numb fingers inside sopping gloves they tried to grip onto the slippery rock-face, concentrating on not falling down the steep steps. There were fifteen – they had counted them often enough as children – and now they counted again, each narrow ledge part of a spiral staircase that could scoot them down to a freezing grave in an instant.

"Take it steady," Rosa instructed from behind. "One step at a time. Let me shine the torch ahead."

Green Man's Cave was unusual in that once through, it immediately descended into a long, natural fissure between adjacent rock walls. Coated with lichen and moss, the cave dripped steadily with moisture all year round. Now though, in the midst of a snowstorm, it provided a haven from the onslaught of cutting Arctic winds; and there were several small alcoves in which to shelter and light a fire.

Once onto the cave floor, Rosa quickly scouted around for twigs and branches, then put her lighter to the snap-dry kindling and lit them both a cigarette. They sat and smoked for a while, coaxing life into their hands and feet. Overhead the howling winds were muffled; the only sounds those of a low whistling through the tunnels, and the drip-drip-drip of water resonating hypnotically as it plopped onto the rock floor.

"If you can feel pain in your fingers you haven't got frostbite," said Marion, taking off her gloves and hat – trying to dry them out over the sparky flames.

Rosa nodded. "How do you feel now? Are you alright?"

"Freezing. Starving."

"I mean—"

"Yes, okay. Thank you." After a few more minutes, Marion added, "How long shall we hole up? Til daylight?"

"Yes." Rosa glanced again at her watch. "How funny, it's started working again."

"So 's mine. Yes, how odd."

"Wrong time, though, it says nine o'clock."

"Same here. I think we've lost hours, Rosa. It's gone midnight, definitely."

"God, what the hell happened in there? I just don't understand it. I feel like I'm going mad or something."

Marion didn't answer.

"Anyway, yes I think we should wait for dawn and then stick to the roads. I'm not going into those woods again in the dark. Ever."

"You know, it's strange," said Marion. "But I feel less tired now. Normally and naturally tired – wind-blasted and exhausted but not—"

"Like you've been given an anaesthetic? I know what you mean. I felt it too. Seriously, Marion, what happened?"

"I don't know."

"I think you do. You said things about dark arts and blood on the ground. You scared me to death."

"Do you think there's anything else we can put on this fire? It's not going to last more than a few minutes."

"I'll have a look. Hold on. Stay there – are you sure you're ok?"

"Yes, I'm sure."

There was scant firewood material to be found and she'd probably already found what there was. Rosa flashed the torchlight around the walls. As children they'd brought picnics up here in the summer – she, Marion and Viv – running around pretending they were part of King Arthur's Castle: Vivien standing at the top of the spiral steps declaring she was Guinevere and the rest of them her ladies in waiting. They never spent too long down here on the cave floor, though – there was something about it; something creepy, Marion said. Even then she'd managed to put the fear of the devil in them with her stories and visions. Some said a horseman had been galloping across the moors when his horse had suddenly stopped and ejected him to his death, and now his green-tinted spectre haunted the place even on the warmest of days. Others said it was a spiritual place and non-conformists worshipped here before the Methodist chapel was built; and then there were stories of darker rituals and those who liked the isolation and secrecy. Rosa pushed away an image placed into her mind long ago of a procession of hooded Satanists solemnly making their way up to the cave. A breath of freezing night air coiled around her neck and she pulled up the collar of her coat as high as it would go, refusing to look at the dark recesses and narrow tunnels that burrowed along corridors to who knew where.

Spying a few more branches, she quickly cracked them into a bundle and carefully retraced her steps back to Marion. Her sister, although the eldest, was by far the most fragile of the three – both physically and emotionally - and also the most secretive. Rosa sank to the floor next to the fire and passed her another lit cigarette. For a while they watched the fire crackle and spit with new life. Marion's face seemed drawn and etched with shadows, her expression glazed.

Eventually, Rosa took a deep breath and asked again. "So tell me what happened back there then, Marion? I hope you're going to because I'm confused and upset. I'm tired and I'm bone-cold. So just bloody well tell me. What was it you said about *them* messing with the order of things? Who? I don't understand. And how come neither of us have seen those graves before?"

Again Marion shook her head. "I told you I don't know."

A tad more sharply, Rosa said, "You did say you'd explain later."

"I'm at a loss." Marion took a drag of her cigarette, then another in quick succession. "God, I'm so bloody frozen I could cry."

"That makes two of us. Now tell me – this stuff about the dark arts and a thinning of the veil? What the hell's all that crap and nonsense about? There was definitely something scary about the graves and the horrible dolls in the trees but why would it make you ill and why would you say you'd never been there before when you seemed to know so much about it?" Her voice had risen with irritation and her fingers trembled as she put the cigarette to her lips.

Still Marion said nothing.

Rosa turned and glared at her, stifling the old frustration. Marion knew things she didn't, as did Vivien, although Viv covered it all up with non-stop chatter and a brilliant social act; whereas Marion painted weird things and drifted around in a dream. But she had appeared to understand what was happening back there, and since they both nearly died this evening and could still do so she decided on the right to know why.

"And?"

"I think we're going to die out here, Rosa. That's what. I can't feel my blood pumping round anymore. They say it's nice, though, dying from hypothermia."

"Marion. We are not going to die. We are going to stay awake. In a few hours it will be dawn – you saw the stars – there'll be enough light to see the way home and we'll keep walking until we get there. Now bloody well tell me what you were talking about – that stuff about ley lines and those damn dolls."

Still Marion gazed into the flames.

"Why won't you tell me a darn thing? Ever?" Rosa's voice had risen to the pitch she used in front of an unruly class.

"Alright then. Because if I told you, or anyone else for that matter, that I hear voices in my head and I know when forces are being used against me or someone else, you'd say I was mad and making it up. Just like my mother, like Vivien, like all of them – the doctor, you, everyone. Even though Mother and Vivien know damn well what I'm talking about. And look what you were all like about Snow! The child can't fend for herself but she hears things too. Just as I do, and bloody Viv does. And Louise… she knows too. She hears them."

"Who? Hears who, hears what?"

Marion shrugged.

"Marion, are you talking about hearing things in your head or dead people or…? I don't understand – what black arts–?"

"Annie! Annie, for Christ's sake – you must know that, surely? Look, I don't want any part of it. They wanted me – to use me as a channel, and they'll want Louise. But now look – see the expression on your face! It says everything."

"Okay, so tell me then. What are they saying? Why did we get lost just now when we both know we were on the right path home?"

"We were on ley lines – song lines or hare paths as they used to be called – magnetic pathways that form a triangle between the chapel in Ludsmoor, Castle Draus and Grytton Forest. Look at the Ordinance Survey map and you'll see you can draw straight lines that form an isosceles triangle between each point. But at Grytton those lines converge and actually cross. The forest is a sacred place, Rosa, which is why there's a holy well there. Because people from a long time ago knew that and picked up on it – they were more finely tuned into the earth's energy and to natural laws than we are now. They worshipped there, you see, and built the well to remind us where to go and to pass on what they knew. It's a beautiful magical place. The spiritual energy is magnified to such an intensity you feel you can almost…" Her eyes took on the faraway dreamy expression they so often had. "Well, it's as if you're transported to a higher consciousness. It's the most amazing feeling. There are places like this the world over and we have one right here on our doorstep; and our ancestors found it. Imagine that!"

"Energy from the earth? Okay, I'll go with that."

"Yes, telluric energy. And it affects every part of us, you see, because we're all made up of energy too. Energy and magnetics. Think about it. It's what makes the planets spin. And it's a tremendous experience to be where the thinning of the veil allows you to pass through to another dimension. You can feel spirits from throughout the ages crowding into your mind and all with stories to tell, it's so powerful—"

"Through the veil and in touch with spirits? Marion—"

"Hear me out! You asked and I'm trying my best to explain even though you haven't a hope in hell of understanding because you've closed your mind. But here's what I think happened tonight: there's a problem when the powerful energy I've described is used for negative purposes. If someone with evil intent has channelled this energy in order to alter the natural course of things – summoned spirits - well, it can be a dangerous thing. And they have. It's not for any of us this time, though. It's for someone else–"

"What do you mean? Who?"

"I don't know who."

"Oh, I don't understand this at all. Just explain to me please, what or who is it you hear exactly?"

"Spirits. I can't always hear what they're saying. It's when they're active that I pick up on it - I just do."

"Active?"

For a few seconds over the dying embers of the fire, Rosa stared into Marion's sombre, grey eyes, so like her father's and her own. She tried hard to make sense of it all but part of her rebelled against what she considered to be fanciful, over-imaginative nonsense. And possibly out and out madness. "How is it you hear things and I don't? How do you know there is evil intent on someone?"

Marion nodded. "For years I didn't hear anything conclusive. It would just be whispering I never quite got hold of. I'd swing around and there'd be nobody there. But then I found if I practiced meditation and cut out all the normal daily noises – you know, be absolutely quiet and attune to a higher vibration - I got my ear in, if you know what I mean? At first it was really faint and garbled but soon the words formed more clearly, and after that I started to hear things outside the normal everyday five senses. Some people like me are more sensitive to it, that's all. But you know…" It was a hollow laugh and she shook her head. "Ah, how can I put this? They seem to sense you after that – they know you found them. And that's when you wish with all your heart you hadn't."

Rosa put her arm around her and kissed the top of her head. "We're Christians, Marion. We can't really believe in all this dark arts stuff, you know? We mustn't commune with dead people and spirits – it's unhealthy and wrong."

Marion's body seemed to sag against her own. "Don't you think I know that?"

Rosa stroked her hair. "Shush, now. I think you're unwell, that's all – very, very unwell. And I'm going to help you. But first let's get through the night. Hold my hands. Let's pray."

***

Chapter Nine
Danby
Hazel Quinn

With shaking hands, Hazel picked up the phone in the hallway. If anything had happened to him, though. *Oh, dear God*! It was one thing coming to terms with the end of their marriage but quite another if…

Her voice came out small and childlike, "Hello, Hazel Quinn here."

There was a slight pause while coins were pushed into a phone box, and then a female voice burst onto the line. "Oh, hello, Hazel? It's Grace Holland here."

Oh no, oh for God's sake, no. He must be trapped somewhere in the snow with this awful, blousy woman in some sort of vile love nest; and now she was about to be told they were together and…

"I wondered if we could meet up?"

She gripped the receiver. A bluish light emanated through the porthole in the front door, casting an elongated shadow along the hall tiles. At the other end of the corridor, the kitchen door was ajar, the rear garden iced white; the only sound the pitter-patter of sleety snow blowing onto the window.

"Meet?"

The other woman sounded impatient, too forthright. "Yes, meet up. I think we ought to talk, don't you?"

"Erm—"

"How about now? Tonight?"

"What? Why? What about?"

Another coin was pushed into the phone box. "Look, I haven't got any more change. Can you get to The Feathers in Danby in say, half an hour? The roads are still open."

Hazel glanced again at the front door. It sounded as though thousands of shrapnel fragments were being hurled against it. Caught off guard, she floundered. "Now? But it's a blizzard." And yet, oh the compulsion to talk to this woman – to find out what she had to say, to know what was going on and have that information. This was her life, her whole future… And where was Max anyway? Was he with Grace? Would the two of them confront her when she arrived? Oh God, she was going to be sick. Or…"Has something happened to Max?"

There was a slight intake of breath, then, "No, no, nothing like that. Look, I'm in Danby now and it's clear – the main road is clear from the end of your road—"

"Hang on a minute, you've been here?"

"Look, Hazel, I haven't any more money and we need to talk while he's away. Can you meet me? It's not far for you to come and we have to talk. It's urgent."

In a state of shock that the woman had been to her home, knew where it was and also that Max was away and still not home - and not only that but that this was urgent - she found herself agreeing, already picturing what she would wear, and that she'd need a spade from out of the garage, some salt and... "Okay," she heard herself say.

"Good. Thank you. I'll be there in about fifteen minutes—" She was talking over the pips. Hazel couldn't hear, expected more coins, but then the line went dead.

In the silence that followed, she stood holding the receiver, her heart a lump of granite. So here she was then – facing what she had to face. She'd known, of course, that it was coming, but just not yet.

Now the end was here, it seemed so sudden.

Trembling violently from head to foot, she replaced the phone in its cradle. What in God's name was this all about? Urgent, she'd said. Endless possibilities criss-crossed her mind as on auto-pilot she walked into the lounge, banked the fire up with coal and placed the fireguard around it; then checked the back door was locked and bolted before hurrying upstairs to change and put on some make-up. Not a chance she would be facing that woman without battle dress and war paint. Fifteen minutes, like hell! Let Grace Holland wait. After all, she held all the cards, did she not?

***

Chapter Ten
Ludsmoor
Louise – the night after the blizzard

When we woke next morning it was to the sound of spades scraping the road outside. Ice frosted the inside of the windows and we dressed under the bed clothes. I can still remember those thick, hand-knitted tights I had, and wearing so many layers of woollens that my grey school pinafore was the devil's own to fasten over the top. I must have waddled.

Downstairs the fire was blazing up the chimney in a furnace blast behind a sheet of newspaper. This was Arthur's job. Once it was hot enough he'd take away the paper and throw on half a scuttle of coal, briefly snuffing out the flames until the sparks burst through. His face would be scarlet and his hands grubby, but he always nodded with satisfaction when it was done. That morning we had breakfast in our overcoats by candlelight because the power lines were down. Best meal of the day, though, and I still love it: doorstep slices of white bread toasted over the fire, spread with butter, topped with Lyle's golden syrup and then cut into fingers. You were allowed to dip your knife into the Lyle's tin once, and whatever came out you could have but no more

– thus, the art was to wrap the syrup around the knife as quickly as possible then trickle it all over the toast. And as always there was a big pot of tea on the table covered in a knitted tea-cosy.

"Still snowing," said Mum to Auntie Connie, who was supposed to live next door but seemed to spend more time at ours.

Connie's husband, Jack, was out clearing the road alongside Dad and some of the other men. Any excuse though, to sit there smoking herself to a wheezy death at our breakfast table. A ubiquitous presence was Connie, eyeing us through a haze of smoke every morning and talking about us kids like we weren't in the same room. She wasn't a real auntie – none of them were except, of course, for Auntie Rosa and Auntie Marion – but back then we called all the local women, 'Auntie' and never thought anymore of it.

Connie was as much a fixture on school mornings as the freshly-filled coal scuttle on the hearth, and the oilskin tablecloth set permanently with teapot, milk and sugar; and it was a small room. There was a high-backed, green leather sofa we all crammed together on, jostling for elbow space, but apart from Dad's armchair the only other piece of furniture downstairs was a welsh dresser in the parlour. The top drawer on the left was for the Co-op dividend book and my mother's purse; the one on the right for my father's business papers. Bearing the sole burden of our family's personal possessions, it bowed under the weight of crockery, framed photographs, and dolls. My mother collected the darn things – dozens and dozens of china-faced dolls in a variety of costumes. She displayed them all pointing the same way but I swear that once, just as I was about to leave the room I glanced over my shoulder and saw the head of one of them twisting round on its stem, its wide blue eyes unblinking.

I still hate them – wouldn't have them in the bedroom even though she lined them up on the windowsill and I got them every Christmas and every birthday. I'd wake up during the night, see them eyeballing me and scream the place down until Dad finally shoved them all into a box and hid it in the back of the wardrobe. After that I'd stare at the wardrobe door waiting for it to open and the dolls to peep out. Such weird things, I always thought, for my mother to keep and collect. And she had them all round the house too. Each had a name, and sometimes a new one would be added and another she'd been calling Lilian, Cynthia or Helena would disappear.

Tacked onto our small living room at the back of the house was the scullery. Leading out to the yard it had a corrugated iron roof that echoed loudly when it rained. The scullery consisted of little more than a free standing cooker, a sink, and a tall, yellow Formica cupboard in which the pans were kept. The cupboard was ingenious now I come to think of it – with frosted glass doors, drawers for cutlery and a drop-down bread board. We had a larder too – for jams, pickles and cans – and a cellar. Fetching the coal up once a day was the worst job of all. At the moment it was Arthur's but when he started his paper round it would become Iddy's. I hoped, really hoped, it would never be mine.

"It'll go on for weeks yet," Connie was saying. "And then—"

"Will we get to school, Mum?" I said in-between mouthfuls.

"What did you think of our Grace last night?" Mum shouted to Connie from the scullery.

"Ooh, wasn't it a beautiful service, though?"

"Oh, yes – beautiful!"

"Mind you—"

"I know."

"That dress!"

"I know."

"Mum, will school be open today?"

Connie lit another cigarette from the stub of the one she was smoking. "You've heard about her and that Max Quinn, I suppose?"

There was a slight hesitation before my mother said, "Yes, flaunting it to all and sundry an' all. Apparently they were in th' Danby Chronicle last week – pair of 'em grinning like Cheshire cats."

Connie tapped the end of her cigarette ash into a saucer. "It's a disgrace."

"Ooh, it is an' all - carrying on with a married man."

"I'll say! And he's been seen in th' village with 'er, you know?"

"Mum, will we be able to get to school?"

Mum, who'd been clearing away the dishes up to that point, plonked herself opposite Connie and poured out a cup of tea, spooning sugar in –one-two-three – stirring and stirring, tapping the side of the cup with the spoon while the atmosphere fair crackled with anticipation, notably from my corner. Eventually she said, "His wife must know, mustn't she? What with him carrying on like that right in front of her nose—"

"She'd have to be blind not to, Viv." Connie took a deep drag on her cigarette, held the smoke in her lungs, then tilted her head back and blew it out in a long plume – all with the elbow of one arm balancing on the palm of the other – just like Lauren Bacall.

I thought, watching her, that when I grew up I'd do it just like that – smoke like a film star. Not that Connie Gibbs looked like a film star, far from it. Although only in her mid-forties she was already what my dad called an old busybody, spending her days dressed like a battle axe in rollers. Pink the rollers were, with one pinned to the very front peeping out of her headscarf. Sometimes she would still have her face cream on from the night before, and most of her teeth were missing at the sides. 'Probably just as well Jack's as vacant as a Blackpool guest house in winter', Dad used to say, 'with her for a missus. Bloody hell, a bloke needs nourishment not punishment.'

Jack had never been the same since returning from the Second World War. At his happiest in The Quarryman playing snooker or digging over his vegetable patch, Jack Gibbs wore the haunted eyes of a traumatised soldier, had been signed off work for the foreseeable, and spent a good deal of time staring at something no one else could see. He was also in possession of a hearing aid, although he rarely used it. Dad and Jack were good friends. The pair of them had rigged up the scullery at the back, with our lean-to being the envy of the street. I found out many years later they'd drilled holes using an iron-hot poker, nicked the piping and somehow fashioned a two-way electric switch. Perhaps it was because they'd been in the war together but I do remember them being very close.

"He drives a very smart car, have you seen? Mind you, apparently…" My mother glanced over at the three of us sitting quietly eating toast with our ears swivelling like radar dishes, and annoyingly lowered her voice, "He used to sell knickers in Leek before—"

"Mum! Will I be going to school?" I shouted.

My mother put her tea-cup down with a clatter. "Louise, what have I told you about butting-in to adult conversations?"

"What are you going to do with them today, Viv?"

"Oh, they'll be going to school," said Mum. "Soon as th' road's cleared."

They made sure we got to school in those days – every single day – even if we had to sit at the desks by candlelight in coats and scarves. And that particular morning a whole load of trouble was taken to make damn sure we were educated. The local farmer fetched Miss by tractor. She was late and by the time she arrived there was a queue outside in the yard, not to mention a snowball fight and several bloody noses. Then it turned out the boiler had broken but that was no barrier, either; lessons were to be given using oil lamps and we sat around a paraffin stove to keep warm, taking it in turns to read out loud.

By mid-morning, however, the day began to darken once more and fresh flakes of snow fluttered from the sky. Jumping up, we ran to the window. "It's snowing! Look everyone, it's snowing!"

It stuck and slid down window panes; softly, silently, icing the skeletal boughs of the shivering trees; and quickly covered the tracks that had only just been cleared until they were white-over once more. Not a single car passed either in or out of the village that day – a situation, although we didn't know it that would last for nearly a month more.

Finally, at three o'clock in another wave of Arctic conditions, Arthur, Iddy and I formed a chain with me in the middle, heads down – sopping mittens gripping sopping mittens – for the slippery tramp home along School Lane and down to Moody Street. The other kids had been sliding and every few steps one us would slam hard to the ground, and once you were down you got pelted with snowballs from the gang behind. My coat, hat, scarf and hair were matted with snow; my face and ears freezing pink; hips and knees bruised. Cold like that never really leaves you; locking into a childhood bank of terror along with dark cellars, ghosts and creaking wardrobe doors.

Bursting in through the back door half an hour later we were grateful to see there was a fire going and ran straight to it.

"Don't drop your wet things on the floor. Take your coats off and hang them up properly."

In our eagerness to get to the warmth we didn't immediately register the fact that Mum was home unusually early. Normally we let ourselves in and lit the fire. But after a few moments it became clear something had happened.

I remember the clothes horse to one side of the fire and steam coming off the wet clothes. And that tea had been laid out for us already; that the aunties were sitting there smoking. But there was something else different too. The wireless was on. Normally that was a treat reserved for Saturday nights when we listened to Valentine Dyal and *Saturday Night Theatre*.

"Quiet now!" My mother snapped. "There's been an incident and we need to listen."

"Mum, what's an incident?"

Auntie Flo and Auntie Connie looked grave.

"Who is it? Did you catch as who it was?" said Auntie Flo, in a low, shocked sort of voice.

My mother, ear to the wireless, shook her head impatiently.

"Mum, what's an incident?"

She turned up the volume. "Shush, Louise. A woman's gone missing. Quiet!"

"Who's gone missing?"

"Shush, Louise!"

I didn't understand what the man with the clipped, urgent sounding voice was saying, but after he'd finished, she switched the wireless off and said, "Well, I never!"

"What?" I said. "What's happened?"

"Who's gone missing?" Arthur said.

"'Ou'd 'ave 'ad a devil of a job in weather like that," said Auntie Flo.

"'Ou must be dead. 'Ou's got to be."

My mother never spoke the local dialect in front of us. She'd been educated at Danby Grammar along with Auntie Marion and Auntie Rosa. The only time she ever used it was to her 'coven' as dad called them, and even then only if she thought we weren't listening. So this, instinct told me, must be very serious indeed.

"What do you mean by, 'dead,' Mum?"

"'Er might've holed up somewhere and then–" said Auntie Connie.

"It were raw out," said Auntie Flo. "Nobody could survive that. Even Crocker up there on th' moors. God knows how he survives at th' best of times, I dunna."

Mum was standing by the back window now, looking out at the yard with a hand over her mouth, just staring, talking as if to herself. "I knew it. I said…Didn't I? I said—"

"Mum, what do you mean by 'dead'?"

Abruptly, she swung round. "Louise, go to the table and eat your tea. All of you, get your tea eaten this instant."

We didn't have to be told twice.

"No more than three slices and that's all the dripping we've got. Then you can get ready for bed, Louise. Arthur and Iddy - get your chores done and then you can go too."

It was four o'clock.

***

I was bawling my eyes out being packed off to bed so early, but Arthur and Iddy were sent up soon after so that helped.

The bedroom was like an igloo and dark already. The only form of light came from the dazzling white expanse outside. It seemed to shine through the curtains like a full moon. And although a watermark had stained the flocked wallpaper from decades of damp, a new high tide was reached that night. Snow spattered and flurried against the window pane and icy water drip-drip-dripped from the guttering. Sparsely furnished, there was one large, old walnut wardrobe between the three of us and a matching chest of drawers – a relic from better days, said my mother – and an old cast-iron fireplace with a tiny grate. The flue was blocked with birds' nests, which was why it wasn't lit, and so the only way to keep warm was to put a heated brick in the bed and then stay there.

Arthur, trailing up behind me, boots clomping up the wooden stairs, angrily threw the cloth-wrapped brick into the bed. "Four o'bloody clock in the bloody afternoon," he said.

"You're not supposed to swear, our Arthur," Iddy said.

"Shuddup, you."

Iddy and Arthur were always fighting. And they kicked and punched each other in bed too with me getting the occasional stray fist. "Stop it, you two."

"Shuddup, Louise."

"Yeah, shuddup, Louise."

Despite Iddy always arguing and fighting with Arthur, he still copied him and ganged up on me whenever he got the chance.

"Ah, look, now she's crying. Cry-baby, Louise!"

A sudden thump sounded on the ceiling from the floor below. Mum with her broom handle. "Be quiet up there. Get to bed this minute or your father will be up when he gets home and then…"

We jumped in fully dressed, fighting over the warm bit where the brick had settled.

After a few minutes, Arthur said, "I'm not a bit bloody tired."

"I'm not," said Iddy.

"I'm not," I said. "Who is it who's gone missing anyway? I don't understand why we've got to go to bed just because someone's gone missing."

"It's because of th' weather," Arthur said. "Nobody could survive out there. They're saying a woman's dead. She'd 'ave frozen to death."

"But who?"

"All blue and purple with icicles hanging out of her nose," said Iddy.

"What do you mean, frozen to death?" I wanted to know. "And who's Crocker?"

"It means she's turned into ice but when she gets warmed up her skin cracks and then her eyes snap open, and then she grabs you by the neck with her long, bony fingers and then she sucks out your blood so she can live again and then she turns into a vampire and then—"

"Shuddup, Iddy," said Arthur.

"And her eyes are all red and she comes for children at night when they're asleep—"

"Shuddup, yer cloth 'ead or I'll punch yer."

They started fighting again after that, but I must have fallen asleep because I don't remember anything else from that night. Just the stillness; an air of something bad having happened, a sadness, and that in some way it was connected to us.

It was to be a long time yet, though – well, three weeks to be precise – before any of us found out what it was. And even then we had difficulty believing it.

***

Chapter Eleven
1908
Annie Bailey

Annie Bailey wandered away from Castle Draus where the crowd still lingered excitedly, and began to pick her way across the moors towards Gallows Hill, from where she would make her way down to the old church.

Watched by her two daughters, Agnes and Ellen, she cut a solitary figure, with long, black Victorian skirts flying around her like the ragged wings of a raven. Although mourning for the late Queen Victoria had long since passed, Annie had embraced the fashion in all its gothic darkness and kept it, wearing well the sombre memory of death and perhaps relishing the wariness she elicited. You didn't cross Annie Bailey, came the whispered advice. There was little, if any, evidence to substantiate this fear, but generally speaking people heeded the warning; intuition cautioning against eye contact. There was something, they said, strange and unsettling about the sallow-skinned widow who lived on the edge of the moors with her two daughters.

No one quite knew where Annie originally hailed from. She had exceptionally dark eyes and jet-black hair shot through with an auburn streak – in marked contrast to that of local folk with their wan, weather-beaten complexions and predominantly light brown or fair hair. Small and wiry, her facial features were also unusual, being in possession of a hawkish beak of a nose, underneath which her thin lips sneered and twitched at the slightest vexation. Local history suggested one of two possible theories as to her lineage. Either she was of Saracen descent – it was well known that local men had fought in the Crusades and returned with Arab captives who had then gone on to farm the land – or she'd arrived with a family of Romanian gypsies. Either way, with a muscular, sinewy physique and long, bony fingers, she was both a capable worker and a gifted healer. She had always found work and never shied from it.

Twenty-three years she had been here now, arriving in Ludsmoor already pregnant with Agnes, from who knew quite where? At the time the village gossip had been vicious and the ungodly woman shunned; but a local man, a widowed sheep farmer by the name of Jed Bailey, had stunned the entire community by marrying her within weeks of her arrival, resolutely claiming the child as his own.

Tongues sharpened. 'Had the foreigner not been with child when she first came here? Had they not all clapped eyes on her at least five months gone and maybe more? It was a scandal. And she'd been seen selling ribbons and buttons at the roadside, no better than a common gypsy beggar. Yet here she was on a wet miserable day in January, just back from Leek Register Office clutching Jed Bailey's arm, and didn't she look like the cat that got the cream? Now a respectable farmer's wife with her own cottage on Wish Lane, was she? Well, she could think again because they'd be buggered if they invited that one in for tea and biscuits, and that was a fact.'

A quiet fury gripped the village: Jed Bailey, a handsome, strong-boned man with a thriving farm, had been widowed for less than a year. It wasn't decent. And besides, there were far more deserving and considerably prettier women in the village. Scurrying past her in the street with their heads down, local women managed to pretend for years that she didn't exist. Where had the strange-looking incomer hailed from anyway? Blown in on an ill-wind that was for sure.

A year later, though, Annie bore another child – this one fair and as different to little Agnes as it was possible to be. Where the first girl mirrored her mother in looks, the second was flaxen haired with the lighter, hazel eyes of her father, and a skin that flushed pink in the fresh northern winds.

Six months after that, however, Annie was a widow.

'She'd poisoned him,' they said. 'Aye, and no doubt worth more dead than alive with his life insurance.' Whispers and rumours were exchanged swiftly over walls and washing lines, from back doors to kitchens, and from pew to pew on Sundays.

Jed Bailey had been a big man – physically robust – yet look how grey and gaunt he'd become of late? How hollow-eyed. Oh, those eyes were haunted such as they'd never seen...And how his clothes hung from his flesh and the skin sagged from his bones... like a scarecrow he was, and all since he'd wedded that witch. Because a witch is what she was and no mistake. Jed never used to miss a Sunday in church yet ever since she showed up he'd not once crossed the threshold, even to baptise his girls. 'Oh, and hadn't she got it all sewn up nicely? Jed's crippled son, Bill, did all the hard work – living up on the moors in that shepherd's hut just a child himself – while she kept the tithed cottage on Wish Lane, taking in sewing and reading palms. Not that they personally had their palms read. No, but they'd heard she made poultices and some silly girls went to her for love potions. 'Oh no, really?' 'Oh, yes...apparently...'

Annie had not remarried, but quietly remained in the cottage bringing up her daughters; keeping a low profile and avoiding further speculation, notably about the rights to the farm cottage. There were ways, of course, of giving folk precisely what they wanted; and ways of reflecting straight back any spite sent her way. Eventually the people came to know that, to understand. Given time.

Twenty-three years it had been thus, but now change was coming... and coming far more quickly than expected.

With her head down against the sharp, spring breeze Annie hurried down Gallows Hill towards the Church of England on the east side of Ludsmoor. There would have been very few in the congregation today and those who had been present would have long since gone home. With luck she would have it to herself.

Ludsmoor Church had stood on the corner where Gallows Hill met Hilltop Road for as long as anyone could remember. Originally a Saxon construction of stone and mud, one wall of herringbone masonry had been preserved down the ages, along with two triangular headed windows and a tower topped with a simple bell-cote. This was all that remained of its medieval origins however, with various improvements added piecemeal over the years and the walls now made of sturdy stone and mortar. Typically gothic additions were the ornate spire adorned with gargoyles at the four corners of the tower; an arched doorway – again with gargoyles either side – and stained glass windows. It was said that during the Civil War, Cromwell's men had blasted much of the church away including the stained glass, the fragments of which had been preserved by the local vicar and later painstakingly replaced in its original form.

The grey stone walls were now smoothly polished from years of being pelted with wind and rain, and the hall attached to the side seemed disproportionately large for the few who still attended. Now it rattled with emptiness – every cough or wrong note echoing self-consciously. It seemed to many that the church was something of a tomb for the Danby family – a relic from days gone by. In a recess at the back lay a large sarcophagus, built for one of the Crusading knights in the eleventh century. Above it, his crest, gauntlet and spurs were still on display along with a brass plaque to commemorate his bravery. The Danby Coat of Arms and tablets dedicated to various family members adorned the church at every turn. Even the eleventh century coffin lids, now a row of six stone benches outside, bore the distinctive deer figures carved along the sides - a feature predominant on their Coat of Arms.

One or two of the more recently dug graves had fresh flowers laid across them, but Annie was heading for the north side of the churchyard, passing her late husband's headstone on the way without so much as a twitch. This was what local's referred to as the Devil's Side and not for 'decent people'– a comparatively neglected part of the graveyard where the boiler house was situated and the masonry left to crumble. Passing wind-buffeted headstones with indecipherable inscriptions – many for children – she walked through unkempt grass sprinkled with dandelions towards the yews at the far end: to where her own family had been buried in unmarked graves.

Tonight, that damn boy had said, they'd be here making plans to build the new chapel. So then, there was no time to lose. She must quieten her mind and focus.

***

Chapter Twelve
Annie – continued…

She lay on the ground amongst quivering clumps of long grass and bundles of late snowdrops, gazing up at a sky brisk with scudding clouds. Under her back the earth was hard from a long, dry winter, and a gentle skein of mist blew over the headstones. In shafts of sunlight daffodils shivered, and crows cawed from nearby treetops. She closed her eyes, soothed by the sheen of soft spring rain on her skin, drifting through layers of consciousness. Hours passed. Until all at once the answer came.

Thank you, thank you. The corners of her lips lifted and her eyes snapped open. *What a delicious and most perfect execution of revenge. Oh, it had been a long time coming but now, oh yes, now she saw the ancient ones had their way of doing things, and patience had paid off. How strangely these things worked.*

Her thoughts darkened, tunnelling excitedly with her prize like a worm through dirt, gathering together all the slights, insults and injustices hiding in every crevice and every corner of her memory - all the better for the power needed. Yes, the time had come. Indeed, what had at first seemed like more doom was in fact a gift from the dark angel himself, in the form of that puffed-up cockerel of a boy. Like a picked sore he had reminded her… disinterring a long-buried injury. How dare he present Odin's Tree as a generous gift of land from the Danbys! How dare he whip up a frenzy of hatred towards all that had gone before!

Pity him, though, oh yes pity him, for he had no notion of the wolf he fed inside her and of what would soon pay him a visit.

The oldest religion had served the people of this village well, had it not? Albeit under cover of darkness the people, almost all of them at one time or another, had come to her in their hour of need and gone away satisfied with the results. Despite going to church the locals possessed an intertwining of beliefs, weaving a blend of Christianity and Paganism to suit themselves, a practice that harmed no one. Only the churchgoing was public, however. Still, the two systems had co-existed down the ages and nothing had ever been outwardly proclaimed against it. Until now. And now it seemed clairvoyance, herbal remedies and love spells were evils to be trounced into the ground. By him! Who the hell did he think he was? Rage curled her fingers into claws that drew blood from her palms. But most of all - what hurt the most, the sword plunged into the very soul of her being - was the plan to wrench from the ground that beautiful, ancient tree; to hack off its branches and axe the trunk. Thinking about it, seeing it happen in front of her as a deed already done, her own blood vessels seared with the pain of gnarled and twisted roots hewed and yanked from the earth; the howling resistance of mandrake roots and all the screeching agony of bottled, stuck and buried curses released from centuries of darkness.

Oh yes, he knew where to build alright – and not just for those reasons. He knew where the power was. *How did he know?*

No answers came. But he did, and he wanted it for himself.

Well then… by the devil himself he would be cursed to hell for this. He should know since clearly he believed in their power, that if witches can foretell futures and proffer cures, they can damn well hex too.

As she lay there lost in her mind, what had been a light drizzle had now become a curtain of fine rain that swept across the fields, turning the earth to mud, dripping steadily from the yews, trickling from the mouths of gargoyles and pooling onto the church path. The day was rapidly draining of light, low cloud brooding over the moors and tumbling into the valley below. Yet even as a cold breeze blew up and the shower intensified, Annie continued to lie silent as the dead, the movement of her lips barely discernible as deliberately and determinedly she formed her intentions.

***

Odin's Tree was as ancient as the village itself, depicted in centuries-old etchings. No one knew exactly when the old oak had acquired the title, but hearsay dictated it was named as such because that's where highwaymen, vagabonds and murderers were strung up and left to swing by the neck, after which they were disembowelled and their throats were cut – fresh blood spraying, saturating and sinking into the ground. The muscular, contorted trunk gave the impression it had firmly knuckled itself down over the years, its great roots resembling a neck jutting with protruding jugulars; the gnarled and knotted limbs so contorted and distinctive they called it, 'Old Man Odin'.

That there had been human blood spilled there, soaking through to its underground chambers, was not lost on the locals. On a winter's night, with its blackened branches sharp as toothpicks silhouetted against a stormy sky, one or two folk, usually those lumbering out of The Quarryman, had sworn they'd seen a decomposing corpse dangling from a noose. There were others, though, mostly those whose ancestors had worked the land for centuries, who said the tree's history could be traced even further back. And then there were those, like Annie, who already knew it could, no matter that occasional artefacts had been found which backed up the theory. The tree's spiritual imprint was clear if you could see these things. Oh, there had been blood spilled there alright, and not just from hanging vagabonds.

The whole area had once been the site of a violent battleground during the Civil War – a war that raged between King Charles I supporters and the Roundheads for several years. And here in remote rural Britain, half way between Leek and the west coast of England, one of the bloodiest battles of all had taken place: in rows of three, men were lined up eyeball to eyeball to fire muskets directly at each other. Cavaliers trampled over heads and bodies indiscriminately on charging horses; and twelve to eighteen foot long pikes were used to impale assailants. As soon as the front lines were down, more men surged forwards to take their place, and in the end tens of thousands had perished in one blood-soaked battle in just one afternoon. What brought it to an end was a cannon loaded with local stone that blasted through the castle walls and then into the battle field. Afterwards, hundreds of corpses – both men and beast – lay in the muddy field for days on end, as the rain came down and washed away the blood, which ran in scarlet rivulets down, down, down into the roots of Odin's Tree; sucked into mud that fed the mandrake, the hardy grass, the sheep, and those with wildly furtive imaginations.

A tiny nerve underneath Annie Bailey's left eye began to twitch involuntarily.

Betrayal, ingratitude, weakness and fear. They were full of it. Those same women, who had stood on the moors this very morning singing praise to the Lord and demanding a chapel, were the same ones who'd come to her in the dead of night. And yet none of them had said a damn word when Aaron Danby 'generously donated' the land on which Odin's Tree stood, so that 'all the wickedness that had gone before could be eradicated and trampled into the ground'. As if the sanctimonious cock believed he was the last word in divine purity; that in his self-appointed position as preacher he presumed the right to dictate what God wanted. How the hell did he know what God wanted? How did any of them – these men in robes who told the rest of them what to do?

Her lips moved faster. But she forced his pious face from her mind, storing the energy for later; and began to concentrate first on the tree. On what was there. On what was buried beneath in the rich, fertile earth along with the twisted bodies of mandrake root - all the little phials of brain, bone, hair and herbs; the love potions that got those women what they wanted; and the curses and death spells burned in oil. Not least, of course, the special one she'd cast for her late husband, Jed - the God-fearing man who had no conscience when it came to pummelling her with his fists on a regular basis, no matter if she was lying asleep or up feeding one of the infants when he rolled in from The Quarryman reeking of ale. She smiled a little. That one had worked pretty well, had it not? But the smile faded quickly. Every single spell had been carefully worked at particular times of the lunar calendar, each as individually designed as the other. Hundreds of them and not only from herself but from those who had gone before. From The Four...Agnus, Meg, Elizabeth and Anne...Their wrath would surely be incited now, too? And they would help her; would come when she summoned Hecate. They were here now, spirits rustling in the green breeze...How many secrets and spells lay beneath that tree? Thousands? Oh, but the blood of life that ran beneath it, the pulsing, telluric power that belonged to them and them alone - that it would now be Aaron Danby's...

Of course, she would not be able to prevent this desecration. No one would prevent it – especially those pathetic and desperate creatures who had come to her because no doctor could help them with what they had – the inability to conceive or the heartache of unrequited love. Oh, how the poor wretches had snivelled into their snotty handkerchiefs, sitting in her tiny front room, eyes downwards, cheeks aflame, as they asked for a magic potion to give them what they desired. *Magic potion*. How silly they felt uttering the words. *No one must know...oh, and how he or she would kill them if they found out...*

Annie's features contorted into a sneer of disgust. These same women were the ones who crossed the street to avoid her. Oh, but how they must have this chapel now they had secured what they wanted: standing in the pews with hymn books and hats, holding the hands of the children nature did not care whether or not they had. She gripped the tiny stones in the earth until her nails began to impale the beds from which they grew, a shock of raw pain tracking up her arm. There was a place in Grytton Forest on the same line as Odin's Tree that would suit her purpose – a beautiful, spiritual spot imbued with the power of water – where The Four were buried. She often visited it for clarity of vision but certain forces guarded the magnetic field and she had only once been allowed into its powerful centre. The Four were with her now, though. And already she could feel her feet carrying her there. It was time. For this was not a simple love spell but a binding hex.

Agnes would make Aaron Danby a fine wife, would she not? Undoubtedly he would prefer to marry a well-to-do girl from the Gentry but that was not what he'd be getting.

Suddenly Annie's eyes flew open in alarm.

More time had passed than she realised.

Murmured voices had roused her from meditation and she jumped up. Several black-cloaked figures were rapidly approaching the church – no doubt in order to prepare for tonight's meeting?

Darting behind a large headstone she crouched low, the grim afternoon and darkly bowing yews shadowing her presence.

Flanking the local vicar as they walked up the path were Aaron and Edward Danby. Her black eyes sparked with a hatred so all-consuming their fate was almost sealed there and then. But not quite. There was much to prepare yet.

***

Chapter Thirteen
1951
Louise

Once, after a particularly harrowing night terror, my mother told me I could and should learn to control them. These were irrational fears without foundation, she explained, and it was possible to tell myself not to be afraid: all children had bad dreams but unlike me they didn't feel the need to scream the house down. It began to occur to me then, through the fog of childhood that she was trying to shut me up, and by telling me I'd be taken away as a mad girl she accomplished this pretty effectively. In all my years I never told a soul about the things I instinctively knew without ever being told, or when I first started to see and hear things that weren't there.

The nightmares and visions started soon after that night my brothers and I had to spend the night at Grandma Ellen's down at Lake View. The boys were put in the bedroom next to Auntie Marion's at the front and never saw or heard anything untoward; but I was at the back in the room next door to Grandma. It must have been autumn because I remember the walk down to the house after school. We were kicking up leaves on a bonfire-scented afternoon and a low sun was slanting through the trees. To the left of us lay Grytton Forest, which we were under strict orders not to enter, but to continue down the lane in full view of any passers-by and go straight to Lake View Villa.

It was deeply tempting to defy instruction. The woods, we had heard, were both ancient and haunted; and hidden deep within them was a magic pond with five pure white stepping stones that if crossed without getting wet would take you to another land – a world without parents. Of course you had to appease the goblins that guarded the holy well, and you had to take no notice of the wood sprites and the evil fairies. All three of us looked across longingly at the leaves, spread like a lavish golden cloth chequered with light and shade, gently rustling between the trees.

"Pixies and elves live in there," said Iddy.

"No they don't," said Arthur.

"Yes, they do. Fairies live in the grass and sit on the rocks. They spin dresses out of cobwebs, and the elves have boats made of leaves that they fish from on the magic pond."

"How do you know all that, our Iddy?"

"I've seen them, Lou."

"No, you haven't," Arthur scoffed. "You saw it in a book and that's not the same thing."

"Can we go and see if we can see them now?" I said. "Please? Arthur, please!"

"No." Arthur quickened his pace in the dying light. He was, of course, as the eldest, responsible for getting us to Grandma's safely and on time. Dad would be phoning from the funeral parlour at bang on half past four to make sure we'd arrived with no dallying.

A stirring of excitement was fizzing between the three of us. We'd been to the big house many times, sat outside on the grass, played on the tree swing, paddled in the lake and been given tea; but never stayed overnight, and we were always accompanied by one or both parents. This was a huge adventure. The main draw, though, was the lake. A vast expanse, it mirrored the shimmering oaks along its scalloped edge and rippled darkly on the horizon. Grytton Mere, however, was not a natural lake but a flooded valley, which had once housed an entire village. They said that during one long, dry summer the water level fell so low the church spire had spiked clean out, and when the dawn mists lifted the bells could be heard ringing out in a funereal toll. In fact, many swimmers vowed never to dive into its depths again for fear of further encounters with the long-drowned dead reputed to haunt its depths. Everyone had a story to tell about the ghosts of Grytton Lake.

We rounded the bend at the bottom of the hill and tramped up the drive, school satchels weighing heavily with overnight clothes and books from class. Bordered with rhododendrons and laurels, the driveway eventually veered to the left for Lake View Villa and to the right for Spite Hall. Spite Hall was far bigger than my grandma's house; a mansion as elaborate as you can imagine with turrets and verandas. You could only see it properly from the opposite side of the lake, shrouded as it was by high walls, shrubs and trees – not to mention an imposing wrought iron gate. My mother's cousin lived there, although we'd never been invited, and their boys went to a private school in Danby. I never met them. They didn't even go to Chapel.

As far as I can remember the rest of the afternoon passed uneventfully. It never occurred to any of us children that such a big house with so many bedrooms stood almost empty while we slept three to a room in our cramped terrace on Moody Street – we were just excited to be there and especially on our own with separate beds. I had never had my own room before and there suddenly was the pure heart-lifting joy of silence. No boys! I shut the door, ran to the window seat and sat there for ages with my knees drawn up to my chest, just staring out at the fiery blaze of an autumn afternoon, and the shadows stealing across the lawn at the end of a God-given day. Far away, from its secret place in the woods, came the sonorous echo of a wood pigeon and I wished with all my heart and soul that the moment would stretch into forever.

In their room across the landing my brothers were playing conkers, but it was a distant provocation and I had the door firmly shut, content to sit and dream – making up stories in my head about how one day I would live in a turreted castle with a view of a softly rippling lake; and how beautiful I would be when I grew up. My hair would be piled on top of my head in shiny, black coils studded with diamante; my red lips would be full, and my eyes feline green. My dress, of course, would be a long, emerald ball gown cut very low indeed because I'll be going out dancing. I'll be wined and dined, and everyone will stare when I walk into the room. Oh, and my bedroom would be just like the one at the front of the house that used to be Grandma Ellen's, with a balcony and a dressing room and a four poster bed.

Not for me a cluttered, sunless back bedroom that stinks of cooking and rattles with street noise. Not for me a damp terrace with condensation running down the windows. No pegging out washing in a cobbled back yard, no scrubbing net curtains until my knuckles bleed and definitely no sweaty, back-breaking factory work. No, you see I did not want to be who I was cut out to be. Not at all.

"Louise? Louise, sweetie!" A soft tap and then Auntie Marion came in.

She was so different to my mother, hovering in the doorway to tell me dinner was ready instead of yelling up the stairs. I wondered why we were having dinner at night time but then that's what they called it. They had luncheon at dinner time and dinner at tea time. And it wasn't bread and pickles either, but soup followed by chops and potatoes.

At the time, none of us wondered why these women, who seemed so pleased to have us stay the night, chose to live in such isolation, especially once the other house was built – the one that took away all their light. I just recall the simple pleasure of being in the large kitchen at the back of the house that evening, with the cast-iron range churning out heat while I played with little milk bottles, dressing them up as dolls with remnants of material. Grandma Ellen had endless boxes of ribbons and buttons– in every colour you could imagine – and as a skilled seamstress was the first to show me the rudiments of dressmaking. I learned how to tack and how to do cross stitch that night; and how to play gin rummy.

It's funny but I don't remember either of my aunties being around much after dinner. But I do remember Snow. Of course! She's seared on my memory and always will be. It must have occurred to me when tiredness began to weigh down my eyelids that we were about to spend the night in the same house as her.

All evening she'd sat in a corner pretty much unnoticed, flicking a ball with a piece of string. Over and over and over. Rocking back and forth she had her back to us, murmuring and mumbling – this great lump of a woman dressed in short, zipped slippers and thick, tan stockings that collected in folds around her ankles. Although she wore the ubiquitous flowery pinafore over a dark green sweater and skirt, and her hair had been tied back, her appearance elicited a sickening lurch to the stomach. You see, from behind she looked like an old woman – a fat, old woman with long, knotty white hair – and that was what you expected to see when she turned round. Only she was not old at all. And when she sensed you looking, her head would suddenly tilt to one side and the humming cease. Then before you knew it she was charging across the room. I saw those hands balled into great fists more than once, and felt the thunder in the floorboards. But on previous visits I'd been shielded by my mother or my dad. I'd never been alone and exposed to her before.

Snow was an albino and we mustn't stare, Mum said; it simply meant the absence of colour in her hair and eyes. But it wasn't that which gave you the fright. It was her expression. There was nothing serene about it. Either she was gazing at something a million miles away or directly into your soul. And when she did that you wished she hadn't because it made your insides flip, like you'd been defiled in some way, as if she had burrowed into your mind and rubbed dirt into it – a slow, malicious grin cracking open her vacuous, pudding face. Mum said that once she'd thrown a grown man across the room with one hand. She said she should be in an asylum, apparently, but Marion said there was nothing wrong with her and so there it was.

That night we were lucky, though. Snow flicked the ball, rocked back and forth, and mumbled to herself. She didn't turn around once and we played cards until late.

But after the candles had been lit and hot bricks put into the beds, I started to wonder if Snow would wander around the corridors at night, and if she would come into my room to hurt me. As the time drew nearer to go to bed and a pan of hot milk was on the range for cocoa, I stared hard at Grandma Ellen.

"What is it, Louise?"

Still I stared, not knowing how to phrase the question.

"Louise, you've got something to say so what is it?"

I banged my feet together, lips pressed tightly, looked down at the table.

"Spit it out, Louise."

"Does Snow get out of her room at night?"

There it was done.

Three pairs of eyes looked at Grandma Ellen for an answer. At least Arthur and Iddy had each other. I'd be on my own.

A moment or two elapsed before Grandma Ellen nodded. Then after a quick glance over her shoulder she leaned forwards and whispered, "Snow has something to help her sleep through the night, don't worry."

I often think about that. I think about how those three women coped with Snow and how they managed to get those tranquilisers for her; but I'm guessing they had little choice. All I knew, at the age of six, was that I felt the uncomfortable prickle of fear that night for the first time in my life; fear of the dark, of the unknown, of a creaking old house, and of a mad woman who could crack my neck like a nut if I so much as looked at her the wrong way.

The house had a generator. One of the first in the area to have electricity at all – many of the farms and cottages still had only one main lightbulb – and even more unusually it had a telephone. Located in the hallway, the sisters had it installed because of Grandma Ellen's 'dottiness.' I never found her dotty. Not one bit. That evening she led me by the hand up the stairs, read me a story and kissed my forehead. And within minutes of her closing the door I was fast asleep, all my worries vanishing with the flick of a light switch. For a few blessed hours anyway.

Fear… Well, I didn't feel real fear – out and out terror – until later that night, and after that it never stopped.

You can control it.

But what if your dream is not a dream even though people keep telling you it is? What if it's real? Only no one will ever admit to you that it's real? Well, then it becomes a nightmare. No, more than that… it becomes a night *terror*. And that, I believe, is what I experienced during all my years as a child from that night on.

I woke, you see, to the sound of a baby crying. Now, there was no baby in that house. I knew that full well. I had no concept of the time, except it was tomb-black and cold enough to see my breath on the air. And a baby was wailing, it's cry plaintive and miserable. For a long time I lay completely motionless, listening. It seemed to be coming from outside the bedroom window. My first thought was that there must be a baby in the garden, and it seemed to be getting more and more upset; impossible to ignore. After a while I threw back the covers and padded over to the window, parted the curtains and peered outside.

An ethereal mist hovered over the lawn. The stone fountain seemed starkly white under what was a full moon, and by contrast the forest so much blacker than I remembered.

Squinting into the murky dawn, I tried to work out where the baby's crying was coming from but couldn't see anything. It's wailing was escalating, becoming increasingly desperate. The woods then? I stared hard in that direction, ears straining. Yes, the woods...

And it was then, as my eyes focused on the dark perimeter, that I saw at first one, then more – *one, two, three, four* - tiny figures dwarfed by the towering trees behind; swathed entirely in black. Just standing there. Staring at the house.

***

Chapter Fourteen
Harry Whistler – Louise's father

Harry Whistler was pretty shaken up and he didn't scare easily.

Whistler's Funeral Parlour was situated at the far end of Moody Street on the T-Junction with School Lane. The tan-painted shop front had a net curtain strung across the lower half of the window; and in the yard at the back stood the hearse, alongside a Victorian horse-drawn carriage. Inside his stall, Mack, the family's grumpy black stallion, shuffled, puffed and pawed at the door; and sleet pebble-dashed the backroom window where Harry had been preparing to finish up for the day.

December had been slow for business but people got old early here, and generally speaking once Christmas was over January picked them off - ground down by hard work in their forties and either wheezing with emphysema or crippled with arthritis by the time they reached fifty. Retirement was something to be celebrated simply because so few reached it; and those in their seventies or beyond were considered 'as tough as old boots'. All of which made Annie Bailey, at ninety one, a walking miracle. Harry was sure she would be absolutely fine, snow storm or no snowstorm. Viv was worrying about nothing. Still, if she wanted him to go out there to the back of beyond and check on the old crone he'd better get a move on because another belt of snow was coming. The afternoon had darkened ominously and the wind was whipping up. He muttered under his breath.

Still, one day he'd be looking down at her in one of these coffins.

Viv usually took care of the embalming side of the business, blessed with a talent for making even the most haggard of cases look peaceful in their eternal rest. By God, she had some energy that woman – working full time, running the house, looking after the children and then coming here at nights and weekends to work in the embalming room. And to his knowledge she'd never had a sick day in her life, even taking the children to work with her during school holidays so she could continue to bring in the wages. That wasn't something he wanted for them – stuck under those long trestles in the dark inhaling dust while knives slashed along the sides. But you didn't argue when you had a nutcracker of a wife like Vivien, and besides she was right when she said they were scraping along the bottom and needed every last ha'penny. At least Arthur was old enough now to take on some funeral work – proper little undertaker he was going to make! Long limbed like his late grandfather, Aaron, he'd shouldered a few coffins already.

What a bloody awful day and it wasn't over yet.

Still in his mid-thirties, Harry's body had begun to stoop at the shoulders; his cheekbones angular ridges shadowing a somewhat lugubrious face. He suited being an undertaker, people said – looked the part as if born to it – which in many ways he was, following in the Whistler footsteps. The embalming though - no, that wasn't his favourite bit. Especially not alone in the ethereal greyness of a snow-locked January afternoon.

It had been Violet Bailey, recently deceased aged three score and ten, who had given him the heebie-jeebies.

The poor woman had passed of pneumonia according to Dr Ferguson, the local GP, but had in reality been dying for several months of pancreatic cancer. The lack of an early diagnosis could not have made much difference to her, with the understanding and treatment of the condition so inadequately treated at the local hospital; although it surely hadn't helped that Dr Ferguson had declared she should expect to feel tired at her age and her ailments were nothing a short holiday with her daughter in Scarborough couldn't fix. As it was, by the time said daughter had arrived home for Christmas, poor Violet's bones were as brittle as kindling sticks and her skin the colour of English mustard. A week later she was dead.

Not a good time of year to die, Christmas Eve. By the time he'd arrived at the family terrace Violet's body was already decomposing, and with the onerous task of removing her corpse from where it had lain since her demise, the thought occurred to him how dreadful it must have been for the family – particularly the grandchildren brought for the festivities. Violet's body was laid-out on a couch in the parlour. The mirror over the mantelpiece had been covered by a black cloth (in case her departing spirit became trapped) and a candle flickered on a small side table. Presumably the rest of the family had continued to eat Christmas cake, sleep and entertain themselves in the other room while Mother's body having first set with rigor mortis, then bloated with gasses and tissue fluids before settling into the flaccid, mottled flesh now steadily rotting into the upholstery.

Liver failure had caused the additional unpleasantness of blood-laced faecal matter, which continued to seep out even after death. The room stank so badly he'd had to cover his nose and mouth with a handkerchief, feigning a cold, to stop himself from gagging in front of the relatives. He and Jack Gibbs had carried her out feet first through the front door, as was customary, trying not to breathe. The stench of corporeal decay had clung to the entire house, a fetid odour that oozed into every corner, permeating the furnishings and coating the walls. Only the bitterly cold temperature had prevented the situation from becoming so very much worse.

Vivien though, well, Violet's decaying body hadn't fazed her one bit. In fact, Vivien had rolled up her sleeves and got straight on with the business of washing and disinfecting. She seemed to enjoy it.

Said it gave her satisfaction to make someone look nice for their funeral, so people could look at them lying there all serene and peaceful before the Service. But as it turned out, even she had been sorely challenged with this one. The funeral was booked for Wednesday if they could get the hearse out. If not, they'd have to use the horse and carriage, something he'd kept on from his dad's day and occasionally came in handy. Some folk actually preferred the slow dignity of the horse-drawn carriage and he didn't blame them for that. It wasn't a day to rush. Not your last day.

Time however, was running out for Violet Bailey's corpse.

The problem was that not only had she been left far too long after death, but that disease had already wasted her body. The skin was so papery thin it broke with the slightest of touches, and tore a little more with every attempt to massage in the embalming fluid. When Vivien punctured Violet's femoral artery to inject the formaldehyde mixture the needle had shot straight through and out the other side, leaving an open zip of ripped skin in its wake. Eventually though, she'd managed to inject enough to lift the colour of the skin to a waxy lemon. Still it hung from the bones, sagged into crevices and seeped fluids; and despite the copious use of disinfectant, soap and talc, and blocking orifices with cotton wool, the stink of putrefaction pervaded the entire building. The sickly stench of death. It got into their nostrils, coiled itself around their tongues and slid down their throats.

After many hours of work, Vivien eventually conceded defeat and decided to use a plastic sheet. In all her years, she told Harry, she had never once had to resort to this and it displeased her greatly, but even she had little option: the relatives had to be presented with a person they recognised and she, Vivien Whistler, was not going to be gossiped about as having proved inept. All of which was why Violet's entire lower body had been encased in plastic, her favourite dress pulled over her head and then her ankles clipped together. In haste, Vivien had popped cloth underneath the sunken eyelids, stuffed the toothless mouth with cotton wool and finally sewed the lips together. By then, however, the weather was deteriorating rapidly, there was Chapel next day, and she'd had enough. Marching home, she threw her coat across the back of the sofa and told Harry he'd have to finish the job.

So there he was on a Monday evening, and after a full workload he'd still to fix Violet's hair and make-up before the family visited tomorrow. In fairness and after a night's sleep, Vivien did say she would have come back to do it if she hadn't to trek down to Grytton this morning to check on her mother. And on top of that the children had been sent home early from school on account of the weather. But it wasn't a big job and had been his last before finishing up.

Violet Bailey's remains, however, had still looked ghastly, especially under the oily glow of the lamp. The facial skin had markedly disintegrated in less than a day and now oozed fishy slime. The slightest pressure and his finger punctured it further. In vain he tried to recall how she used to look but could not for the life of him conjure up an image of where or when he'd last seen her alive. Thus, with the acrid stench constantly hitting the back of his throat, he tied a handkerchief around his face and got on with the task, praising the Lord she couldn't see and be offended.

Wind soughed under the window frame, and a feeling of being utterly alone crept up on him, as slowly and methodically he worked as delicately as possible. It had been a while since he'd done this, using wax, applying rouge to cheeks and lips, brushing hair, spraying perfume, packing the casket underneath so the body looked fuller. Oh, there were lots of tricks but still nothing that could transform this festering corpse into anything that resembled what had once been Violet Bailey.

In the end he took off his gloves and threw them into the bin. No one could do more. And had been about to close the casket lid when the lamp snuffed out.

That was odd.

The electricity had been cut off since last night but this was paraffin. Puzzled, he walked over to the desk to fetch his torch and returned to the casket. But just as he was about to close the lid something feathery brushed against the back of his neck and he swung around, letting it drop with a slam into the frame.

The room was now utterly dark.

He shone the torch into every corner, sweeping the light over the coffins. Six in a row. All of them with the lids closed.

A prickle of unease crawled up the nape of his neck and he backed out of the room, floundering for the door handle. Once he had hold of it he shot through and pulled the door shut, turning the key with a firm click. Shivers goosed up and down his arms. Nothing like that had ever happened to him before. Nothing. It was as if a fear hitherto unknown had suddenly found him.

Once outside in the street, Harry's claustrophobic terror instantly dissipated. The icy coldness felt wonderful and he lifted his face to the falling snow, inhaling lungful after lungful of sobering fresh air. *What in God's name had happened back there?* He squeezed his eyes shut tightly, trying to make sense of the incident, waiting for his heart to steady. *Bloody hell, my hands are still shaking.* But after a minute or so the arctic chill forced him to start walking and besides, he'd not had much sleep last night thanks to Vivien. Maybe it was just that he was tired then? Imagination playing tricks or something? Anyway, there were still the old witches to check on or Viv would play merry hell, so best get it over with. Frankly, though, a shot of whisky right now would be a hell of a lot more preferable. He shook his head. *Bloody hell, though, bloody hell… Talk about shaken up…* Perhaps a little detour to The Quarryman? God knows he needed it and she'd never know.

Moody Street, cleared only this morning, was once again white over; and snowflakes spiralled from the sky. Blinking at the wintry scene like an animal emerging from an underground lair, he marvelled at the depth of it. There must be a foot or more laid down already. Curtains had been drawn in every house down the street, the amber gleam of firelight escaping through the gaps. His lone footsteps creaked in the crumbly snow. What if he went straight to The Quarryman instead? Seriously, would she ever find out?

Course she bloody would. That woman's got eyes up her arse.

Right, he battled with himself, well best get this over with then maybe he could nip to the pub after – just for a quick half. There was another reason for wanting to pop into The Quarryman too. Something had come on the wireless earlier about a woman going missing in the blizzard, and there might be some who'd know more about it. He wondered who the woman was. Too much to hope it'd be Agnes, he supposed, a smirk spreading across his face. Nah, he didn't have that kind of luck. Besides, they said the devil looked after his own, so it definitely wouldn't be that old bitch.

***

Chapter Fifteen
Harry – continued...

Alders Farm stood at the end of a long track on the edge of Ludsmoor, at the point where the moors became too barren and boggy for human habitation. Isolated and uncompromising, its gritstone walls had weathered the drear, dank weather for centuries, and the pitted dirt-track down to the farm led only to the house itself with no one except the occupants or visitors to the Hollands ever using it.

Deep snow now covered the unlit lane and Harry stumbled in and out of potholes, slipping and cursing with every near fall. A raw northerly sandpapered his face with icy sleet, his hair was pasted to his skin, and cold drips trickled down his neck. The hedgerows had petered out half a mile back, leaving nothing to counter the fierce wind that rushed over the clifftops and down over the desolate plateau, flattening everything in its path. Not much survived out here – a few hardy sheep, the rawk-rawk of a lone bird on a summer's day...but there was nothing out here on a night like this...

Another half mile still to go and up to my knees. Damn and bloody blast Viv asking me to do this.

So much for getting it over with quickly and scooting off to the pub! His legs were beginning to ache and his face was numb. It wasn't until you got out here on your own, he thought, that the vast sense of space really hit you. It must be seriously lonely. God knows they were cramped on Moody Street but he could never live out here. Bent double and with the wind howling around his ears it wasn't until he got much closer that he heard the five-barred gate repeatedly banging against the drystone wall at the end of the drive. Relieved to be almost there and gasping from another belt of sleet, he secured it properly then hurried down to the house.

That was odd: there were no lights on. He flicked on the torch. Alders Farm squatted low and dark, its blackened walls gleaming wetly, the outhouses weighted with snow. The double doors to the garage were closed and there were no tyre tracks. Downstairs the curtains were open and the rooms in darkness.

Great. No one was home so he could go straight back and tell Viv he'd tried.

He made to turn around but Viv's voice chipped away in his head. *Well, did you knock? How do you know she wasn't lying dead in the yard at the back? What if she'd slipped and was knocked unconscious? You'll have to go back, I'd never forgive myself...*

Harry sighed. It was a long, long time since he'd been here and the place didn't feel any less hostile. If he never saw it again it would be too soon. Well perhaps he should knock on the door and then at least he could honestly say he'd done all he could?

Eyeing the front steps packed with several inches of untrodden snow, however, he hesitated. A person could break their neck on those. On impulse he looked up and scanned the bedroom windows. *Someone's inside watching me.* All the curtains were drawn upstairs and the house stood dimly silent yet there had been, he was sure, a fleeting movement from within. For several more minutes he stared intently at the upstairs windows but no, it must have been his imagination. He really must be overly tired today.

With the overriding urge to leave as soon as possible, Harry decided to have a brief scout round the back and try the kitchen door to say he'd done his duty, then he was bloody well going home. It was freezing and clearly the old crone wasn't here. She'd be at Annie's on Wish Lane. He'd call in there since it was on the way back. Well, it wasn't really but it was on route to The Quarryman.

Rounding the corner of the yard, a fresh blast of wind knocked the breath out of him and he slipped, awkwardly saving himself with the palm of his hand. Cursing loudly, he slid down to the back door, rattled the handle and rapped on the glass panel. "Agnes? It's Harry! Just checking to see as you're alright, duck!"

No answer.

Rubbing his hands together, he glanced over his shoulder at the yard. The wind whistled and whined around the outhouses. A pile of firewood lay half-chopped, the logs iced with snow. Again there came an uneasy feeling of being watched from inside the house. Was someone in there or not? Pulling his coat collar up higher, he cupped his hands and stared through the glass into the shadowy kitchen. A movement then caught his eye, so sudden it caused him to draw back sharply.

For a full few seconds he lost the power to move or think clearly. Inside his chest the anvil banging of his heart pounded into his ears. Every nerve in his body shrilled with alarm. The movement had not been from inside the house, but rather in the reflection. *So whoever had made it must be...*

He whirled around, back flat to the door and flashed the torch across the yard. The weak ray of light caught on a discarded spade, an empty wheelbarrow, bolted stable doors. But the yard was quite empty.

The second he realised nothing was there his limbs relaxed and began to shake violently. Bloody hell this place was spooky. Right, that was it, anyway. Duty done. It was time to get the hell out.

Hurriedly he retraced his footsteps. There was a bridleway half way down the track that would cut across to Annie's place on Wish Lane and then he was done. The two old hags would be there anyway, probably sitting by the fire knitting effigies. Viv was bloody going to have to make it up to him for this... *Yeah, well that would be the day.*

For some reason, and he couldn't quite say why, once safely at the end of the drive by the five-barred gate he stopped to get his breath and glanced back at the house.

One of the upstairs curtains twitched and immediately fell back. So there was someone in! Agnes or Grace? Well, they were the only two who lived there so it had to be one of them.

***

The return journey was not as arduous with the wind at his back. Not only that but it was buffeting him along as if hustling him to leave. All he had to do was make sure not to miss the turnoff for the bridleway, which could be easily overlooked if you didn't know it was there. Un-signposted, it was now also covered in snow, but he'd known the place since childhood and knew where to spot the boulder. The inscription etched on the front of the rock said, 'Wish Lane 0.3 miles' and the mystery of a hand imprinted into the granite remained just that – a mystery; but meant it was distinctive enough to be the right one.

Even to this day it still rankled with many in the village that Annie had the Wish Lane cottage at all. Jed's family had worked the land for centuries and by rights it should have been left to young Bill when his father died. Yet Crocker Bill, crippled by polio and now in his seventies, lived in a shepherd's hut up near Kite Ridge, occasionally frequenting The Quarryman and working as a gravedigger to make ends meet. Most of the time though, he stayed up there on his own. It seemed a strange and peculiarly harsh life. Not much was known about him apart from the fact he'd never gone to school, had a built-up shoe, played a neat game of snooker and never spoke to his step-mother. They said he was simple, a bit behind the door, but Harry didn't think so. Crocker Bill was smart as a brass tack. Behind those shuttered eyes he knew everything. No, he bet Bill stayed up there with good reason.

It wasn't long before the lamplight of Annie's cottage window came into view and Harry sighed with relief. A quick knock on the door and he'd be away. Job done. It should be that fat, bone-idle bugger, Vic Holland, looking out for his mother and grandmother on a night like this; but of course he'd be lording it on his fat arse down in Grytton, probably swigging a fine port by the fire. If he couldn't get the car out he wouldn't be budging. Bloody awful family he'd married into, he really had, and with a history he could never get his head round. The thing was, Annie's younger daughter, Ellen, had married brilliantly well – to Aaron Danby of all people. They should have been wealthy and set up for life. Yet it seemed the marriage had been cursed with rotten luck because first Aaron, a fit, healthy young man, had died within three years of the wedding; then Ellen had been crippled with rheumatoid arthritis and now didn't appear to know one end of the week from the next; Marion, her eldest, had been ostracised because of an illegitimate child, and now Lana had turned out to be…well to put it like everyone else did, as mad as a shithouse rat. On top of that there was the huge fall-out between sisters Agnes and Ellen, with neither ever speaking to the other again.

Was it a coincidence that Agnes' husband had also met an untimely end within a couple of years of marrying? Dr Fergusson – good old Dr Fergusson – had shaken his head, listened to the previously fit, young man's chest, and declared it was nothing a good holiday and some sea air couldn't fix. And his life insurance had, just like Annie's husband's, been considerable. For a time Harry had worried for his own longevity, but luckily it seemed Vivien was not of the same ilk as that half of her bloodline. Some wondered why he'd married Vivien at all, when she came from such a family. Why take the risk when all their husbands died? The black widows they called them. And as his own mother said, Viv wasn't exactly a looker, but a fog of confusion wrapped itself around his memory. He couldn't even recall how they'd met except she'd been in the same class at school and they'd been to the flicks once or twice. Oh yes…the night they'd walked back through Grytton Forest…ah… He laughed.

The thing was, why were these old women so embittered? You'd think Annie would have been thrilled her youngest daughter had married the richest man in the county. He scowled, not for the first time wondering what in God's name had happened to all that inherited land and wealth, because it hadn't come his way that was for sure, and those women down at Lake View Villa slept in threadbare sheets. Viv told him!

Vivien's closeness to Agnes worried him too, now he came to think of it. Viv's closeness to a lot of people worried him. And now little Louise was beginning to worry him too. Partly it was the child's growing resemblance to the coven – that dark hair with its distinctive copper stripe and the knowing eyes. But mostly it was the things she saw that weren't there – the way she'd watch something invisibly work its way across the room – and the disturbing dreams she woke the household up with in the early hours. He shuddered inside at the thought of her being enticed into this...well, not to put too fine a point on it...witchcraft; because there was absolutely no doubt in his mind they practised it and frankly, Louise's imagination was troubling enough already.

Harry clicked open the wooden gate to the cottage and was just about to knock on the front door when it flew open. Agnes stood there and his heart missed a beat. She was not an easy woman to look at. Even with the light behind her, her face seemed set to stone and her eyes burned with malice and loathing.

In the name of self-preservation he feigned concern. "Just checking as you're all alright, duck?"

She nodded. "Yes, I'm 'ere looking after Mother. What with the weather–"

Clearly she had no intention of inviting him in. He nodded and made to leave. "Right you are then, duck. I'll be off home."

"Been up to th' farm, 'ave you?"

"Aye."

"Our Grace there?"

He shrugged. "I think so. She didn't answer but I saw the curtains move so—"

She nodded. "Daft time for 'er to be in bed – keeps all hours 'er does. Anyhow, thanks all th' same. Good of you to come. Much appreciated."

She'd shut the door in his face before he had time to reply. *Ungrateful cow.* She could at least have asked him in out of bloody decency. Not that he'd have accepted but she should have asked. With a shrug, he walked back down the path, deciding that yes, stuff the lot of them, he would pop into The Quarryman for a quick pint to see what was happening. He deserved it and Viv would have to lump it.

With luck, Bill would have made it down and be able to help with grave digging tomorrow. They were going to need pick-axes to break the ground open. His mind moved onto thinking about the iron-hard earth and the task ahead. And deep in thought he'd almost got to the end of Wish Lane, about to turn onto Moody Street, when he suddenly remembered where he'd last seen Violet Bailey and his mouth dropped open.

It had been there, hadn't it? Inside Wish Lane Cottage? Bloody hell, aye…last autumn when he'd come to find Viv one Saturday afternoon. She'd taken Louise to visit Annie, 'for half an hour to play with the kittens'.

Only they'd all been there – about seven or eight of them sitting round a table in the parlour.

***

The snow was coming down thick and heavy now and the village had merged with the landscape in a cotton wool ball of white. It was probably stupid to think of tramping up to The Quarryman in this. In a moment of indecision he paused at the corner, when suddenly a dark shadow materialised from out of all the other shadows and moved rapidly towards him.

"Who—?"

He let go of his breath.

"You look like you've seen a ghost!" said Vivien. "Not thinking of hopping up to The Quarryman, were you?"

Shoving his hands deep into the pockets so she couldn't see them jumping about like marionettes, he laughed. "No, of course not. Sorry, duck, I wasn't expecting to see you there."

"I'll bet!"

"What are you doing out, anyroad? It's freezing."

"The lines are still down. I went out to th' phone box to ring Mum but there's no dial tone. Then I saw you'd locked up and thought you'd be checking on our Annie and—"

"She's fine," he said. "Who's looking after the kids?"

"They're in bed. Anyhow, look, I couldn't get down to Grytton this morning. I made it half way along Hilltop but I was up to my waist in it and 'ad to turn back. I'm just praying the road 'll be cleared tomorrow. I'm worried sick. I hope Rosa and Marion got home. Honest, I'm that worried about Mum. I don't suppose you'd be able to get down tomorrow morning, would you? What if we took Mack? Tonight?"

The two of them began to tramp back towards Moody Street. "He'd be even worse in this than us, and he needs new shoes. Look, if Ellen stayed indoors she and Lana will be fine. I think it's Rosa and Marion we need worry about myself, but I'm sure they'll be back by now. The snow makes everything take twice as long and there's no reason they wouldn't have got home eventually."

"But what if—"

"Viv, we can't go in this tonight, and the kids are on their own. Anyhow, I think I'm going to 'ave to delay Violet's funeral until we can clear the path to the church so let's see what we can do tomorrow, eh? If it stops bloody snowing for five minutes I'll get down to Grytton, I promise."

"Alright. First light tomorrow, though? I'm really worried."

"Maybe your mother could ask that lard-arsed cousin of yours next door for a bit of help?"

"I don't know why you don't like our Vic. I'm sure he'd help her out if she asked him—"

Yes, and I'm just as sure he wouldn't, Harry thought. What was wrong with that side of her family? And why couldn't Viv ever admit it?

***

Chapter Sixteen
Lake View Villa, earlier that morning
Ellen Danby

The long night fused into dawn and Ellen woke from a fitful doze at the kitchen table. Something was badly wrong, but what?

At barely five on that January morning the blackness of the kitchen seemed to have folded in from the corners and boxed her in. Panic snatched inside her chest. There wasn't a sound. Not a single stirring of movement. Blindly she stared through the window until her reflection faded away and silvery-white shapes on the lawn began to emerge – a familiar landscape... shrubs, a fountain... She rubbed at the ache in her neck. Still alive then. Still here.

But why was she in the kitchen? There was a vague recollection of drifting around the house, moving from room to room. Had that been a dream or real? The answer came rushing in with a sickening lurch: her girls, her daughters - they hadn't come home last night. *Oh dear God in heaven - this was real!*

What had happened? What? What? She searched around in the mists of her memory. They'd gone to Chapel, yes that was it, but had never returned.

She'd been to check on Snow. The girl was having one of her funny turns…but after that what had she done? She closed her eyes and tried hard to remember. It had been going dark and the girls should have been back. Was she sitting at a window last night or way back in the day when, transfixed, she'd be here in the kitchen willing them to burst out of the forest – just children – breathless and brimming with things to tell her about what had happened that day at school.

But this time they never came.

The first time….they never came…

Vivien had phoned, hadn't she? Yes, shouting into the receiver, dropping coins into a call box. "Don't cry, Mother, they're grown women and very sensible. I'm sure they'll be alright. They've only to keep warm and put one foot in front of the other. Now, 'ave you 'ad something to eat? You need to get a fire lit and make you and Lana some tea. I'll come down in the morning… Hello… hello? Oh, the line's terrible - it'll probably come down th' weather's that bad. Look, don't worry, keep warm and I'll be there soon—"

Static had crackled in her ear and after a while the only sound was that of the rafters creaking and snow flying against the windows. It must have been shortly after that she'd begun the night's vigil of walking around the house not knowing quite what to do. Iciness shivered into her skin, permeating her bones to the marrow but she found she could not rest. An ethereal whiteness from outside shone through the windows, somehow managing to make the interior seem darker; her footsteps echoing starkly as methodically, room by room, she wandered in and wandered out again.

At midnight the grandfather clock in the hall chimed twelve and abruptly she stopped pacing. Wasn't there something she was supposed to do?

Oh God, Snow...

Climbing the stairs again, her knees almost too rigid to bend, she was half in mind to go straight to her bed, so weighed down with fatigue she could have slept where she fell. But Snow's incessant humming, once she became aware of it above the noise of the storm, drew her on, further down the corridor and back to Marion's room where she had left her earlier.

As soon as she pushed open the door it was clear the girl's state of mind had worsened. So much so that Ellen stood in the doorway wide-eyed with her heart skittering in her chest. *If only Marion was here. Where was Marion? Where was Rosa? Where did they keep her pills? Could she get her to take them?*

She bit her lip and clung to the door handle.

Snow was rocking to and fro but so violently the chair seemed likely to tip over. Saliva drooled from the corner of her mouth and her eyes had rolled back in her head so far that only the whites were showing. There was a pool of urine on the floor as she ranted and raged in an unfathomable tongue;

and with every swing of the chair her head snapped from side to side like that of a plastic doll.

Paralysed with terror, Ellen's throat moved but the words lodged and stuck fast. Even if she could find Snow's pills she wouldn't be able to get her to take them when she was like this. If only Marion and Rosa would come home. What was she to do? What did her daughters do with the girl when she got like this? Should she be restrained? And did she interrupt or just leave her to exhaust herself? It occurred to her then, how shielded she had been from the severity of Snow's condition. The girls had protected her, even though she lived in such close proximity. Not only did Snow have a sedative at night but so did she. Ellen wrung her hands. *Oh dear God, what should she do? If only they would come back...*

The storm raged around the corners of the house, the metronome ticking of the clock on Marion's mantelpiece hypnotic as she inched into the room and sat on the edge of Marion's bed, wringing her hands and wondering what to do. How sheltered she had been all of these years - first by the nurses, then by her daughters. She set the lamp on the floor. This was a strange room; more noticeable when sitting here alone in the darkness. In the dim glow of the oil lamp it seemed as though Marion's paintings had begun to take on altogether different meanings. The bedroom walls were covered with her artwork – landscapes mostly – of trees, flowers and ferns, graveyards and churches, skylines, lakes and moors.

But all had something in common, and it was only when you noticed one that you noticed them all. When you looked closely a darkly shrouded face appeared. Surprised and somehow excited by the find, an observer would stoop to examine the painting more closely only to find the image was no longer there. Turn away, however, and back it came... sometimes more than one face... in the corner of an eye and almost as if trying to catch the viewer out. How Marion could sleep in this room with all these spooky paintings she didn't know. It was bad enough walking past them in the hallway or down the stairs.

Quite suddenly Snow's frenetic rocking and humming stopped dead.

Ellen gripped the quilt.

The girls' limbs had twisted into the rigidity of a lightning-struck tree, with fingers outstretched from claw-like hands. Her head had ratcheted to one side and was now stuck at an unnatural angle, her features contorted into a gargoyle grimace. But the chanting, thank God, and the rocking, had stopped. It seemed the trance or fit was finally over. And for that she was thankful.

Unable to move the girl, who seemed to have set to stone, Ellen pulled the bedspread off the bed, draped it over her and put a pillow under her head as best she could before tip-toeing from the room. What else could she do but keep her warm until the girls came back? Marion understood these seizures of Snow's but no one else did. Even Dr Fergusson, the old family doctor with his little black bag, would shake his head and advise that after a tot of brandy and some hot broth, she'd be right as rain.

There was a hiatus in memory after leaving Snow. What had she done next? She had left the room...but what then? She shook her head. No, there was nothing but a dense fog with no recollection at all of how she came to be in the kitchen slumped at the table.

At some time during the night, the storm must have abated because now there was only the soft hush of new snow. And for a while Ellen sat in silence as she tried to piece together events from the night before. In the hallway seconds ticked solidly into minutes on the grandfather clock, and it was around then that she started to notice a new sound. Something... a wailing... like a fox?

She tilted her head to one side. *No, it couldn't be...* Straining her ears into the stillness she tried to make sense of it. That wasn't a fox but quite definitely a baby crying. Well, how very odd. Perhaps she'd drifted into dreams again? Had she drifted off? It really must have been a dream because... no, wait... there it was again... And her children were missing!

Now she listened intently and with purpose. In between the dock-dock....dock-dock...of the brass pendulum in the hall... there it was again and quite definitely... a baby. The wailing child seemed closer now too - from directly outside the window, in fact.

Dizzy with fatigue and confusion, she pulled on wellington boots with shaking fingers. The child could die out there. She fastened up the old tweed coat kept on a hook by the back door. Someone was out there with a baby. And weren't there children she had to look for? And all this time she'd been asleep! Ellen grabbed the torch from the shelf over the sink. Children were missing. Children of her own.

With her hand on the door handle and just about to leave, something flickered on the edge of her vision – a movement – and her glance flicked to the window ledge. Legend had it that death portended when a lone raven appeared and she nodded now, at the black, ragged creature that eyed her knowingly through the glass, pecking at the frame.

Then she stepped outside.

The temperature was mortuary-cold, her footsteps a solitary line imprinted on the snow as she crossed the lawn to the little gate leading onto the lane. Every step plunged so deeply into snow that it crumpled and oozed over the top of her boots, trickling down her legs.

Forgot socks…

The orb from her torch bobbed ineffectively in the night air, picking out one or two feet in front at the most.

Forgot gloves…

"Rosa! Marion! Are you there? Is that you?" Her breath clouded in the wintry dawn, her voice feeble, a wobbling old lady's voice. Yet still the baby's crying grew louder. And she stumbled on. "I'm coming. You wait there, d' you hear? I'm coming…"

***

He is so close…the dewy musk of his skin in the swallow of his throat, the gentle warmth of his hands caressing her back. He is dotting her all over with kisses – shoulders, arms, breasts – ever more urgent… opening her blouse, tugging at the cloth, popping the buttons, sinking his head. He cannot stop, he cannot speak. She is gazing up at him from the dappled grass into the blue-grey of his eyes, and her arms reach out, pulling him down… And they roll over and over, lost and half mad until the birdsong fades and the breeze stills.

"Mum? Mother?"

He is real; far more real to her than the tea being placed into her trembling hands and the dry slippers pushed onto her feet. In the harsh light of daybreak, her mouth quivers and a steady stream of tears tumble down her crumpled-tissue cheeks.

The pain was still as desperate and raw now as it had ever been – the love every bit as inflamed and insecure as the very first day, and it had stayed that way for nigh on forty-three years. He'd fallen in love with her right there and then, the morning the foundation stones had been laid for the new chapel – on a fresh March day shivering with clumps of bright daffodils. Everyone in the village had been there when the largest stone etched with the words, 'Hitherto Hath the Lord Helped us Build This Chapel, 1908' was lifted into place. He'd stood in his white shirt sleeves for the camera, the proud smile faltering only when his gaze levelled with her own – all at once crumpling and helpless. She actually saw him fall, as if he had lost his very soul and she had caught it. And it seemed to them both that the rain clouds drew back from the sun for that one inexplicable moment, and that there was nothing anyone could do about it.

From the corner of her eye, on the very edge of her vision, a part of her saw the sourness of expression on her mother's face and the dark glower on her sister's; but she had paid no heed, returning his smile without hesitation. And two months later they were married in the very same chapel.

And yes, she'd known there would be a curse. Her mother was always mixing hexes and Agnes helped her. But why it should have angered her mother and sister that she had married so well was beyond her. Perhaps it was because Agnes, as the older sister, should have been first? Or was it jealousy? She'd tried, really tried, to make them both a part of her good fortune but it only seemed to incite further fury, the hatred growing stronger every day. How had it got so bad, though; so evil, prolonged and relentless? And surely her belief in God should have offered protection from such malice? A curse would work if you let it, she knew that much. If it quite literally worried you sick you gave your enemies the power to reduce you, but not if you were resolute and prayed daily for His protection? Surely?

Although she possessed strong intuition and a gift for clairvoyance, however, she did not and would not dabble with magic. Not even counter-magic. Sorely tempted to use it she refrained and chose instead to attend Chapel regularly and pray in earnest. Alas, it became clear very quickly that those who had stooped the lowest had won.

It took them three years. After which there was nothing left.

"Mother?"

Dazed, she looked around at a large, gloomy kitchen as if from the end of a very long tunnel – at flames flickering in the grate, at the honey-glow of an oil lamp on the table, and at a woman's face she felt she should know, peering into her own.

How had she got here?

"Mother, we're home and we're both safe. You'd fallen down outside. Can you feel your legs? We found you on the road—" The voice seemed to come from a long way off, trailing away; then suddenly amplifying again as if she had surfaced from the bottom of a well – everything too loud, too bright...

"Hurry up with the brandy, Marion. It's on the top shelf behind the flour."

***

Chapter Seventeen
1908
Annie Bailey

Their haste was downright indecent.

Annie stood with her arms folded and her face set to granite, watching Aaron Danby's men hack down Old Man Odin. With ladders and ropes they scaled the ancient oak as nimbly as monkeys, and proceeded in a frenzy of glinting axes to slash, saw and splinter it apart with great, savage cracks that severed the tree limb from limb. It seemed to Annie that a murderous gleam burned in each man's eye, a fever of determination and self-righteousness as they worked hour upon hour, until at last the job was done and all that remained was a stump.

They stood back admiring their work, panting and sweating, abruptly released and staggering with near delirium. It had taken the best part of a day and now all around them, everywhere they looked, were stacks of logs and chunks of timber, piles of branches still budding with leaves, and bundles of twigs strewn on a carpet of sawdust. There seemed enough, they said, to build not one but two or even three new houses – look how much fresh wood they had from just one tree! The gang of red-faced men flopped to the ground dabbing at foreheads and necks with handkerchiefs, swigging from hip flasks. *By God, it had taken some felling, had that!*

Annie waited a while, wondering if they would attempt to pull up the stump itself or if the roots would be left in place. The men were cooling off in the breeze, discussing the matter, while wives arrived with bread and cheese and a few children began to play fight with sticks. Those roots, all agreed, had snaked under the ground for centuries, hooking round boulders and anchoring into the earth. They wouldn't come out easily. They'd need a couple of carthorses. It'd be another day, maybe more…

As the sun dipped behind the clouds and muscle fatigue set in, they started to collect together their tools. A local farmer had arrived with a horse and cart and the timber had to be loaded on before nightfall. It would take many loads but then they were done, and whatever was left would serve as firewood for the locals – many of whom had already turned out to scavenge.

Annie held her breath. It looked as though the roots would be left intact after all, which at least was something. But just as she made to turn away, Aaron and his father, Edward Danby, clattered down the lane on horseback.

She recoiled into the shadows as the horses cantered over the common and the two men quickly dismounted. Wearing the long, leather boots and riding habits characteristic of the well-to-do, their presence immediately commanded authority, dissipating scavengers and playful children in one swoop. And it soon became apparent that the Danbys weren't happy. Voices were raised as dusk fell, carts were loaded and bonfires crackled. Annie strained to hear. The Danbys wanted the lot ripping out even if the men had to work all night: the building of the chapel must start tomorrow. In fact they were surprised, nay horrified, that the roots were still there 'infesting' the earth. Working speedily to clear the area, the men were telling them it would take longer, and even then the roots were so deeply embedded they could never truly be removed. Not in entirety. The horses could pull out the main stump and they'd hack at the rest the best they could, but not the roots and even then, it would take another day, maybe two. The chapel could still be built, but if they wanted it done quickly...

They did.

Then the roots would have to stay.

A few harsh words later the matter was finally decided and hands were shaken. Tomorrow morning a supply of stones and equipment would arrive along with a dozen men from the quarry. They would be well paid but after a good night's sleep work must recommence at dawn. The Danbys then called for their horses, and in sombre mood the men finished loading up the last of the timber by lamplight.

When the sound of thudding hooves had died away and all that remained was the spit and crack of twigs on the bonfire, Annie crept from her hiding place unseen. So then, they meant to do it! Overhead, the March clouds sweeping across the new moon were brooding with rain and in an agitated state she began to hurry across the common towards Grytton.

The forest, when it came into view, wore the tail end of winter like a rag in the wind, its ancient sentinels skeletal against a bruised night sky. She did not need to think about which path to take – her feet seemed to lift and guide her with a rhythmic pull along a trail older than time. A light breeze stirred the leaves in her wake, and soon the air turned sweet with damp earth and pungent verdure, the track beginning to taper. There was a feeling of spiralling inwards towards the centre of a labyrinth, and her body grew weightless, her senses exalted. The veil between this world and the next was gossamer fine.

They were letting her in...

Her heart began to flutter like that of a dying bird. Her steps quickened. Her breath came dizzily. Almost here... to the druids' tree grove... to where the power would flow. Tonight magic would be made and The Four were waiting as she knew they would be. The door was open and her feet flew; and then finally it was there before her and she stood dazed, out of breath, and entranced. Was the dark side not a wonderful thing? There when no one else was - to give you everything you desired. All you had to do was invite it in.

The small clearing buzzed with static, and everything she touched, including her own dress, sparked with electricity. A light mist hovered over a pool of still water, brushed at the edges with the fronds of a weeping willow; and the burial stones, which she had only had the privilege to see once before, radiated fluorescent light. *One...two...three...four...* Meg, Agnus, Lizzie and Anne.

Annie fell to her knees, brushing away fallen twigs and leaves from one of the graves, in order to recite words of thanks and pay homage to the wise old women who had been persecuted by churchmen centuries before. Hanged then burned at the stake, each woman was then buried face down in the woods with pitchforks through their backs and boulders rolled over them lest they ever dare to walk the earth again. Such was the fear. Such was the cruelty and the ignorance. And so it was again.

A few large drops of rain spattered onto the rocks, big flat splats, and the air stilled. No birds sang and no sounds came from the forest as Annie took from her pocket the small effigy she had made of Aaron Danby and placed it on the ground by the base of the weeping willow, making sure to thank the spirits that dwelled within the tree, for their help. Fashioned from a mixture of wax and clay before being melted into a grotesque mask, the poppet was further enhanced by several strands of hair taken from the coat he'd hung in the church porch, and bound with one of his handkerchiefs spotted with blood. What a happy find that was. Had he suffered a nose bleed or grazed a finger? A lucky addition indeed.

Meddling with the natural order of things was never to be taken lightly and her fingers shook slightly as she cast a circle of protection and lit the candles, knowing how this may well come back to haunt her as she prepared to focus her intent and invoke Hecate – the triple goddess found where the energy lines crossed and the magnetic force was strongest. The new moon was in Taurus, which meant the spell would last the longest and be hardest to change; followed by the waxing phase during which the power would grow daily as the spell come to fruition. Tomorrow the foundations for the Methodist Chapel would be laid and within days the first stones would descend on all that lay beneath. There would be a celebration and an opportunity for Aaron Danby to lay eyes on her daughter, Agnes – who would appear to him as a captivating beauty – and to whom he would then be irrevocably bound.

Once fully prepared, and on the hour of Saturn at three a.m. she summoned the dark moon goddess, Hecate.

"Crossroads Goddess!
Scared fire!
I invoke the Hecate!
This dark hour
Grant the Magick
Bind him with fright

Call of my familiar owl in flight
Bind my enemie
Make him weak
With spells of woe and curses bleak!"

Her eyes shone with an unearthly fire as finally, with the full might of Hecate behind her, magic crackled through her veins and she set to work.

Driving the first silver pin through the doll's head, she then drove another into the right arm, the third into the left and the fourth to where the heart should be.

"As this pin is driven into the heart of this image, so may love of Agnes be driven into the heart of Aaron Danby, so that he cannot sleep, wake, rest, stay, go - until he burns with love for her."

The fifth pin she stuck into the navel, the sixth in the groin, the next into the right side, then the eighth into the left side and so on until every part of the body had been pierced and every pin accompanied with an instruction. "I command as follows – your head, your hair, your eyes, your ears, your organs, limbs, sides and ribcage, your whole self…"

When every part of the poppet was pierced with pins and every energy line of the body committed to purpose, Annie stood and raised her arms to the sky. "I command Aaron Danby, your whole essence, so that you cannot sleep nor settle nor rest nor have any skill at anything until you have fulfilled this erotic purpose."

When it was done, she sat back on her heels and lifted her face and hands to the fresh, clean rain emptying from a burst of cloud. It dripped from the leaves and plopped onto the bare earth, and she closed her eyes in awe. Excitement filled her; and she knew as sure as she had ever known anything, that the deed was done.

"This is my Will…so mote it be."

***

Chapter Eighteen
1951
Louise – two days after the blizzard

When we woke the next day it was snowing again – steadily and solidly, the air thick with snowflakes settling onto the packed layers already there. On and on it snowed, several feet deep in the drifts and still it kept on coming, entombing the landscape as far as you could see in glacial whiteness. I don't think any of us had any inkling at that point, just how long it was going to last and how totally isolated we would become. To us children it was still exciting: we built snowmen using lumps of coal for eyes and carrots for noses, threw snowballs, and took tea trays up to the slopes for sledging.

That morning Dad cleared the front path before setting off early for Grytton to check on Grandma Ellen, and we kids were at the table having breakfast, eyed as always by Auntie Flo and Auntie Connie.

"Not another one," my mother snapped at Iddy. "One dip of syrup per slice. What have I told you about being greedy? There's others you know, not just you."

Iddy grew red in the face as he always did when he was told off, although he still crammed the toast in his mouth.

"Greedy guts," said Arthur, watching the excess syrup dribble down his brother's chin.

Iddy couldn't answer back because his mouth was full so I took the opportunity to swipe one of the illicit fingers of toast left on his plate, and the next minute he had me pinned to the floor. "Spit it out, Louise." He was trying to get it back out of my mouth before I swallowed it.

"Cut it out!" my mother shrieked. "Get back on your chairs and sit at the table properly or you'll all three get a good hiding. Now behave!"

There was a funny atmosphere and everyone was fractious. At eight in the morning it was still dark and the coal fire was blazing, flames leaping up the chimney as if it was night time. None of us wanted to go out into the freezing, wet day but we'd tried tummy ache and 'feeling sick' to useless avail. So we sat suitably chastised, lingering over the last dregs of tea, delaying the moment we'd have to go out into the cold again.

"That's not fair, he—"

Arthur shot me a look and put his fingers to his lips. It seemed something was wrong – something important – and he wanted to know what it was.

Mum was certainly very preoccupied, as were the aunties, with waiting for the news broadcast on the wireless. All of a sudden the pips sounded.

"Shush," Mum said, turning up the volume.

The man with the urgent sounding voice was speaking. There was still no word about Hazel Quinn, the woman who'd disappeared in the blizzard two nights ago. Last seen leaving her home in Danby by car there had been no further sighting and the police were becoming increasingly concerned for her safety. Driving conditions on the night she went missing had been atrocious with many roads unpassable. Local police speculated she could not have got far and people were urged to keep their eyes open for a car stuck or abandoned in the area, and for a lone woman who could have become lost or disorientated. The longer time went on, said the man, the more unlikely it was she could survive. Interviewed by police, one of the neighbours had described Mrs Quinn as keeping herself to herself and rarely going out, if ever, on her own. It seemed odd, the witness said, that she'd attempted to drive in such dreadful weather too. Not only that, but she'd been dressed in heels and evening dress with nothing more than a fur stole to keep her warm.

My mother's face was white.

"Well ou couldna 'ave got far," said Auntie Flo. "Not in this weather."

Mum nodded. Danby, although in a valley, was surrounded by moors on all sides and was only escaped by steep winding roads, all of which would have become blocked with snow very quickly.

"Still snowing an' all," Auntie Flo added, somewhat unnecessarily.

We watched as she took a long drag on her cigarette. Sometimes the smoke came out of her nose nearly a whole minute later. Arthur said he could do that too – talk with the smoke still inside his lungs and then let it out later – without coughing.

The man with the excitable voice went on to announce that the woman's husband had been taken in for questioning by the Danby police.

Mother and the aunties all said, "Ooh!"

"Fancy setting off in this, though," said Auntie Connie.

"I bet 'er got th' car stuck and then 'er came a cropper."

Their accents were getting thicker the more animated they became.

"Mum, what's a cropper?"

"Never you mind, Louise. And what have I told you about listening in to adults' conversations?"

After the news finished she turned off the wireless and took a cigarette from Auntie Flo. "Ta, duck."

"Well then—" said Auntie Connie.

"He'll 'ave murdered her I reckon," said Auntie Flo.

"'Er 'usband?" said Auntie Connie.

"Oh, aye, it's always th'usband."

"Mum, what's murdered mean?"

"Be quite, Louise. Aren't you done yet? Get down from the table and get your clean socks from the warmer. Arthur, duck, get them ready for school or you'll be late."

It snowed for the rest of the week with no let-up; and every morning Dad and the other men in the street began the process of digging out a path, the sound of shovels grating on the road a sound we became accustomed to waking up to. That scraping, the darkness, the freezing air and the sooty smoke of the coal fire will always haunt snowy mornings for me. I remember the painful numbness in my itchy, swollen toes, and the sight of the bedroom wallpaper peeling away with damp. And two doors down the wailing of Uncle Lloyd's euphonium and Auntie Flo's coughing. Above all though, I remember the light: the blinding, brilliant clarity of blue-white light.

On and on it snowed. Until food supplies started to run low and the shelves at the Co-op were almost bare. There'd been no bread or fish van round for weeks. The milk delivery that usually came by pony and trap, ladled directly from the churn into a jug, Mum fetched from the farm on her way home from work; and the hens in the back yard had stopped laying. Although we had plenty of coal in the cellar, only one scuttle of it was to be used per day in case the next delivery couldn't get through. Arthur said he could see the stone floor of the cellar now and was shovelling up more coal dust than coal. Few people had cars back then but not a single one had passed through the village in weeks – everyone was on foot and even then the going was slow with people slipping, bruising hips and twisting ankles. Phone lines were still down and a raw wind blasted off the moors, drifting the snow into hazardous piles that had you up to your neck before you knew it. And on the lanes cleared by tractors the edges were now too high to see over. We were land-locked.

Dad did manage to reach Grytton that morning, though, and when he returned the relief was palpable. Mother did that dramatic collapsing into a chair thing with her hand on her chest. Auntie Rosa and Auntie Marion had made it home sometime in the early hours, although he said both had horrible colds; but Grandma wasn't at all well after falling on the ice.

"Falling? What do you mean, falling on the ice? Why was she outside?"

"I don't know, Viv. She had some vague idea of going out looking–"

This set Mum fretting, wringing her hands and pacing up and down. "Oh, if only it would stop bloody snowing I could get down there…"

But we couldn't get down to Grytton or anywhere else outside of the village after Dad's first visit, because the roads and lanes became completely impassable. Everything was postponed or cancelled because of the treacherous conditions. Apart from Chapel. And would you believe – school? Much to our dismay they managed to keep a single track dug out every single day so we could get there and back. Even in the absence of heat and light, and long after school dinners ran out, we were simply told to bring candles and sandwiches and get on with it.

My mother still got to the mill for work too. If the workforce didn't go they didn't get paid so she made sure she got there and set off earlier. But Dad spent much of his time digging other people out and helping those who were too old or sick to look after themselves. Brittle bones could not afford to slam and fracture on the ice. And there were no funerals held for three weeks in total. 'Apparently', Mum said. 'The bodies were piling up.'

Bodies piling up.

Well, that gave me, Arthur and Iddy something to think about.

A week later, though, two full weeks after Hazel Quinn had originally been reported missing, an abandoned car was sighted up at Castle Draus. Buried in deep snow only the top was visible, its metallic roof spotted glinting in a rare shaft of sunlight.

"I can't believe it," Mum said to Dad. "I mean, how the dickens would she have got the car right up there? It's a trek at th' best of times…"

Dad shrugged.

"And it is definitely *her* car, they say? Why, though? Why up there? It's in the middle of bloody nowhere. Why would anyone in their right mind go up there?"

"Perhaps she weren't in 'er right mind?"

I struggled to understand. "What's happened?"

"She must've driven up there that first night," said Dad. "Not impossible if you keep going in a good car like that."

"Mum, what's happened?"

"I suppose they'll have to dig it out and see if she's still in it? Dear Lord, she must 'ave been buried alive."

"Mum, what do you mean by, 'buried alive'?"

"We're going up first light," said Dad.

"Who? You and who's army?"

"Me and Jack, Lloyd, Handel, Bill—"

"And who were it who saw th' car? Must 'ave been Bill, then?"

"Aye, and purely by chance an' all. He were out searching for sheep, most of th' poor beggars dead and buried like, but anyhow he'd been out all night – got as far as th' castle walls when he saw a flash of metal."

"And it were 'er car? Up to th' roof in snow? Well I never, and then…"

"It's looking that way, duck."

"But they said she left after dark? It were a raging blizzard up 'ere, though. You couldn't see a thing. Marion and Rosa couldn't even get 'ome in it. So how the divil she got a car up there I dunna know. Folk have got stuck on a fine day—"

"Or why," Dad said.

"Yes and why? Do you reckon as it were suicide?" Mum wailed.

"What's suicide?"

"Shut up, Louise!"

"We'll know more when we get up there tomorrow," said Dad. "Bill only came down and told us all an hour ago—"

"Lucky you were in th' Quarryman then?"

"Very," said Dad, with a tiny smile. "Any road, he and Jack are on their way down to Puffer Jud's now. It'll be a police job, like…Mind you, they'll not get a motor up there—" He frowned. "And Puffer Judd won't make it on foot will he, the fat sod?"

"Mum, what's Puffer Judd?"

"Oh, my Lord, it doesn't bear thinking about – what you'll find, I mean. Have you thought? Have you thought about what you'll likely find?"

"Mum, what's a Puffer Judd?"

"Louise, pipe down, duck," Dad said.

Arthur was the one who explained it later, after dark.

The three of us were in bed buried under a weight of covers. He flicked on his torch.

"Right, what's happened then, our Arthur?" I asked.

"All I know is it's about a woman from town called Hazel that drove off and never came back. It were on that night we 'ad that really bad snowstorm, do you remember – when we walked 'ome from Chapel after Grace Holland were singing? It were that rough we could 'ardly walk?"

Iddy and I nodded. "Yeah, it were an' all."

"Well, then after that no one could find 'er and they started to think as it were th' usband as killed her and put 'er somewhere. But now Crocker Bill's seen a car up at Castle Draus and they think as it's 'ers. But nobody can get up there to find out, and if it is 'er then she's been buried alive."

"You mean like she's alive but stuck in the car? Won't she be cold?"

"Lou, it means she'll be dead. Gone. Kicked th' bloody bucket."

"How do you mean? What bloody bucket?"

"He means dead and all blue and mottled purple," said Iddy, who had once seen a corpse being brought into the funeral parlour and never forgotten it.

"Has our Dad got to dig her out, then?"

"All the roads are blocked from town," said Arthur. "So he's going to go and see if she's in th' car. Me an' all."

"Are you going, our Arthur? Really? Aren't you scared?"

"Course not."

"She'll be all blue and purple patchy and her eyes will be wide and staring and her fingers like claws, and then she'll see you and suck your blood to get her life back… and then float into the night looking for more children—"

"You're daft in the 'ead, our Iddy."

"Why, though?" I said. "I mean, why did she go up there?"

Arthur shook his head. "Could be suicide."

"What's suicide?"

"It's where they chop their own heads off," said Iddy.

***

Chapter Nineteen
Lake View Villa
Ellen Danby

Where, she thought, did dreams end and reality begin? And how had she floated so seamlessly through the veil – from deep involvement in another life – to this, a calm, powder blue bedroom laced with spidery shadows? It looked as if it might be late afternoon. At first, with the house so piercingly quiet, Ellen wondered if she was still alive at all or had in fact, become a spirit trapped between two worlds. But then a confetti-hand of snowflakes blew against the window and a gust of soot wafted down the chimney, filling the room with the acrid smell of coal dust.

She closed her eyes. Yes, she was still alive. Nothing in heaven could surely feel this cold and dead?

There was no strength in her arms to either pull up the covers or turn her head, and sleep weighted her down once more, a surge of memories and fears rushing into the void. Helpless to stop it, she cried out in her sleep. "No, not to that place again. Don't take me there. No…" In vain she fought to surface from the depths of her nightmare, the feeble fingers of her rheumatoid hands clawing at the sheets, dimly aware of faces peering down at her, of voices gurgling her name in a pool tide of ripples. Again she called out but it may as well have been from the bottom of a lake because no sound came from her lips, and now the current was pulling her along, to where it was warmer and easier to simply float away.

He was there in the sunlit dapples among the gently swaying reeds, more real to her now than ever, reaching out with the softest of touches...brushing tendrils of hair from her face, caressing her brow, stroking the oyster smoothness of her eyelids. A frisson of pleasure tingled through her whole being and she swam into his embrace as naturally as a mermaid. "I love you, come to me, it's time—"

"I want to but I'm afraid."

"There's no need. I'm with you, Ellen. I've come for you."

He was wrapping ribbons of reed around her ribs, tying them into bows and she was laughing, river water in their hair, droplets trickling from eyelashes...*Now this was heaven, this was joy, ecstasy...*

Suddenly, like a rip-cord the ribbons were yanked so forcefully she was propelled out of the dream and straight back into the cold bedroom, sitting up lunging desperately for breath. Every inhalation was a knife to the chest, her frail ribs almost cracking with the strain.

"Mum?" A voice resounded through her head. "I'm trying to get Dr Fergusson out to you urgently. Can you hear me? We need to–" Interrupted, the voice paused and a wracking cough broke out. "It could be pneumonia."

She tried to work out who was speaking. *And who is it who has pneumonia? Aaron's mother had it. Clara had it...*

"Clara?"

"Mum, it's me – Rosa. You're a bit confused. I can't get hold of the doctor because of the weather." A hand spanned across her back, and something was held to her lips. "Try to drink some of this."

Scorching brandy burned her throat and she spluttered, flopping back in the crook of Rosa's arm, a bundle of rags.

"I've put a hot water bottle in, can you feel it on your feet?"

Ellen nodded.

"Good. Marion's still really poorly. She's in bed with a nasty cold, probably flu. We spent the night on the moors after we got lost in the blizzard, do you remember me telling you? Anyway, we've all of us been asleep all day and now it's evening. Mum, can you hear me? Do you know where you are?"

Ellen nodded, slumping back onto the pillows.

"We found you outside on the lane. You must have fallen but you're back in your own bed now and I'm looking after you. You'll be okay, Mum, but you've a bad chest and probably need some penicillin."

Ellen winced at a sudden stab of pain in her hip, a fuzzy recollection of slamming sideways onto the ground. "Lost?"

"Yes, in the forest. It was the strangest thing but we couldn't find the path – couldn't see a thing. To cut a long story short we ended up on the moors again and sheltered in Green Mans Cave until daylight. At least by then we could see the way home. Anyway, it doesn't matter now – we got back safe and sound....freezing and exhausted but..."

Ellen tried to move her head but couldn't.

"Mum, are you in pain? Is it your hip?"

She nodded, the slight movement causing a swell of dizzy heat to rise in her throat from the liquor.

"We've got plenty more aspirin if you need it, and I've put a dressing on your leg so that's what you'll feel pressing on there. Can you manage some soup, do you think? I'm going to make some for me and Snow."

Ellen frowned, her last vision of Lana at once stark in her mind.

"Mum? Could you manage soup if I brought you some?"

She shook her head.

"A dry biscuit, then? And a glass of milk with some aspirin?"

Her head lolled to one side, eyelids dropping.

"Alright. Look, I'll go and make something for me and Snow, then I'll pop back and see if you'd like a cup of tea. You need more rest. It's going to take some getting over that's for sure. Are you warm enough?"

"Mmm..." Ellen tried to push away the blankets as nauseating heat spread rapidly into her neck and face.

"No, keep the blankets on. It's freezing in here. The generator's not working again and all the lines are down. We've no electric and the pilot light went out on the range. Stay in bed and keep warm. I'll be back in a while."

The bedroom door clicked shut and Rosa's footsteps tap-tap-tapped down the corridor. After she'd gone, Ellen inwardly recited her daughters' names over and over - *Marion, Rosa and Vivien, Marion, Rosa and Vivien* - holding onto reality for as long as possible until all the years she had blocked out for so long began to crowd angrily forwards once more, baying to be heard.

Fuchsia spots blazed on the crests of her cheekbones, a slick of sweat on her skin. The hot water bottle in the bed was scorching her legs and she kicked at it; mumbling, clutching at the air as if falling backwards from a great height.

It was the strangest thing....but we couldn't find the path...couldn't see a thing...

"No, no, no....please, don't take me there again... Don't let me see..."

***

She is eight months pregnant with Vivien when she wakes on top of the sheets in a sheen of sweat. Already the heat is up and it will rise and rise until there is no air even in the shade. By three o'clock, that most intense point of the afternoon when the ticking grasshoppers and droning bees finally still - time seems suspended and even the hardiest of souls will sag with fatigue. If only the sky would crack and break – spark a dousing, bouncing downpour; but this July is topping all records and no end is forecast.

After splashing her face with cold water, Ellen walks straight out of the back door in her voluminous white nightdress and heads to the coolness of the forest, relishing the dewy grass beneath her bare feet. Without even the wisp of a breeze, the water in the lake behind her is at such a low level the bell tower spikes out in the middle. People had taken to bathing in it, including herself, but now it lies glistening and untouched, fright tales of coming face to face with the long-drowned dead having circulated rapidly, along with accounts of being pulled underwater by cadaverous hands. Thus she heads for the dappled coolness of the woods.

Beneath the sylvan shade, baked earth crumbles between her toes, a blackbird sings a sparkling fountain of song from the sunlit canopy, and a mellifluous stream trickles from deep within the moss and trees. Deeper and deeper into the woods she wanders, sleepily and dreamily, drowsy in the hazy dawn of what will be a blistering day.

Soon she will turn back.

Although he left at dawn and will have been at the mills for many hours already, Aaron frequently rides home to check on her; keeping a close eye now that her time is nearly due. She must not worry him by not being there. She smiles, picturing his concerned, steady grey eyes searching hers for any sign of worry or pain. His are the arms that cannot but enfold her, the hands that constantly reach for hers, the lips compulsively searching her own; the kind of love so intense, so all-encompassing it has knocked them both blind. They crave each other's company, words, looks, caresses... dazzled at what they have found, disbelieving and a little bit afraid. After all, what was given could just as abruptly be snatched away...and with it the essence of life itself.

It catches her totally unaware, time dissolving so suddenly it's as if a switch is flicked. Without her noticing any transition it is now absolutely dark – as dark as night, in fact - and deathly quiet. There is not the faintest of sounds – not from the stream, the blackbird's aubade or the foraging of any small creature. And the air is as damp and chilly as November – smoky and swirling with mist. Instinctively she looks up to find the canopy no longer green but as black as a starless night. Bewildered she assumes she must have fallen and hit her head; that she has been unconscious and he will be out looking for her. Or did she sleep too long? And yet she is still standing. What madness is this?

At once the ground begins to roll beneath her in a turbulent sea and from somewhere nearby a baby is crying; whimpering at first but quickly escalating into open-throated screaming for attention. She holds out her hands in front of her, feeling her way in the dark towards the howling child, but the ground is as insubstantial as a flying carpet and she stumbles. It seems the nearer she gets to the child the further away it moves. *Where is it*? The trees are now spinning around her in a bonfire of screeches and wailing.

Still the baby cries and in desperation she calls out, "Where are you? Where are you?"

"Mum, it's okay."

And then they are everywhere: babies – only not babies at all, but dolls - staring unseeingly from pinned eyes and cracked china faces; melted wax effigies with grotesquely distorted features; blood-soaked bandages unfurling from poppets, nails hammered through foreheads, limbs dangling from trees...Not dozens of them either, but hundreds.

Reeling, her heel catches on the corner of something and her spine slams down hard onto stone. The wind is knocked from her lungs and a sickly wave threatens to engulf her senses; but from far, far away her name is still being called. She opens her mouth to respond but no sound comes and no words will form.

There is only the nightmare in front of her. A nightmare from which she cannot wake. A male doll, definitely and obviously male with its phallus fashioned into a mangled, gargoyle caricature of a man, swings by its broken neck from the bough of a weeping willow. Squinting at the hideous effigy that is stuck with pins through every part of its waxen body, the neck snapped at right angles, she slaps a hand to her mouth. But it doesn't stop the screaming. Nothing stops the screaming.

"Mum? Mother, wake up. Are you alright? It's Rosa."

Eventually Ellen quietens and her breathing steadies, wheezy and tight, but slipping once more into the oblivion of dreamless sleep.

***

Chapter Twenty
Ellen – continued…

That same morning, Aaron was thrown from his horse and died instantly from a broken neck. On hearing the news, even though on some level she knew what was coming, Ellen doubled over in agony, her waters broke and Vivien was born some five weeks prematurely.

She never ventured into the woods again, not once, preferring to lie stonily on the marital bed staring into a void of despair. Unable to move, even to turn her head when the new baby was shown to her, she had to be fed, bathed and tended to by a nurse. But the years had passed; and in a state of dissociation she eventually began to drift around the house again, gradually mastering the marionette motions of her role as a mother. Six months later the nanny Clara Danby had hired for her moved on, and one by one the girls started school.

With Ludsmoor Primary School directly on the other side of Grytton Forest, however, naturally enough the girls wandered into the woods. She hadn't realised. Had never thought. And one day while deadheading roses in the back garden she looked up and saw the two oldest burst from out of the darkness in a tumble of apple cheeks and curls, duffle coats and satchels. A vague fear clutched at her but she couldn't quite say why that was.

She should tell them to take the lane to school, but why? Bouncily happy, they were running across the lawn to tell her everything they'd learned that day.

"I don't want you taking short cuts through the woods."

Their joy visibly drained away. "Why?"

"Just don't go in, that's all."

"But why–?"

"There are bad things in there—"

Well, what bad things, they wanted to know.

"Evil things."

"Like what?"

Ellen frowned so hard her forehead ached with the wrenching worry of how to explain it. What could she say about a terror hidden in a vault so far down the corridors of her mind, so heavily bolted and chained, that its very existence could never be acknowledged, much less discussed? And so she'd had no option but to frighten them with fairy tale readings of child-eating witches and hungry wolves. Rosa, dear sensible Rosa, had heeded the warning, sticking to schoolwork, attending Chapel and helping to look after Vivien. Marion, though... Well, she just had to go looking, didn't she?

Ellen drifted in and out of dreams. Occasionally, she called out and a woman's face hovered over hers, feathery hands smoothing away tendrils damp with sweat. "She's getting worse."

Another one further away, coughing – a sore, nasal voice. "Could you get to Dr Fergusson on foot, do you think? Do you feel well enough?"

She tried not to groan. *Dr Fergusson... Don't they know yet?*

"We could ask Vic and Nell, I suppose?"

Was that Rosa? Was that Rosa asking about Agnes' boy? She tried to shake her head.

"No!" said the other voice in between sniffs and coughs. "No, we absolutely cannot."

"I don't see why—"

"Just no. Not ever. Rosa. We have to fetch Dr Fergusson."

So Marion knew... Marion knew...

"...and still snowing..."

She faded in and out of consciousness. Snowing? Was it? Good God, how long had she been lying here? What year was it now?

And the girls...they'd still gone into the woods even though she had strictly forbidden it, hadn't they?

The slap had stung her palm and Marion, still in her school pinafore, was falling sideways onto a kitchen chair... her cheek smarting scarlet in the shape of a handprint.

No, they had not found anything in the woods... just trees and a stream... a beautiful place where sunshine danced off the spray and the rocks were shiny, and there was a magic pool with stepping stones. They'd played there all day... Marion was clutching her face, tears swilling into her eyes.

"Until it got dark? Did it not occur to you how much I'd worry? You know I told you not to go in there, yet you even took Vivien with you too. And I expressly told you not to linger after dusk. How dare you disobey me, Marion! How dare you!"

Marion hung her head. All three girls stared at the floor, their happy day snuffed out.

"Tell me one thing – just one thing. Did you find an odd place – anything unusual? A place that scared you? Is there anything you want to tell me about?"

All three shook their heads most vehemently. 'No, no, they really hadn't.' Their eyes shone with honesty. 'Nothing. It was just a place to play.'

At first it came as a relief her children hadn't found anything untoward; but on further introspection this only served to deepen her own confusion. Maybe then, she had imagined it all….and in the white, static space between sleeping and waking, where dreams merged with reality, maybe… maybe… that was where her mind had made it all up? Perhaps to make sense of what happened to Aaron? Some said it was the trauma of a birth brought on too soon by shock. Others said she had clearly suffered a head injury. So had she slipped on the rocks that day and fallen? Perhaps she was mentally ill and just as Dr Fergusson diagnosed, suffering from 'nerves'? After all, there was nothing in the forest except trees and a stream, rocks, grass, and a picnic spread of bluebells in May – the ones the girls had picked bundles of for the kitchen windowsill. Just as they said: an enchantingly beautiful forest in which to play.

She spent a lot of time gazing out of the window after the confrontation with her daughters; the slap forever imprinted in the echo of the house. And in the midst of her pain and bewilderment she had called Clara Danby once again, for help. Fearing Ellen might tip once more into depression, Clara suggested the girls could be schooled privately in town now they were a little older. The Danbys had paid for a cleaner too. After which the years merged into cotton-wool corridors with Ellen drifting through arranging flowers for Chapel and gazing out of windows at the woods. There was not a room where she didn't gravitate to the view and stay there, motionless and transfixed. Was there anything to fear in there or had she had a vision, like the ones she used to have as a child? In other words had everything, in fact, happened inside her own head?

It was just a feeling, albeit a strong one however, that she had not been mistaken at all. Piece by piece and often when least expected, fragments of memory floated to the surface to catch her off guard. Did this or did that, tie in? What was it she was missing?

On the day of Aaron's funeral, her mother, Annie, and sister, Agnes, had sat at the back of the little chapel as if magnetically challenged to have crossed the threshold, both dressed in the same long, black outfits they had worn to her wedding.

With faces veiled, they inclined their heads as she walked in; each with the tiniest pin-prick smile, the slightest upturn of sour lips. And only because she knew them both so well had she noticed.

She had chosen his favourite hymn, 'The Day Thou Gavest, Lord, Has Ended.' Beams of light streamed through the stained glass window he had personally chosen, radiating through the dust mites of gloom. How her heart had swelled, her stomach hollowing, as the pain wrenched through her in convulsions of a grief she could not contain.

The Danbys kept their poise but a small hand had slipped into hers and she held onto it. Marion – a toddler who miraculously seemed to understand – had looked up and squeezed her hand without question and without words. Looking back, she realised the child had seen her through that dreadful day, the last day she was seen in public for nearly a decade.

The coffin had been taken out through the porch into a summer's day bursting with life and song; and she had to let the congregation file out ahead in order to regain composure. Although she'd hung back for only a few minutes, by the time she emerged both her mother and sister had vanished. She glanced around several times, before having little choice but to be helped into old man Whistler's black carriage. The glossy, plumed manes of the horses bounced in the sunshine as the procession clattered smartly down the track to Ludsmoor Church, but it was not until they rounded the corner and levelled with the lychgate that she saw Annie and Agnes again. Her gaze settled on two dark silhouettes by the grave prepared for Aaron's coffin. So they couldn't wait, she thought, to see her husband lowered into the dirt.

By then Agnes was pregnant with Victor. She'd married a miner, a strikingly handsome man of considerable brawn. Sam Holland had thick, black hair he combed back with brill cream, and dazzling emerald eyes. No one could quite understand what he had seen in Agnes – a sallow, mean-tempered stick of a girl with a long aquiline nose that gave her the same hawkish appearance as her mother. And unlike Annie she possessed no hidden skills such as tarot reading for lovelorn girls. No, Agnes was a woman who slinked in the shadows, watching, lurking, and oozing malice. It was said that in the classroom many a child had been fixed with one of her murderous stares and subsequently been signed off ill for weeks on end. Some had even contracted a disease or taken a chain of misfortunes home to their families.

By God, but that girl should be hanged as a bloody witch...

They all said it, underneath their breath mind, but they all said it.

Born first, Victor would turn out to resemble Annie's own father to an uncanny degree: short and squat with a great beak of a nose, he was as bald as a pickled egg by the age of twenty-three. Grace, though... well, Grace had inherited her genes straight from Sam, with raven hair, flashing green eyes and finely sculpted features....the only resemblance to her mother and grandmother being the copper filaments in her hair, just visible on a bright day if she let it swing loose. An angel, the villagers called her - a beautiful gift from God with a voice to match.

She must have slept. When Ellen opened her eyes again the wintry day had dimmed to dusk and a fire was flickering in the grate. The heat didn't reach her bed in the corner of the room, but shadow flames leapt along the walls and when her eyes were closed they leapt across her eyelids too.

There was a cup and saucer on the bedside table but her hand had not the will to reach for it. Heaviness compressed her lungs...impossible to move...and so quiet now... just the crackle of a log...Which is when the memory came. Suddenly and with all the shock and precision of a laser beam.

She looks around startled. It is a night from long, long ago – the smoky taproom of a public house. There is an explosion of laughter... the click of snooker balls potted into corners... clump-clump-shoot... clump-clump-shoot. Her eyes are stinging in a cloud of tobacco smoke and she wants to go home... but the men are fixed on a game of poker long after time is called and the bolts have been shot.

Aaron's hand is a good one and he winks at her. *Not long now.* He knocks back another tot of whisky.

Fear lodges in her swollen belly and shivering breaks out across her arms, her legs, her back. A knowing. Rain lashes against the leaded windows.

Sam's hand is better.

Oh, God...

A lurch inside.

The hand laid on the table is a Royal Flush. The look on Aaron's face... all the blood draining away...

***

Chapter Twenty-One
Harry Whistler

Harry paused and squinted into the dawn fog, shovel in hand.

The sound of footsteps creaking in the snow and wheezy breaths expelled in short grunts meant Jack Gibbs was on his way, but with visibility so poor he was almost upon him before he could make out his face.

"How do, Jack? Give us a hand finishing this, will you? I just want to clear th' path and then…"

Wordlessly, with a cigarette still balancing on his lower lip, Jack started digging. A sinewy, broad-shouldered man with raised, snaking veins, he now delivered coal having been laid off from the pit due to chronic bronchitis and emphysema. Jack still wore the miners' uniform, though, and probably always would – a long dark jacket, flat cap and lace-up leather boots.

Spotting Arthur letting himself out of the back door, he shook his head. "Tell me as th' nipper's not coming, Harry? It's a bloody long walk and one of us is going t' end up carrying th' little beggar."

Harry went on shovelling. "Fitter than th' rest of us put together, is our Arthur."

"But what if—?"

"No, dunna worry he won't be going near th' car. You've got the crowbar, 'ave you?"

Jack nodded, indicating the rucksack he'd thrown down.

"Lloyd coming?"

"Aye – on his way."

They'd been through a lot together – Harry, Jack and Lloyd – serving in the same unit during the war. Jack had never fully recovered, remaining partially deaf and often cowering in a cringe if something took him by surprise - like a horse and cart speeding past. Flo's husband, Lloyd however, rarely spoke at all – silently letting himself in from a day working underground still tarred and filthy with coal dust, to clomp straight upstairs and play the euphonium in the back bedroom. Thus avoiding Flo altogether. Jack said it was a good thing to be deaf seeing as he was right next door to that racket – Lloyds's warbling brass notes and Flo yelling up at him to, 'get thee bloody sen weshed.'

It was speculated that Harry had fared the best out of the three because he was used to death and seeing dead bodies. There may have been some truth in that, Harry agreed, but somehow they'd all made it through, only to find when they returned that the women had got on frighteningly well without them. Word had it Flo and Lloyd had never openly acknowledged each other since. Yet still they managed to share a house.

Clearing the last of the snow away from the gate, Harry propped his spade up against the wall. "What did Puffer say about it last night then, Jack? Who else is coming or is just us three?"

"Bloody useless fat bastard," said Jack. "Took me and Bill over an hour t' bloody walk down there and then he says likely it's a car that were left up there from before th' snow set in. Likely we'd bust a gut climbing all that way up and then it'd be nowt to worry about. Didn't seem like he was interested in going himself."

"The divil he didn't!"

"Aye. Sat there supping tea like we were taking up his time – me and Bill standing there sopping wet while 'is missus is asking us if we're stopping for supper, like…You wouldn't credit there'd been a lass missing these two weeks. Bill 'ad steam coming out on his ears."

"I can imagine."

"Anyhow, Bill made a statement, and that was th' last I saw on 'im. You know how he is – just vanishes. Reckon he's lost a lot of sheep this time."

"Aye well, we've not 'ad owt as bad as this in years …not as I can remember. Purely selfish, like, but I hope he's coming back down again – I've funerals piling up, if thee'll pardon th' expression."

At the sound of approaching footsteps they both squinted into the fog.

"Aye-up, if it inna our Lloyd! 'Ow do, Lloyd?"

Lloyd, nodded and said quietly, "Our Handel's coming."

Handel was Head Master at the local primary school and also conducted the chapel choir. Small, slight and bespectacled, he had a fringe of ginger hair around the back of his pink, domed head and an air of being permanently excited with magnified eyes goggling and glinting behind bell-jar bottomed glasses. The mood lifted to hear he was coming along. Handel would be a good person to have on an expedition like this, his professional credibility invaluable when recounting whatever they might discover later that day.

A grim expectation hovered between them as they waited for the fifth man. *Just what were they going to find up there?*

"Did you bring th' sandwiches, Arthur?"

"Yes. We've got cake and tea an' all."

Jack tapped his jacket pocket. "Something a bit stronger than tea for me."

Harry laughed. "Me an' all."

Eager now to get it over with, as soon as Handel arrived they collected spades and rucksacks and set off – a darkly coated posse quickly swallowed by the freezing fog and another belt of snow.

***

From Hilltop Road, the climb up Gallows Hill was slow, arduous and hazardous. Once a formidable fortress, Castle Draus had been built on the highest point of Kite Ridge, blasted on all sides by the elements and accessed only by a single, winding track.

The most popular reason to visit would be for a picnic on a summer's day, in order to catch the breeze and enjoy the four counties view. People made an occasion of it, taking picnic baskets, table cloths and games to play. Even then, with the earth warm and dry, they parked at the base of Gallows Hill and walked the rest of the way. Few attempted to drive up for fear of getting stuck and consequently being unable to turn the car around on what was a narrow, pot-holed lane with a sheer drop on both sides.

On the western horizon, at the far end of Kites Ridge, an outcrop of large rocks stuck out bizarrely at a toppling angle like a stairway into the clouds. They called it Luds Throne, and no one knew or could fathom how it got there. Seen from the road far below, Luds Throne made a striking silhouette. On the other side, however, it overshadowed a brooding, dark pool of water reputed to be inhabited by the ghost of a girl accused and subsequently drowned for being a witch. Over the years many a lone shepherd or farmworker had mysteriously been dragged into its depths after swimming on a hot day – lured by the sound of her beautiful singing voice. Singing Sally, they called the lake. And if you heard the singing you would just as surely walk towards it as if hypnotised, wading up to your neck before you felt her cold, cold clutches. Such were the fireside tales told to while away the dark evenings. And on a bleak day like this with the wind whistling across the moors, a sense of isolation and insignificance consumed man and boy alike as they climbed steadily upwards, the old stories becoming more believable with every foothold.

Half way up, the group paused to get their bearings. It was a white-out. At this level the fog was a dripping cloud and a raw north-easterly now slashed sideways in sleety squalls, doubling the peril since they could barely see where to put the next step. In the near distance now, Luds Throne was all but obscured and Singing Sally's Pond indistinguishable from the miles of snow covered heath stretching out as far as the eye could see.

Harry shouted to the others above the noise of the wind. "Everybody alright?"

With headlong blasts constantly buffeting them, each fought against fatigue and Harry's gaze lingered on Arthur.

Arthur nodded.

"Right. Not long now then. Stay close, Lad."

By the time they reached the summit it was almost midday and time was now short if they were to be home before dark. The trip had taken far longer than any of them thought it would and the force of the wind at the top was breath-taking, howling around the ruins, wailing through the gaps in the walls.

"Careful now, don't lose your footing," Harry shouted to Arthur.

Arthur was struggling to stay upright, his reply lost on the wind.

Unable to hear, Harry beckoned to them all to follow. Cupping his mouth he shouted and gestured, "Other side of the wall! Car's on t' other side."

Seen from surrounding fields the walls were crumbling stones not difficult to scale, and fun for children to jump on and off on a summer's day. Today, however, they were lethal – ice-coated and unstable. With no chance of a safe foothold, the only course of action was to walk the long way around, which meant trekking west for a good ten minute before the wall was low enough to scramble over. It seemed the weather was taking a turn for the worse, too. Belt after belt of clouds laden with more snow rumbled over the moors and blasted the rocks.

Harry led the way, pulling Arthur over with him onto the lea side of the castle wall. The others clambered after them, grateful for what was an instant respite from the wind.

"Bloody hell!" Jack said, swigging from a hip flask. "I'm buggered."

Handel, crimson faced, crumpled against the wall frantically searching his rucksack for the flask of tea Vera had made. His short, rotund frame was not made for this kind of escapade and his feeble legs had set to shaking quite violently.

Lloyd slapped him on the shoulders and offered a rare word of encouragement. "Shape up now, thee'll be alright."

He nodded, close to tears. But after a short break they were ready again to continue the journey. The walk on this side was sheltered and they made quick progress.

Suddenly, Arthur, the only one still as sprightly as a springer spaniel, yelled at the top of his voice, "I can see it. Look! Dad – look!"

With the sky darkening rapidly, urgency gripped them all and they pounded towards what Arthur had spotted. Yes there was a car there. The roof could clearly be seen.

"Right, you start digging at the back end," said Harry, handing Arthur a spade as they drew near. "Just clear the snow away from th' boot and then give me a shout." He gestured to the others. Whoever uncovered the windscreen would be the first to see a body inside and it ought to be himself.

"Thee do that bit at th' front, Harry," Jack shouted, reading his mind.

Harry nodded, already shovelling and indicating the other three should get cracking too. They all began to dig.

After a few minutes Arthur called out.

The men carried on digging, in rhythm now and determined to get the job done.

Arthur shouted again and Harry looked up. "What is it, Lad?"

"It's a Jag," said Arthur. He was trying to run towards them, skidding and stumbling. "I've seen it afore an' all. It's a bloody Jag."

"Bloody hell! That's 'er's that's gone missing."

"It bloody is an' all. They said she 'ad a Jag, didn't they?" Jack said.

"Nobody's in it, though," said Harry. "No one's in th' car. Look."

All five peered into the interior. An opulent walnut dashboard and cream leather seats were entombed in igloo whiteness.

They stood breathing hard.

"I think we ought to set back now," said Handel. "At least we can say it's definitely her car and leave it to the police. It's quite definitely police business now. She must have managed to get here, then maybe got stuck and decided to try and walk home?"

All five looked across at the vast open plain of snow-covered moorland – a death trap of hidden bogs, crevices and gullies in sub-zero temperatures.

"She may have had hypothermia and become confused," Handel said.

Harry frowned. "I suppose it's possible."

"How else could it be explained?"

Another Arctic blast threatened to lift them clean off their feet and Harry shouted across the tumultuous roar. "Okay, well let's just check the boot and then get off home."

Jack nodded, following him. "That lazy bastard, Judd, can come and get th' car later. We've done what we can," he said, getting the crowbar out of his backpack.

"Don't damage it," said Arthur. "It's beautiful, is that car."

Jack hesitated, looking over at Harry. "Shall I?"

"It's a bloody murder case – we'll 'ave to check."

All four referred to Handel for the final word.

He nodded, keen to call it a day. "Yes, there could be clues in there – clothing or a suitcase for example – that we could report back. Yes, go on, Jack."

"Good point," Harry agreed. "Lloyd? Speak now or—"

Lloyd nodded.

"Hurry up, then, Jack," Harry shouted. "We don't want to be 'ere any longer than we need."

The boot was wrenched open.

All five stared open-mouthed.

And Arthur was copiously and violently sick.

***

Chapter Twenty-two
Louise

The day after Dad and Arthur went up to the castle it stopped snowing for the first time in three weeks. I knew because the light had changed. Knew even before I popped my head over the covers and drew in the first icy breath. And outside, above the sound of shovels scraping on the road, people were shouting to each other in excited voices. Something had changed: a lift in energy.

I ran to the window and looked out at a blinding blue sky. Suddenly the glass looked grubby, and when the curtains dropped back dust mites fizzed in columns of light. You could hear the change too – in the guzzling drains and the drip-drip-drip of icicles thawing under the eaves. It was like waking from a long, dark dream.

Those in the know had another purpose that morning, though, which I was yet to discover. Arthur had returned home very late the night before. Only vaguely aware, I'd heard the click of the latch on the bedroom door and shifted uncomfortably when his icy body pushed between me and Iddy, but soon fell back to sleep. I never heard Dad come in. All I knew was that the neighbours seemed to be scraping away more frantically than usual out there and that there was an air of renewed optimism, of expectation. Meanwhile, downstairs my mother and the aunties were making no effort to keep their voices down. *Odd. Unusual.*

Leaving Arthur fast asleep, I tip-toed downstairs and sat on the middle step listening-in. The wireless was on and I soon got the gist: the main road from Leek was now passable. Council workers had been working since the early hours so the police could get through with the help of local farmers. Apparently, a woman's body, presumed to be that of Hazel Quinn, had been found at Castle Draus last night and the news desk would keep us informed of further developments when they came in.

At this my heart flipped inside my chest. Dad found her! Dad and Arthur!

I crept further down the staircase, ear pressed closely to the railings. In the meantime, people were being told to stay home unless it was absolutely necessary to travel, said the urgent-sounding staccato voice. Phone lines were still down and the power was still out. If anyone was sick or elderly we were to check on them. Supplies of food items were at an all-time low and…

"I wonder who did it?"

"I don't know, Connie," said my mother.

"Have you got th' blood off th' steps?"

I slammed a hand over my mouth. *Blood on our steps*?

"Louise, are you on the stairs?"

My mother's telling-off voice never failed to fill my body with dread and I clung to the stair rail, already mid-turnaround and with every intention of reappearing several minutes later in a normal manner. But she'd swung open the door before I had the chance and grabbed me by the elbow.

"Get in here this minute."

I wriggled from her clutches and darted to the breakfast table, staring down at my place mat with my cheeks burning.

"There's a boiled egg! Now get it down you. I've knocked the top off and done you some soldiers. Eat up and then you can start the cleaning. We've chores to do on a Saturday."

"I've never seen so much muck on th' windows," said Auntie Flo.

"It's going to' take me all ruddy day to do mine, and then…" said Auntie Connie.

I wondered if these women ever sat in their own homes because honestly, they were always here.

"Good of you to go and fetch th' milk for us, duck," Auntie Flo said to my mother. "You're lucky, Louise – your mother's been going to th' farm every day so as you can have your milk. You want to thank her."

"Thank you," I muttered, still without looking up.

Mum poured more tea and Auntie Flo lit another cigarette.

I didn't know what to say. The aunties were always so stern and I never knew why except that I was lucky to have a mother like mine and she suffered a lot because of me and my brothers.

"Have you 'eard anything from Harry yet, duck?"

My mother shook her head. "He didn't come to bed. Sat down here supping brandy til first light and then he was off again. Arthur's still fast asleep."

"Did he say owt? Your Harry?"

"I didn't hear him come in, duck. I only know as he was 'ere at all because we've no brandy left and the fire was stoked up. At a guess I'd say he's gone down to Puffer's."

"But it is 'er, they reckon?"

"Looks like it. I don't know any more than you do, Connie."

"I wonder who put the…" Here Auntie Flo cast a sidelong glance at me and stopped short. "The you-know-what–"

"On our doorstep? I don't know but I've a mind it's to do with ousit being found…"

Suddenly Mum put down her teacup with a clatter and glared in my direction. "Louise, have you finished?"

I nodded.

"Good. Well Saturday chores time, young lady." She plonked a duster and a tin of beeswax on the table. "Drink up and then you can make a start."

My job was to dust the downstairs furniture – an onerous task, which involved taking every ornament off my mother's welsh dresser in the parlour and cleaning each one with a damp cloth. All the china dolls must be brought to a shine and their faces polished; and after that the shelves had to be dusted, making sure to get into the corners and use a chair to reach the top. It was hard work for a six year old and I never replaced the ornaments and plates exactly as they were so my mother was rarely pleased – tweaking and adjusting things when I said I'd finished.

Meanwhile all morning, Iddy, whose job it was to clean the windows with newspaper, speculated on what had happened up at the castle and what Dad and Arthur must have found inside the buried car.

"Shuddup, our Iddy," I kept hissing. "I want to hear what they're saying."

"What about?"

"The doorstep."

Iddy lowered his voice and came over to whisper in my ear. "Whatever it were it's in th' dustbin now, wrapped in newspaper. I'll 'ave a look when I go out to th' bins in a bit."

"Don't let her see you. She'll go berserk." Berserk was my new favourite word. It always conjured up the image of an angry bee.

"Aye, I know."

We sprang apart at every door creak or lull in conversation next door. But Iddy, who'd had his head out of the bedroom window that morning so he could listen-in, had heard the neighbours saying the woman who'd been found up at the castle was definitely the lady from Danby, and that Dad had gone down to the police station with Jack, Lloyd and Handel. That's where they were now. They were saying the woman's husband had been 'seeing to' Auntie Grace, and when she found out she'd driven up there in the snow. With grief, he added solemnly.

"Why would she do that, though?"

Iddy paused from cleaning the glass and inched over to me like a seasoned spy. "The lady froze to death in her skin. They said she was found like a mottled, purple statue just staring out with dead eyes, and she was as cold as an icicle and they had to chip at the skin with a chisel to get the body out."

"Is that true?"

He nodded. "And now she'll haunt the moors forever and her dreadful moaning and crying will always be carried on the wind. She's filled with rage and terrible grief, you see, and wants revenge."

All morning Iddy continued to fill my head with images of an iced corpse with fingers that when prised from the steering wheel had cracked like gingersnaps, and eyeballs that popped out of her skull and rolled down her cheeks. I didn't know what bits were true and what bits he'd made up but I did know it was very serious, and I craved to know what had really happened.

"What are you two doing in there? You're taking a long time. Haven't you done yet?" Mum shouted.

"Nearly!"

"Well, hurry up because one of you needs to fetch the coal up."

I didn't want to be the one to do that so my dusting slowed while I polished the oak dresser to a high shine, delaying the laborious process of replacing the plates and china dolls.

"Maud…you know Maud, don't you?" My mother was saying. "Works at the bakery in Danby? Fat as a lardy cake but ever such a nice woman?"

"Oh, aye? Married to Colin?"

"Aye, that's 'er. Well, 'er sister lives over th' road from Hazel Quinn. Apparently, the neighbours all heard 'er car go off and it were slipping and sliding then."

"Daft of 'er t' go out on a night like that."

"She must've had good reason, like?"

"Aye, well apparently…" My mother's voice trailed off abruptly. It's like she had eyes up her rear end. "Louise, are you listening in? What have I told you about listening in to adult conversations? Nobody ever hears anything good from eavesdropping."

"I wasn't." I lied, shuffling away from the adjoining door.

"Have you finished that cleaning or do I have to come in there and check?"

"In a minute. Nearly done."

"You're taking your time. Make sure you put those ornaments back where they were and then you can go and do some knitting in your room."

"It's freezing. Can't I do it downstairs?" I wailed.

"And don't answer back."

"Iddy, go and fetch the coal up."

"I've just to put the newspaper in th' bins."

"Leave that in th' kitchen and go and get th' coal."

"But—"

"I'll put th' newspaper out."

The day stretched ahead. And it seemed like a very long time before we heard anything more about the lady from Danby. Everyone was waiting. The aunties stayed on and on and more tea was made. Iddy scraped the cellar floor for the last few lumps of coal but there wasn't enough, and as the afternoon light began to dim the familiar chill hovered round our backs.

"We've some spare logs in th' yard if you want them, Viv?" said Connie.

My mother nodded. "Ta, duck. Iddy, go and fetch the logs from next door and mind you thank Auntie Connie."

"Well, I wonder where they've got to?" Flo said.

"They've had a long day," my mother agreed. On cue, the clock pinged rapidly. Five o'clock.

"Well, I'd best get back and then," said Auntie Connie. "Our Jack 'll not be that much longer, I'm sure."

"Me an' all," said Auntie Flo. "Have you anything in, Vivien? Only I've a bit of tongue left if you'd like it, duck?"

"I wouldn't say no. Come back with it and then I'll make us all a bit to eat."

Decisions made, the aunties stubbed out their cigarettes and heaved themselves up from the chairs they'd been welded to all day; and my mother began closing curtains and lighting lamps while Auntie Flo disappeared for the plate of tongue she still had in the pantry.

It was the moment I'd been waiting for all day. With the adults occupied I slipped into the scullery to look for Iddy. I had to know about the contents of the bin and if getting that log had given him a chance to look. I couldn't see him in the yard though, with it now being lighter inside than out, and cupped my hands to the window.

"What are you doing, Louise?"

I'd forgotten all about Arthur and nearly jumped out of my skin. He didn't look at all well. And it was as I was staring at him, at his wide, hollowed eyes and the dead expression in them, that we both heard a clatter from outside and leapt flat against the wall.

The back door creaked open.

Dad was standing on the step, framed by a starlit night. Shoving Iddy in ahead of him, he called out, "Viv? I'm back."

Mum came busying into the scullery, thankfully ignoring Iddy and the clear lack of a log, and ushered Dad into the main room, tugging the coat off his back as he walked. "Go and get his thick jumper, Louise, and fetch a blanket off our bed. Pushing him into a chair by the fire and thrusting a cup of hot tea into his hands she couldn't wait, though.

None of us could. I raced upstairs so I didn't miss anything, praying Dad would drink the tea first.

Happily, he weathered my mother's intense stare while he drank the entire cup straight off, holding it out for another before he was ready to speak. I thundered back down the stairs and handed him the sweater. My mother grabbed the blanket and laid it around his shoulders. He took another slug of tea then flicked a glance at his children, deciding whether or not we should hear this, I suppose.

"And?" said my mother. "Was it 'er or not?"

Dad seemed to make up his mind, sighed and put down his cup on the hearth. "Well, I suppose you'll hear soon enough – it'll be all round th' village. She was in th' boot."

"Alive?"

"Don't be soft, Viv."

"Was she all purple and cracked and mottled? And was her skull sliced in two with one eye hanging out and—?"

Mum's hand shot out and gave Iddy a clip round the head. "What have I told you about putting the fear of God into folk?"

"No, duck, .it were a lot worse than that. Somebody'd taken an axe to her."

Iddy paled. For all his graphic descriptions he was by far the most squeamish of the lot of us. And something was happening to him. His face was crumpling and he was shaking all over, starting to whimper. We none of us really knew why and stared at him in surprise. But my mother put it down to excitement and tiredness and packed us all off to bed with an early supper.

Both my brothers were ill that night and we never did get the tongue. No doubt Auntie Flo was hearing the same news as us; and Connie would be too.

After that there was a tangible shift in atmosphere. The grown-ups talked in whispers and the police came knocking on doors. The thaw was well underway by then with streams of melted snow racing down the roads into gobbling drains. Anaemic light refracted through dwindling icicles and the beads of dew trapped in cobwebs. Mounds of dirty slush bordered the narrow lanes. Mud squelched over boots and splattered up coats, swilling into yards gritty with coal dust. And in saturated fields miserable ponies and moorland sheep stood hock-deep with their backs to the wind, stoically waiting it out.

Over the next few days more and more information trickled through and the mood became evermore grave. Nobody laughed or joked, and conversations with police officers were conducted in parlours behind closed doors. Practised as I was in eaves-dropping, and even with my ear pressed flush to the keyhole, it was difficult to catch all but the occasional word. But I did manage to glean some important facts. The police had indeed recovered a woman's body from the boot just as Dad had said. This had then been taken to a funeral parlour in Danby, and then yesterday the car was towed down Gallows Hill by tractor. Very little was known about the murder itself, except – and this was on the wireless – that the husband was the main suspect as his whereabouts on the night Hazel disappeared were still unaccounted for and no alibis had come forward.

Desperate as I was to ask my mother what an alibi was I didn't dare, and the only person I could ask was Iddy, who said it meant a Turkish man, which only left me more puzzled than ever.

Far more disturbing than anything I overheard from the adults, however, was something that came from Arthur. Albeit unwittingly. On the night we children were sent to bed with an early supper, he woke up in the early hours with a horrible blood-curdling scream, thrashing around with his fists and bearing his teeth. I'd never seen anything like it.

Mum and Dad came rushing in.

"Mum, what's wrong with our Arthur? Mum, what's wrong with him? Why's he doing that?"

Neither parent answered, hauling him out of the room, telling me and Iddy not to mind but to get back to sleep.

After that, Arthur slept in the same room as Mum and Dad for a long while – maybe weeks, maybe months; and Dr Fergusson prescribed him sedatives. He didn't go to school or fetch up the coal or kid around like he used to. And sometimes I heard him through the walls. I heard what he was shouting out, night after night before he was soothed and shushed.

The lady had had her head chopped off, and all her arms and legs.

***

Chapter Twenty-Three
Lake House View
Ellen Danby

When Ellen next opened her eyes it was to glaring daylight. The bedroom curtains had been drawn back to reveal a whipped-raw day, the grate lay black and empty, and thawing snow was dripping steadily from the eaves.

Her breath frosted on the air. Mid-morning and the house was quiet, with just the wind rattling at the windows. Her throat was parched and her head thudded. Noticing a cup of steaming tea on the bedside table she tried to prop herself up but hadn't the strength; forced instead to lie inert and helpless. Someone was looking after her; the blankets were piled high and something hot lay against her feet... but here she began to fade away once more, eyelids weighted and closing.

He was so close to her now that the scent of his skin lingered from dreams as if he lay beside her in bed, the shivery touch of his soul brushing against hers.

Ellen...

She reached into the empty air.

Ellen...

Her heart swelled. She tried to mouth his name.

"Mum, can you hear me?"

Jolted, confused, she tried to open her eyes.

Three faces hovered over her, and shadows of monsters loomed along the walls. Where was she and who were these women? Candle smoke… the faint warmth of firelight flickering on her face. Was it night time? Already? What day, what hour, what month? She tried to sit up but nothing happened, to speak but no words came.

An arm slipped around her back and cool water trickled into her mouth and down the sides of her chin. She gulped and coughed, and more was tipped down.

"You have to drink. Try again."

This time it was easier and a cool rivulet tracked down her throat. Gently she was eased back against the pillows.

"Mum, the road's been cleared from Ludsmoor and Vivien's been for Dr Fergusson. He won't get down tonight but he'll be here tomorrow first thing."

"Doctor Death," she croaked.

Had she spoken out loud? Vaguely aware of a collective puzzlement, she allowed one of the women to lift her head again while another put a glass to her lips. But the weight, oh, the weight of her head, like a stone boulder lolling backwards. Lowered onto the pillows once more she lay wheezy and breathless while they fussed with her nightdress, and a damp sponge was dabbed at her face, neck, and hands. Her head was lifted again and a clean pillow popped underneath; a brush smoothed her hair and the aroma of lavender wafted over her. *Oh, stop, stop...*

"Mum, you've got to take some more water. You've only had three sips."

But the energy needed to swallow was too great, and she hadn't the will. Once again the crush of darkness was folding in, the room dwindling to the end of a tunnel.

And when she next came round it was to the distinct sound of a man's voice booming inside her head. Clear and concise. A command. *Time is running out.*

Hazy moonlight now bathed the room and downstairs the grandfather clock chimed a solid three o'clock in the morning.

Time is running out... but why? Whose voice was that? And why would time run out? Fragments of a half-remembered reverie fluttered like a moth in the dustbowl of her head, just out of reach. The voice had not been one she recognised, rather it was clipped, displeased and quite definitely Scottish.

She turned her head and with a rush of huge relief, clearly recognised one of her daughters, who was sitting beside her, chin bent to her chest, snoring softly – the fairest, the oldest - her first. And the question came on the spark of an impulse. Her cracked lips parted. "Marion?"

Initially, Marion appeared not to hear, but the energy between them quickened and she knew deep down, that on another level, her daughter was surfacing from sleep. Determined to stay alert now, Ellen summoned all the strength she had and repeated her daughter's name until at last, Marion jerked awake.

A moment to recollect where she was, then Marion lunged forwards. "Mum?"

Every word cost her, each syllable croaking in her throat, but this pinpoint of lucidity after decades of confusion suddenly seemed vital. She'd had the gift but never acknowledged it. Had known the black arts were used but tamped her knowledge down with grief as if it never happened. Now though, it was happening again and besides, there was no choice: if she didn't speak now then this would follow her to the grave and beyond.

"In the forest. Did you see it?"

Marion's eyes held hers for several seconds while she clearly decided whether or not to feign misunderstanding. Her hands had clasped her own and Ellen managed a weak but definite squeeze, tacitly telling her to have courage, that this was their last chance to speak the unspeakable.

Almost imperceptibly, her daughter nodded.
"When?"

Marion checked over her shoulder then bent closer, her voice a whisper, "The graves?"

"Yes. When?"

Marion's hands gripped Ellen's ever more tightly. She had the air of a frightened pony, eyes darting around the room. Then, as if making up her mind, she leaned in so close her voice was little more than a sigh. "Just a few weeks ago when Rosa and I got lost. It was like being pulled into a maze and we couldn't get out. It had a bad feeling. So you know what that place is, then?" She shook her head, bewildered. "But I don't—"

"Were there dolls? Effigies?"

Marion's eyes told her what she needed to know.

"So it is happening again."

Marion continued to stare. "You knew about it. So that's why you always warned us not to go? But I scoured those woods when we were children. I knew every single inch of it."

"It wasn't time."

"I don't understand. Mum, what are you trying to tell me?"

"They...The Four...have to be–"

Again Marion shook her head and Ellen summoned all her strength. "Summoned. Somehow...You go to Annie's. Should have stopped you... But she's not there anymore... I'm lost... I can't see... a veil drawn–"

Iron clamps gripped her lungs and she fought for breath, lunging for air with great gasps.

Marion's glance darted to the door then back again. "How did you know? Mum, how did you know I went to Annie's?"

Motioning to be lifted up, Ellen felt strong hands haul her up the bed as if she weighed little more than a bag of feathers, Pillows were packed behind her back. "Do you need water? Honey? Linctus?"

She shook her head, frantically fluttering her hands at her daughter. She had to speak, had to say this. "And Snow? You took her as well... but it's too dangerous... to use such as her—"

Marion's eyes swam with tears and she flung herself onto her mother's chest. "Oh God, I didn't know, I swear. They said we should use our gifts. I didn't know. I honestly didn't know——"

"Who?"

"Agnes."

Ellen's mind cut to black then resurged in a jarring, sickly swirl. No breath would come. Her lungs were a casket of stone and anguish plunged into her heart.

"Mum?"

A full minute passed before her chest moved again and she gulped at the air, clutching at her daughter's hand. All the things she should have said, should have noticed, could have stopped. *Time was running out...* But what...what warning to give? What was it? Every word would matter and she must choose wisely.

"Try not to talk for a minute." Marion's cool hand pressed her forehead, smoothing the hair back from her clammy skin. "I only went up there a couple of times. I took Snow but she hasn't gone there alone, I'm sure of it."

Ellen's eyes were closing again, her words murmurs. "They used your energy, your medium...Annie's too weak now but I thought...I thought it was over—"

Marion suddenly gripped both her hands and shook her. "Oh God, Oh my God...They used black witchcraft on Dad, didn't they? And on Grandad Bailey? Oh, my good God, it's real—"

"Don't ever, ever say anything, Marion."

"How can I with no proof?"

"Mad... They'll say... you're mad. And it's happening again, you know it."

"But who? Why?"

"You saw—"

"I thought it was a séance. I blanked out...I don't remember, it's all a blur...Oh God, to think I helped them do something terrible. I had a bad feeling....something's come to fruition...Mum, I didn't know."

Ellen drifted along on a tide of dreams... Bill Holland, that young fit man with jet hair who liked to dance rock and roll at the miners club; how he'd been carried out of the pit one day shouting like a madman that he'd seen demons jumping out of the rock face; snakes slithering down the mine shaft; and great squelching black creatures materialising from the earth. They said it could happen to miners after long periods underground, and that was what had caused his heart attack. *Digitalis more like... Annie... Agnes...* Why, for God's sake, though? Why?

Downstairs the grandfather clock resounded around the house with the hour of four o'clock and Ellen's breathing became that of painful, rasping Cheyne Stokes – the gaps between each lunge for air lengthening ever further - her passing now near. Clustered around her bed, all three of her daughters sat helpless and miserable, knowing Ellen would not see the dawn of another day. It seemed to them that after every long, drawn-out inhalation there would not be another, their mother's body too frail and weak to fight a moment longer.

A full three minutes passed before another wrenching gasp arched Ellen's body in painful contortion. All bowed their heads and prayed for a gentle release.

Four full minutes passed before Marion leaned over to feel her carotid pulse, expecting to say she'd gone. But just as she bent towards her Ellen suddenly reared up. Staring wide-eyed at the open bedroom door she was pointing at the white-haired girl hovering on the threshold.

"You! You brought them!"

All three women swung round to see Snow suddenly rush across the room with inhuman speed.

Although Rosa was quick enough to grab hold of the girl before she reached the old lady, the other two were staring open-mouthed at what had followed her in

Behind Snow, a line of black shadowy figures had glided into the room. *One, two, three, four…*

Ellen slumped back on the pillows. Turning to Marion, her gnarled hand shot out and grabbed her wrist. "She brought them back…The Four…"

***

Chapter Twenty-Four
Louise

The police came knocking time and time again. Normally my mother got out the best china and served cakes on doilies for visitors, but Puffer Judd seemed to annoy her.

A red-faced man with bristles down the sides of his face and three or maybe four chins, he sat at the table eating biscuits while the aunties stared at him through a fug of cigarette smoke. Within minutes of his arrival my mother began scrubbing pans in the kitchen. And after that, when he still hadn't gone, she ran a bucket of soapy water and started cleaning the hearth, while he talked and slurped and spat crumbs.

Had we, he wanted to know, seen anything unusual three weeks ago on the night Grace Holland sang in Chapel? No matter how insignificant it might be, what we remembered could be very helpful. He dunked another biscuit and we looked at him blankly: three curious children and two middle-aged women in headscarves and rollers.

His mouth resembled a small bushfire in the middle of a thicket. Red-lipped and busy, it gnawed and nibbled, chewed and puckered.

Had there been a car parked outside then? He looked at Arthur – at the boy's eyes, which seemed to have sunk into bruised pockets of tiredness. Arthur shrugged.

Okay, well were there any strangers in the congregation? Or maybe there was someone missing who would normally have been there? He stared at the aunties. They tapped ash into a saucer, shrugged and stared back.

Alright then, when we were walking home that night, did we see or hear anyone acting suspiciously? He looked at me and I shifted on my hands, wriggling.

"What's suspiciously mean?"

Another time we were all questioned individually – even us children – taken into the front parlour and spoken to in turn. But none of us had seen a thing untoward and everyone had been in Chapel who should have been.

The last time he clomped round to our house my mother had been making pastry in the scullery and stood barring the door, rolling pin in hand. "I don't know what you keep coming round 'ere for. You want to try asking that husband of 'ers. It's always the husband," she said, taking care to pronounce the, 'h'. "You mark my words."

"I can assure you, Mrs—"

"And her neighbours? I mean, where did Hazel Quinn intend to go exactly when she left that night? Have you followed that line of enquiry, Officer Judd?"

Peering round her at the crackling fire and teapot on the table, he said, "Ah, now that I can tell you." He waited for her to invite him in.

My mother had her arms folded.

"If I could come in a minute I could enlighten you?"

She stood back, brushing her hands off on her apron and followed him to the table with a cup and saucer.

"Very kind, Mrs Whistler. Very kind."

She banged the cup down and poured him what was left of a tepid, stewed brew so crossly it splashed. "Go on then."

"Thank you. Ooh, a biscuit. May I?"

She grabbed the remaining few Rich Teas and twisted the end of the packet. Holding onto it, she said, "You said you had more information?"

"Patience, Mrs Whistler. Dear me, we are in a hurry."

He laughed and I can tell you that was a big mistake because my mother's nuts and bolts were tightening incrementally, the sinews of her facial strings taut with the strain of not slapping him.

But social awareness was not Officer Judd's strong point and he bided his time. Took a long slurp of tea. "Ah, that's better. Yes, well, and this should interest you, Mrs Whistler, because it now transpires that Mrs Quinn met your cousin, Grace Holland, in a local hotel on the night in question." He slurped his tea noisily, eyeing her over the brim of the cup, as the uncomfortable atmosphere cranked up another notch. "The Plug and Feather, it was, yes… for a chat." He flipped a page of his notebook, looking for the entry he'd made.

My mother stood over him with her arms folded. "Oh, I see. So that's as 'ow you think we're involved, is it? She met our Grace and so you think we know summat about it – me with three kids and a house to run and two full-time jobs and a sick mother?"

"This is a very small place," said Officer Judd. "And gossip stops here by all accounts, Mrs Whistler. Now what would Grace Holland be doing meeting a lady from Danby on a night like that - during one of the worst snowstorms in living memory?"

My mother shook her head.

"Have you ever met Hazel Quinn?"

My mother eyeballed him right back. "No."

I remember I was sitting by the fire, supposedly knitting. But when he asked that question I was glad he hadn't got me alone again in the parlour, because her lie thumped into my head. With picture-clear recollection I could see her - Auntie Grace dressed in white at a restaurant and a lady at the far end of the table with blonde hair. That same lady we saw again at Wish Lane Cottage because all the way home it had been, 'Hazel this and Hazel that…' Right there and then though, I knew not to so much as flinch because my mother's entire body was rigid.

Puffer Judd eventually nodded, slurped the last of his tea and stood up. "Well, if any of you think of anything, you know where I am. I should, however, remind you that this is a murder investigation and something happened to that poor woman between meeting your cousin, Grace, Mrs Whistler, and ending up at Castle Draus dead in the boot of a car."

That was it. My mother snapped.

"I don't know what the hell you're insinuating, Officer Judd, but me and my family all attended Chapel that night and we had the devil's own job walking 'ome an' all because a ruddy great blizzard was blowing up and we've been trapped 'ere ever since. Now I don't know 'ow the bleeding hell she got 'er car up there and I don't know how she ended up in the boot either – that's *your* job. But I do know it's nowt to do with us." Behind the horn-rimmed glasses my mother's eyes had turned to flint, and her face was crimson.

"And don't you," she continued, now pointing at him, "don't you, 'Mrs Whistler' me! I've known you all my life and it was my Harry who found that poor woman for you or she'd still be there. So think on."

By that time he was backing out of the door with my mother in pursuit. She picked up a spatula from the sink. "Coming round 'ere accusing me of being the village gossip, an' all! You've a bloody great cheek. I'll 'ave you, I really will."

Watching my mother lose her temper was like watching a match put to a paraffin-doused rag.

Everyone jumped back. I'd seen her blow up like that a few times but honestly we thought she'd take his head off.

He had both his hands up in the air, half tripping into the yard.

"How do, Judders?" My dad said, letting himself in through the back gate.

I've never seen a grown man look so relieved. The great bear that was Puffer Judd had been cornered against the drainpipes by a woman in hair rollers who stood all of five foot one and weighed seven and a half stone.

"Oh, ah, yes, very good," he said, nervously eyeing my mother as she stomped back inside and slammed the door so hard it rocked in the frame.

None of us children dared speak. My mother's fists were balled up and only after she'd thundered her way upstairs did we look at each other and motion towards the window. Dad and Puffer were talking and we needed to know what was being said.

The net curtains started half way down the sash window, so we huddled as close as possible to listen-in without being seen. Puffer was telling Dad that Grace Holland had gone back to Alders Farm after meeting Hazel Quinn at The Feathers in Danby. The two women had a couple of drinks together, according to the landlord, before leaving the establishment separately and peaceably.

Dad must have guessed we were eavesdropping because he moved away from the house and motioned Puffer Judd to do the same. So we heard no more.

Later that night Iddy and I lay in bed speculating.

"He murdered her," I said.

"Who murdered her?" Iddy said.

"Do you remember that night we went to see Auntie Grace sing in that big music hall and there was that woman who had a bad cold and fell asleep at the table in the restaurant? She had blonde hair all frizzy in a nest on top of her head? Well, that was the woman in the boot. We saw her another time at great-grandma Annie's, don't you remember? Anyway, it was her husband who killed her."

"How do you know?"

"It's always the husband, Mum said."

"They've got to get evidence."

"What's evidence?"

"Don't you know anything? It means they have to collect her belongings."

"Oh. But why did Mum tell Puffer Judd as we hadn't seen that lady before when we had? Why would she lie?"

"Shush!" Iddy hissed. "Don't let 'er hear you. You've got a really loud voice, our Louise."

"But why, though?"

"What I don't understand is how he could've got away from up there. He must've got a sledge. Maybe it's not him but a vampire ghost on a sledge that haunts the moors at night?"

"That chops people into pieces?"

"Into pieces? What do you mean, into pieces?"

I didn't want to tell him I'd heard Arthur screaming through the walls. "Oh everyone's talking about it," I said. "It's what they do to witches, apparently. They chop women's heads off if they think they're a witch, so then they can't rise from the dead and walk again."

Iddy went quiet.

"Oh yes," I added. "There are lots of them buried under the chapel, too. In bits. In bags I expect. Or boxes."

"And hearts stuck with pins in?" said Iddy.

"What?"

"That's what was in the bin the other night. And a dead dog all split open. Mum said it 'ad been run over. I shouldn't have telled anybody…she said not to. Don't tell 'er I said owt, will you? Promise!"

We lay quietly for a long time after that. Listening to the hissed voices that rose and fell from downstairs. And Arthur moaning and crying in the room next door.

***

Chapter Twenty-Five
1908
Annie

On the day Aaron Danby posed for the camera when the first chapel stones were laid, the look that passed between him and Ellen Bailey did not pass her mother by.

The whole village was out in force. Saturday morning and trestle tables had been set up for kegs of ale, sandwiches and home-made cakes. Broad-beamed matrons, rose-bud girls and harassed-looking mothers all busied themselves with plates of ham, sausage rolls and jugs of squash. Every able-bodied man was now helping to get the chapel built on time and they'd be here until sundown day after day, week upon week until the job was done. Children ran along the common with brown-paper kites streaming behind them – the day remembered by all as heavenly, bright with quivering daffodils and the hope of spring.

Annie had been hovering on the perimeter of the scene, her stare fixed on Aaron as he stood chatting. Oh, didn't he know how to work it? Back-slapping and glad-handing with an easy smile that spread like melted butter. Every now and again he'd flick back the pony flop of a fringe falling into his eyes and run a hand through his flaxen hair – a disarming, boyish habit on a mature man. He was so like his father in the bullish breadth of his shoulders, and those stormy-sea eyes that occasionally flashed with silver like a break in the clouds

She narrowed her eyes, focusing all her intent. The moment the photograph had been taken Agnes would walk towards him – a vision straight out of every romantic and erotic dream he could ever imagine – and he would be paralysed, struck dumb with a desire he could not contain. The blacks of her eyes dilated, distant chatter fading; every nerve cocked and loaded. Time stilled…

What happened next, however, happened fast. The photographer ducked beneath the dark cloth surrounding his camera box. There was a brief flash. Polite applause. The photograph was done. But Aaron, who had been poised to walk towards the cameraman and shake his hand, suddenly jumped and swirled around as if bitten on the nape of his neck. Puzzled, he looked all about him, no doubt expecting to see an early wasp. Alas, there was no wasp or indeed any insect causing the arrest in his attention. Instead, with one hand still clutching his neck he was staring into the middle distance as if hypnotised.

Annie followed the line of his vision. *Oh, no…no, no. This could not be.*

Aaron Danby was gawping slack-jawed at the insipid, simpering face of her youngest daughter.

And Ellen was gazing straight back in what could only be described as a cherry-flush of rapture.

Sharply Annie averted her head.

The struggle to regain composure was immense. She focused on the morning mist rising from the moors. How had this gone so badly wrong? He was sick with love and erotic emotion all right, but not with the right daughter. In a flash of needle-piercing clarity the future was shown to her: the virginal bride throwing back her veil, smiling into the loving eyes of her groom. There, it was going to happen and she had seen it. Not with Agnes but with Ellen. And Ellen, sure as the fires of hell, could not be trusted to carry out her wishes. Ellen would let her down, would be loyal to this man. A vision was laid before her of three healthy girls for her youngest daughter and a whole-hearted passion for this man who would ride home on his horse several times a day just to see her face. Every part of him, and only she knew how much this was true, was now bound to Ellen for the rest of his life or he would sicken and die.

No! No! No! This could not be! It would have to be reversed. The whole carefully planned sequence of events could not take place if this course of action was permitted to unfold. Why Ellen and not Agnes? What had she done wrong?

"Mother?"

Slowly, she turned to face Agnes – the older and far less attractive sister – and for a good few seconds the rage inside her boiled so explosively she couldn't speak. Aaron should have been bound to this one and no one else. He should have seen what Jed saw in herself – a voluptuous, raven haired beauty with a sexual magnetism he could not resist, and would fight for, die for…

She looked now at her sallow-faced daughter, at the peevish expression and the hawkish nose, but mostly at the reflection of herself in those watchful eyes. If the eyes were the window to the soul then this one had one of the blackest she had ever seen. Agnes was the one who would do her bidding and not because of duty, but for pure pleasure. In short, Agnes had no lightness within. Annie's light had long ago been extinguished and the darkness had become her friend. But Agnes had never known or wanted any light.

Tacitly they exchanged coded information, each taking in the other's thoughts.

"There's more ways than one to skin a cat," she said.

Agnes raised her eyebrows.

"Would you like to be married, Agnes?"

The girl began to shake her head, to smirk.

"Not for long, don't worry. Just long enough."

"For what purpose?"

Annie's stare gleamed with malevolence.

The girl nodded. It would be done.

***

Most satisfyingly, she hand-picked Agnes's prospective husband from Aaron and Ellen's wedding party in May. To crown the almighty insult to her the happy couple had married in the new chapel on the very day it was finished – two months and two weeks after hacking down Odin's Tree to carrying in the altar cloth.

The Danbys had sent their own workers in order to expedite the build. And once the wedding had been announced the sound of hammering, sawing and chiselling escalated, becoming a daily rhythm from dawn through to the very last rays of sunset. Hedges were planted, a path laid, the lychgate painted. And on the eve of the marriage ceremony, in the blue-haze of a morning buzzing with the promise of a hot day, the brand new altar was carried inside. Carpenters were still at work until nearly ten o'clock that night while busy biddies bustled around with arms full of flowers. May blossom, wild violets, honeysuckle and lilac, filled the tiny chapel with heady scent, and daisies in jam jars from the children lined the window ledges.

Instead of her own flesh and blood, Ellen had chosen four young girls from the village to be bridesmaids; her bouquet a cascade of exotic hot-house blooms paid for by Clara Danby. And with each passing day the bride's tie to her mother and sister had become a slackening rope until finally she slipped away altogether and out of the cottage door, leaving behind the brittle curtness of their comments and accusations. She became untouchable, unreachable, drifting around in an ethereal vacuum; casually informing her mother that she would no longer be working alongside Agnes at the factory, that Clara was having her measured for a dress, that the Danbys were sending a carriage for her...

It was as if, Annie thought, watching everyone spill out of the chapel following the ceremony, her daughter had stepped across an invisible threshold and entered an entirely different world, discarding like a cloak her own flesh and blood. All without so much as a backward glance.

Once or twice, Ellen looked over to where she and Agnes stood alone by the side of the lane. Her attitude, it seemed to Annie, increasingly detached and dismissive ever since the day she'd set her sights on a Danby. Standing there in the cottage she'd grown up in, haughtily declaring she was marrying Aaron for no other reason than she loved him.

"That and you're up the spout."

"How dare you! We're Christians. We believe in the sanctity of marriage."

Annie had laughed at that. Thrown her head back and let rip. The girl was never baptised but she wouldn't be telling her that.

Of course, she couldn't mingle with the wedding guests. Whatever had Ellen expected? And she was quite aware, thank you very much, of the condescending looks thrown over shoulders, of the whispers and the smirks; not least from those who had come begging to her not so long ago for the man of their dreams to requite them in passion. Bitches and whores the lot of them. They mattered nowhere near as much as they thought they did –full of their own importance and all exactly the same as each other and their mothers and grandmothers before that. Just look at the headstones in the churchyard – at all the other Charlottes and Janes and Margarets now dead and buried, withered to sinew and bone, just as they would be too.

Into her third eye came the image of a dark, foul hag – one she recognised of old: a faceless creature with a large owl perched on her shoulder. And she beckoned her forth. An evil crone hanging from the skirts of Hecate she had appeared for the second time in her life on the night of the curse, and would bind and torture the mind of her youngest child. Did she want that?

Beside her, Agnes reached for her hand with the tips of her fingers and a spark of ice shot through the thin fabric of her glove. And even before the bride had settled inside the carriage amid a shower of confetti, she and Agnes swiftly took their leave, vanishing into the dusk unnoticed by the cheering, waving crowd.

It had been a profitable day and she'd done what she came here to do. Chosen the boy. A laughing fool who held his handsome face up to the sun, ran his hands through glistening brill-creamed hair and flashed those emerald eyes at the girls. A vain poppet who spent his evenings in The Quarryman, who played poker and worked as a hewer in the mine. Sam Holland's mother had once told her all she needed to know about her family, and yes, with a squirrel sized brain in his head he would be perfect.

A half-smile lurked around her lips. A change of plan, that was all. It had been given to her for the asking and silently she thanked the old hag. *Come to me...* What a sweet joy it was to know the dark ones walked with her once more. There would be a payment expected, of course, but that would be later. Much later. For now the two women walked home in silence, the only sound on the evening air that of their own breath.

"First night of the full moon," said Agnes. "A red sky too."

She nodded. "And on the third it will be done. This way will be better. More slowly savoured, more drawn-out."

"Yes, I think it will."

The dark side had ways of working you sometimes didn't foresee, Annie thought. But now she had...And it would be so very much more gratifying than anything she could have conjured herself.

***

Chapter Twenty-six
February, 1951
Harry Whistler

On the day of Ellen Danby's funeral, rainwater dripped from trees, slush lined the lanes and muddy streams gurgled into drains. Cowpats of white lay strewn across the moors with the melting snow emptying thousands of gallons into brooks that rushed down to the River Danby, swelling its banks to bursting point. The bare landscape was wet, boggy and cold; and everyone complained of constantly sweeping away filthy water from front doors and yards. It spattered clothes, horses and cars; and a raw wind laced with sleet added to the misery. Would winter never end?

Today, though, Harry thought, it seemed fitting.

The thaw, once it started, had set in quickly; and as soon as the roads were passable he'd made a start on the backlog. A total of twelve old folk had passed away in this sparsely populated village in less than a month.

The first funeral had been for Violet. He'd kept her body in the basement after the family had viewed her; not only because the parlour was getting overcrowded but because despite the embalming process, her corpse had continued to disintegrate at an alarming rate.

"I don't believe that," said Vivien when he told her. But one peek under the coffin lid a couple of days later, and with a hand over her mouth she let it slam on its hinges and nodded her agreement.

It really was most bizarre and neither had an explanation. Violet's eyes had caved into the depths of the sockets; her hands had desiccated to knotted claws tipped with long, talon nails; and her skin emanated a green-tinged mustard hue that festered over the sheen of bone. And on each occasion Harry had entered the basement room where he kept caskets and tools, he'd noticed the distinct and overpowering aroma of Lily of the Valley mingled with the stench of human decay. As far as he was concerned, the sooner she was off the premises and six feet under, the better. Even no-nonsense Vivien seemed spooked. Having gone down there alone prior to an embalming she'd come back up looking quite pale. Violet used to wear Lily of the Valley, she said. It was the only scent she ever used.

Fortunately, the family had only requested to see her that once, and despite the delay she was now, at long last, safely interred deep inside the family plot. There were few mourners for the old lady, just her daughter and grandchildren, and a cluster of lifelong neighbours, which had made the appearance of Agnes and Grace Holland surprising and not a little incongruous. Both dressed in black, mother and daughter had stood under the yews at the far end of the churchyard just as the coffin was lowered into the ground, and disappeared shortly afterwards.

It was a blessing, he'd thought at the time, that these women wore veils because Agnes had a stare every bit as unnerving as her mother's – if not more so. He'd thought Annie might be there, but at ninety-one and in this weather, highly understandable that she wasn't. Grace, though, ah, Grace. She'd still managed to knock him silly. Dressed in a short black swing coat, seamed stockings and stilettoes, her funeral outfit was more Kings Road than pit village, and it seemed to him her effort was wasted with so few to appreciate her. She'd given him the glad eye, though and smiled from under her eyelashes so maybe not. He shook his head. He really shouldn't feel stirrings like that when he had a wife at home, but by Christ that woman could raise a man from the dead for one last go. Strange how his thoughts had strayed to Grace yet again. And thoughts like that too – on the day of his mother-in-law's funeral. Oh, the shame. The disgrace. He should give himself a sharp talking-to.

While the Service was being concluded he stood outside the chapel smoking a cigarette, holding it as was his wont, between the thumb and forefinger of his right hand. Beside him, Crocker Bill took out another Silver Service and cupped a match against the wind. Beyond the chapel roof, high on the moors, clods of snow still clung to tufts of grass, the sky a grumbling grey. Damp seemed to crawl under the layers of their clothes, sinking into bones.

"Thanks for coming down, Bill. I don't know what I'd 'ave done."

Bill nodded. He seemed particularly morose today, his rheumy eyes bloodshot.

"Nice lady, if a bit away with the fairies," Harry added. "She was always nice to me, any road."

He took another drag of his cigarette. There had been such a difference between Ellen and her mother and sister. You wouldn't credit her to the same family. And not just in looks – Ellen being tall with light brown hair and hazel eyes, the other two small and swarthy – but in temperament too. Ellen had been a kind and gentle soul, ladylike and gracious, if a little vacant. She didn't always focus, but would turn her head to the sound of your voice and murmur what she thought you wanted to hear. You got the feeling, he thought, that she was living a very full life somewhere else and this one was just something on the periphery she occasionally tuned into.

He thought about her father, Jed Bailey, and the gossip surrounding his marriage to Annie all those years ago. Maybe Ellen had taken after him? Mostly his understanding had come from Vivien, who had never seen her grandfather, but also from his own family. Mostly though, it had come from Crocker Bill.

Harry was the only person Bill ever confided in. Bill talked to no one apart from some of the blokes he played snooker with, and even then only with nods and grunts. They said he was illiterate. And backward. Some went further and said subnormal or worse. Maybe he talked to Harry because of all the time they spent silently digging graves together, breaking for a cigarette, then back to shovelling dirt, hour after hour before going to The Quarryman? Maybe because he'd worked with his father? Whatever it was, he'd opened up to him a fair bit.

The strains of Ellen's favourite hymn, *He Who Would Valiant Be*, carried on the air. In a few minutes the Service would finish and they would need to carry out the coffin.

"How come as they're so different?" he said now, almost to himself. "Ellen and Agnes? Makes you think. Same mother - same upbringing—"

Bill had one elbow on the wall, his face a pock-marked mass of weather-beaten wrinkles. "Different fathers. Me and Ellen – we had th' same one."

"Aye, and it were all th' talk at th' time, weren't it? Like as how Annie 'ad come ready knocked-up? Beats me how your dad took 'er on? Good-looking an' all, weren't 'e, your dad?"

Bill nodded, ground his cigarette stub into the dirt and buried it with his built-up shoe. "Handsome bugger, aye. Big bones - a gentle giant 'e were. Mind you, I remember 'er on th' first day he brought 'er 'ome. Me dad 'ad such a daft look on 'is face. Like 'e coudna believe his luck. I were about six, maybe seven…and I looked at 'er, like, and thought, thee's a bloody witch. Thee's bloody tricked 'im. I just bloody knew it, like. She were up th' duff then, an' all."

'To be a Pilgrim...'

"Tricked him? How come?"

"Like as 'e saw summat different to th' rest on us. Kept saying, like, as 'ow beautiful 'ou were – skinny and yellow-skinned with a ruddy great hook of a nose? And it weren't 'er personality that 'ad 'im neither." Bill flicked a glance out of the corner of his eye and a rare glimmer of humour passed between them. "Anyhow, I really knew it were tricks because of th' way 'er looked at me – just a lad – like she knew I saw right through 'er. I knew I'd 'ad it right from th' start."

"Who was the father?"

"On our Agnes?" He shrugged. "Aye up, they want us back in."

Harry quickly stubbed out his cigarette and like Bill, scuffed it into the mud with his shoe before ambling back up the path to the chapel. While he walked alongside the clomp-clomp-scrape of Bill's footsteps he kept his voice low, "And did she? Have it in for you, like?"

"Polio and then smallpox? What do you think? Still 'ere though, as long as I keep me distance. Mind you—"

"Bloody hell, I didna realise! I thought you'd got th' polio afore 'er showed up, like?"

"Took me up to th' lake. Swimming on a roasting day."

"Singing Sally?"

The two men drew level outside the porch, waiting for the vicar to finish.

Bill edged closer, keeping his voice low. He looked every bit as wild and unkempt as you'd expect, Harry thought, wondering how on earth he'd managed to extract his own teeth because there were only three or four left.

"Aye. I reckon 'er were determined t' finish me off. After me dad died I were only about six, but it weren't long before I got sick. 'Ou left me in th' back bedroom and locked th' door. It were one of th' teachers who sent for old Fergusson. And I were lucky – 'e 'd got th' flu and the one that came sent me down to th' 'ospital in Danby or I wouldna of made it, Harry."

"So Annie wanted you out of th' road altogether, like? You've to wonder why, though, I mean you were only a nipper. What harm—?"

"Aye, well… thing is, Harry, I'm beginning t' suss it out now—"

Cut short by the necessity of entering the hushed chapel it was to be another forty-eight hours before Harry would find out what Bill had been referring to.

***

The shock of Ellen's death resonated around the village. While not unusual for those in their sixties to perish in a hard winter, they were usually ex-mining or factory workers already struggling with lung disease, malnourishment and exhaustion. But for a lady in Ellen's situation it was a sobering event. And to the villagers Ellen was almost gentry, having been a Danby for over thirty years. She lived in a very comfortable house, her daughters had all been to Danby Grammar, and two of them still looked after her. Ellen never did her own baking, cleaning or laundry – not for her steaming suet puddings, scrubbing floors or pulling washing through a mangle, because a local woman did all that for her. No, as far as they knew she'd spent her days flower arranging, helping with Chapel duties, and generally floating around.

'Of course, she'd never been the same since the accident.' Many shook their heads here, muttered what a terrible thing it had been, leaning close to whisper over the pews. 'And wasn't there a granddaughter who wasn't quite buttoned up right? Marion looked after her. Oh, did she? And that was something else as had never rung true, either…

'Ellen Danby, though! I know – and she could only have been sixty-two? Slipped outside apparently, and no one found her until the next day. So where were the daughters? Got lost in the snow, apparently! What - in the woods they know inside out? Aye… and with poor Ellen lying out on the lane all that time. It was how she'd caught pneumonia, must have… What about the nephew next door? Aye well, you'd have thought…'

Every head in the congregation turned to watch her coffin being carried down the aisle and out to the Victorian funeral carriage, from where she would be taken to the Danby plot at Ludsmoor

Church and interred next to her late husband, Aaron.

They'd held their tongues for the duration of the funeral, but a degree of anger and speculation about the circumstances of her death, and the no-show of her own sister, mother, nephew and niece, now began to bubble under the surface as they walked the short distance from chapel to churchyard. The horse's hooves clattered down the lane, Ellen's coffin inside the glass chamber immersed in flowers. She'd wanted the same Service and send-off as Aaron, and Harry couldn't help but be reminded of that occasion, even though he had only been a child at the time. Aaron's funeral had been shocking and devastating, with people openly howling in grief, not least his widow. He glanced around as the procession made its way to Ellen's final resting place, half-expecting to glimpse two small, darkly clad figures watching from the shadows. But today there was nothing, just a sharp breeze that flapped the black skirts and coattails of the mourners about them, whipping up the undercurrent of their discontent.

'Victor lived next door, didn't he? Yes, and what a disgrace it was to have built that monstrosity and taken all of her view – a nice woman like that. Just nasty. Spite Hall indeed! Well, no doubt he was proud of himself? And what about Nell, his wife? Where were they when those poor women needed help – with no power and no phone and the old lady fallen in the road? No, and you never saw them in chapel, neither. And how come as he'd had enough money to buy those mills? Oh, didn't you know? Yes, Vic Holland owned the lot now - the mills, Alders Farm, Wish Cottage, most of Grytton, and Danby Grange too... He never? Well I didna know that.'

Ellen Danby was well-liked, never failing to provide flower arrangements for Chapel or cakes for fund-raising events, and she often read the Sunday Service. Everyone was of the opinion she'd been a real lady, quietly spoken and kind. Oh, they all had stories to tell. Many of the workers had been unable to read or write, never having been to school or only until the age of eleven, and Ellen had patiently given up her time to teach them. They found out only now just how many she'd helped. Something of a sad creature who had never recovered after losing her young husband so tragically, she would be greatly missed.

On the Danby family plot close to the south west wall of Ludsmoor Church, Ellen's coffin was lowered into the ground, and the mourners now silent, bowed their heads until the burial concluded.

"Forasmuch as it hath pleased Almighty God of his great mercy to take unto himself the soul of our dear sister here departed, we therefore commit her body to the ground; earth to earth, ashes to ashes, dust to dust; in sure and certain hope of the Resurrection to eternal life, through our Lord Jesus Christ; who shall change our vile body, that it may be like unto his glorious body, according to the mighty working, whereby he is able to subdue all things to himself."

Marion, Rosa, and Vivien threw handfuls of dirt onto the coffin and with handkerchiefs pressed tightly to their faces, waited for the rest of the mourners to trail away and leave them alone for a few moments. Sherry and sandwiches had been laid on at the village hall, and it had been a long, cold, miserable few hours. But there was gossip. They could hear it still, trailing on the wind.

'Something doesna sit right. Agnes should have been 'ere. And where was that granddaughter? Wouldn't she be about twenty now? Old enough to attend her grandmother's funeral, any road. You could excuse the old woman – she were ninety-odd, but what about Victor? What's his excuse? And Grace? Yes, and it's funny as that one's not 'ere when 'ou went to Violet Bailey's funeral but not 'er own auntie's less than a week later. Is she at home, then? Oh aye, been seen with that fancy man of hers, as well. Not the husband of the woman who was murdered? Aye, been out with him since it 'appened an' all. Well, that's disgraceful. I think as there's something amuck, don't you?'

***

Chapter Twenty-Seven
Marion and Rosa Danby

Marion and Rosa were the last mourners to leave their mother's graveside. The dull, grey afternoon had finally given way to sleety rain and their smart, black court shoes sank into the mud. Neither had realised just how highly their mother had been regarded and sadness hung over them in a cloud as they walked across the churchyard and out through the lychgate. Neither spoke.

Half way up School Lane towards the village hall, Marion stopped and shook her head. "No, I'm sorry, Rosa, I can't face them."

Rosa hesitated, in two minds. What to do? People would expect them to show their faces and Vivien would already be there, handing round trays of sherry, ham and tongue sandwiches, sausage rolls and home-made pastries. All those sorrowful eyes on them, though – all that pity. And the questions - face to face nosy-parker questions about Lana and Grace and Vic. And was it true they got lost in their own woods? What a shame the old lady wasn't found until too late.

She looked at her sister's stricken face and nodded. "Neither can I. To be honest, I'd like to go straight home. I want to feel the sadness and let it all sink in – to give in to the grief, if that makes sense?"

Marion reached for one of her hands. "It's all those eyes. All those searching eyes. All the staring and people waiting for us to cry."

"Don't get upset, Marion, dear. We'll not go. People will just have to understand."

"What about Vivien? Do you think—?"

"What about Vivien?" came their sister's voice.

They wheeled round, surprised to see Vivien so close behind.

"We were just saying, we can't really face the stares and the questions," Rosa explained. "Would you mind if we didn't go - if we just went home instead? Only we've both been ill recently too, and Marion's still not feeling too good." Her eyes suddenly welled with unshed tears.

"It's catching up on us," Marion added quietly. "Trying to look after Mum when neither of was well, and Lana too. And now this—"

"Actually," Vivien said. "I was coming to find you. Our Vic's invited us to his place for a drink instead of the village hall. Apparently Mr Caruthers is there."

Marion and Rosa stared at their younger sister aghast. "Caruthers? Caruthers as in the solicitor, Caruthers?"

Vivien flushed slightly, such a faint sheen of rosewater pink that no one other than those closest to her would ever have noticed. She shrugged. "Nell came to the funeral. I didn't spot her until right at the end of the Service as we were leaving. Anyway, she was the one who gave me the message."

"Nice of his wife to turn up, at least," said Rosa.

"Sent to do his dirty work, more like," said Marion.

Vivien ignored her. "Vic's had a bad chest, apparently."

"Where was Grace? Has she got a bad chest as well?"

Vivien shrugged. "Agnes didn't want her to go and she does as she's told, as you well know, Marion."

"Oh, so you've been to see them, then?"

Vivien looked right through her.

"Honestly, you'd think they'd let bygones be bygones, wouldn't you?" Rosa said. "At a time like this and after all these years? Agnes was her sister, for God's sake."

"Well, it's not up to us to judge, is it?" said Vivien. "We don't know what really happened before we were even born, do we?"

"I know our mother was dropped like a hot stone when she married Aaron Danby. And I know it's because Agnes wanted him for herself. She couldn't stand that her younger sister was pretty and likeable and kind; that the richest and most handsome man in the county chose her sister instead of herself. Despite the witchcraft."

Vivien's eyes flashed. "Witchcraft? What witchcraft's this, Marion? What are you talking about?"

"Oh, don't give me that, Viv. You know what Annie and Agnes get up to. In fact, you're cheek by jowl with them. You've been going up there to check that they're all right when you could have come down to help us look after Mother—"

"I did come down. I can't be bloody everywhere, and don't you—"

"And you're not averse to a bit of witchcraft yourself, either, are you?"

"Stop it!" said Rosa. "Just stop it. We buried our mother today and she's not cold in her grave yet. Have some respect."

Marion and Vivien both looked away, at anywhere but each other.

After a few more moments of uneasy silence, Rosa sighed. "Come on then. We'd better go. It's getting dark already and we're soaked through. I don't know why Mr Caruthers is at Vic's house and not ours, but I should imagine it's important or he wouldn't be."

The three sisters walked along the rest of School Lane towards the village without speaking. The light was fading quickly now and the houses lining either side of Moody Street lay in darkness. There were no stars or streetlights to light the way, and their court shoes thudded dully on the wet road. Ahead lay the gloomy silence of the woods and the fork turning down to Grytton. As they drew nearer, Marion searched out Rosa's hand and gripped it meaningfully twice in quick succession. Rosa responded in the same way.

Something was coming they weren't going to like. Something that would change their lives irrevocably. And there was no choice but to keep walking towards it.

***

Chapter Twenty-Eight
Spite Hall
Marion and Rosa Danby

The unmade lane was pitted with potholes, the surface awash with running water; and with the forest on either side the evening plunged into gloom, chilled and dank with the smell of mud and moss.

The sisters' unspoken words lay heavily between them.

"It was a nice Service anyway," Rosa said, to break the silence.

Neither Marion nor Vivien replied.

"A good turn-out for her?"

With no response Rosa sighed and tried again, "Is Harry not coming down with us, Viv?"

"He's still working or he would have done."

Rosa blinked back the tears, realising her gaffe. Harry and Bill would at this very moment be burying their mother. "Yes, of course. Stupid of me."

From the edge of the woods a barn owl screeched, its cry raw and unearthly.

"Who's got the children?" Rosa said.

"Arthur's old enough now. They'll be fine 'til I get back and then…"

"Yes, yes of course."

The gulf of silence opened between them once more and they walked on for a further five minutes or so, until finally an ink swell of water loomed ahead, and a cool breath of air wafted off the lake.

"We're almost there," said Rosa.

Marion stopped, forcing the other two to turn and look at her. "I can't stand all this bloody small talk. Vivien, just tell us what the hell's going on because I'm not going in there unless you do. Why are we here – what's the real reason? Tell us!"

"Tell, you what?" said Vivien.

"You know very well what. We had an appointment with Caruthers next Wednesday in Danby, a full week after Mum's funeral, so how come Vic couldn't wait until then? It's downright bloody disrespectful. He didn't show up for the funeral but he can get the solicitor in quick enough. So what's in it for him that he hasn't had already? Isn't he rich enough?"

"How the bloody hell do you expect me to know?" Vivien snapped.

"Shush, keep your voices down," Rosa hissed.

A matter of yards away the lion-topped gateposts to Spite Hall were clearly visible, behind them a long, shrub-lined driveway tapering away in a tail of vapour.

Regardless of the proximity, Marion fired straight back at Vivien as if Rosa hadn't even spoken. "Of course you know. You know everything. Only here's the thing, Viv, so do I! I don't want to but I just do, and yes, you know damn well what I'm talking about. Something very unpleasant is about to happen to me and Rosa, not to mention Snow, and you know what it is. We've done nothing to deserve this, but if you know what's coming you should bloody well say so – we're your sisters. Where the hell's your loyalty?"

"And I told you I don't know anything. Are you calling me a liar? And what about Snow, anyway? She's illegitimate and she's mad and she should be in a home. If anyone's been lying it's been you. About her."

A sharp crack caused all three to physically jump and wing round.

A white faced girl with deadpan eyes was standing on the fringe of the woods, staring directly at them. Her stocky figure seemed to be rooted in the ground, moon-silver hair long and unkempt.

"Snow! You made us jump," Marion said. She held out her hand. "Come here, darling."

Vivien pulled her coat tighter to her chest. "Bloody, spooky mare." She glared at Marion. "You're surely not bringing her in here with us?"

"Oh, I am," said Marion, as Snow lumbered over. "She's my daughter, and besides, her grandmother will have left her something."

"So why didn't you take her to the funeral, then? Why didn't she go to school? If she's so normal and you're so proud of her. Or shall I spell it out? You're in denial, Marion, and you always have been."

"People stare at her as you well know. Why would I put her through that? For Christ's sake, Viv, have a heart. Oh, I'm sorry, you haven't got one, have you?"

"Cut it out, both of you. This isn't doing anyone any good."

"The dumb bitch should be in a home, Marion. And you know it."

A bank of fog had rolled in across the lake and begun to curl around the stone pillars, sinking into the driveway. Marion took hold of Snow's hand and yanked her forwards. "Come on, let's get this over with."

***

Vic and Nell Holland had been living comfortably in Spite Hall with their three young boys for the past ten years. Vic, at thirty-seven, had swelled with the years into a rotund figure with several rolls of belly fat. Like his mother he sported a hawk's nose and blackcurrant eyes; although unlike his mother he wasn't in the least bit sinewy. Nor was he one to skulk in the shadows. Vic smirked and swaggered, eyeballing women straight in the chest, letting his gaze wander all the way down before slowly working his way back up again with a contemptuous sneer, as if he found them sadly wanting. And Nell, who had been in service as a maid, waited-on him and the three boys as if she was still employed. Rarely did she make eye contact with anyone outside the immediate family, and if she spoke at all her gaze always flicked to her husband first. It was said that for much of the year she hid away because of the bruises to her face and arms. 'Always covered up she was,' said the villagers, 'always wore long sleeves and high necks, did that one....very suspect....'

Today she answered the doorbell so quickly it was as if she'd been waiting behind it. Ushering them inside, she offered to take their coats and indicated the library. It was funny, Rosa thought as they followed her down the oak-panelled corridor, she'd never noticed how tiny Nell was – less than five feet tall and so narrow across the shoulders that from the back she could easily be mistaken for a child.

The library was the last room they came to, opulently furnished with an imposing marble fireplace and a large bay window heavily draped with swags of burgundy velvet. By daylight no doubt it would afford a spectacular view of the lake.

Vivien marched straight in, nodding to Vic before shaking hands with Mr Caruthers – an elderly man with reptilian eyes that peered over the top of his bifocals. "How do, Seth?"

Seth? Frowning, Rosa followed her sister's cue, albeit less enthusiastically. "How do you do, Mr Caruthers."

He held out a waxen-white, slender hand and she touched the ends of the fingers as if it was a wet fish. Normally an advocate of the firm handshake it gave her some small pleasure to withhold it. The atmosphere, she thought, with or without a gift of clairvoyance, was charged with a foreboding even she could feel. For once she could empathise with Snow, who had melded seamlessly into a corner by the window, and now gently rocked back and forth. Best place to be right now, she thought, noticing the look on Vivien's face as Marion walked in.

Marion deliberately avoided contact with both men, choosing instead to perch on the brim of a high-backed chair.

She addressed the solicitor sharply, "What's this about then, that it couldn't wait for our appointment next week? It would have been more respectful, would it not?"

Rosa's eyebrows shot up to her hairline. Vivien's eyes flashed and Nell, weighed down with a tray of drinks, hesitated in the doorway.

Mr Caruthers looked over at his client. "Victor?"

Vic had his back to the fire and took his time, letting his full attention roam all over Marion's body.

She waited for his eyes to level with hers before continuing, "And you! We've not seen hide nor hair of you in all these years, dear cousin and neighbour; and you were apparently unwell enough to attend your aunt's funeral, yet here you are looking as fat, hale and hearty as ever."

Astonished at the appearance of fuchsia starbursts on Marion's cheeks, at the trembling hands gripping the armrests, but mostly at a forthright aggression she'd only ever witnessed once before, Rosa was rendered speechless.

The fire crackled and sparked, and no one spoke as Nell put down a tray of quivering, tinkling sherry glasses and proceeded to hand them round one by one. Clearly Vic was waiting for her to leave. Her hands shook under his impatient gaze and once everyone had a glass she hurried to the door and closed it behind her. Shortly afterwards there came the sound of running footsteps and doors banging upstairs – the boys evidently being kept out of the way.

"And what about Grace?" Marion said. "Where's she, then? Do we have only the one cousin now? Only I remember there being two?"

He was using silence as a weapon in its own right, Rosa thought, watching Victor sip his sherry once, twice, three times – each with a little slurp and a little gulp.

"Did you not hear me?" Marion said.

Rosa took a deep breath, about to ask him the same question, when suddenly he decided to speak. "Alas, my sister is poorly with the flu, hence why neither she nor I could attend our dear aunt's funeral today."

"Miraculously well enough for the Will-reading though, aren't you?" said Marion.

Snow started to hum and Vic glowered from under his brows.

"Come on then, Caruthers," said Marion. "Spit it out. You're keeping us waiting with your master's bidding and I've got things to do."

Rosa scrutinised her sister's profile. Since when had Marion become so confident and domineering? She looked around the room, almost expecting the real Marion to appear any moment now. The only other time Marion had ever come out and fought like an alley cat was when the Danby family tried to persuade her to have Lana cared for in a home for mentally handicapped children.

Vic knocked back the dregs of his sherry and smiled. The smile was that of a higgledy-piggledy graveyard crammed with too many headstones and went nowhere near his eyes. "Well ladies, we seem to have dispensed with manners and formalities so perhaps Mr Caruthers would indeed prefer to get on with it? Seth?"

"The reason for your haste being?" Rosa said to the side of his face.

He ignored her. "Seth, we may as well proceed."

Mr Caruthers stared first at Marion and then Rosa, long and hard over the top of his glasses, before retrieving a collection of papers from his briefcase. Pulling up a chair, he then sat down, crossed his legs and took a sip of sherry. He swallowed noisily - the Adam's apple bobbing up and down in his turkey neck - then sipped and swallowed again.

Marion's stare bored into him. *Making us wait.*

Finally, the solicitor put down his glass and cleared his throat. "Good evening everyone and thank you for coming on such short notice. Now, many years ago as you may or may not be aware, I was instructed to issue the late Mr Aaron Danby's Will only on the death of his wife, the late Mrs Ellen Danby, who was informed of the situation at the time of her husband's death in 1912."

Snow's humming was becoming more noticeable, the rocking a repetitive clunk on the floorboards. A few heads turned but mostly everyone remained focused on Mr Caruthers, forced as he now was to raise his voice. He eyed Snow over the top of his glasses, glanced down at his papers again, audibly sighed, then looked again at Snow. Her humming had escalated and was getting louder by the second. "Could someone take that woman out? Would it be possible?"

About to protest, Marion's voice was instantly quashed by Vic, who shouted for Nell. She appeared in an instant, her face pinched and pale. "Yes?"

"Cake or biscuits for the girl? Glass of milk? Use your initiative, Woman."

Nell looked stricken. She glanced over at Snow, who was busy working herself up into a fit - drool oozing from the corners of her mouth, eyes rolling back in her head.

Quite suddenly, Marion said, "Actually, I will take Lana out - don't worry about it, Nell." She turned to face Rosa. "Let me know exactly what he says. I can't stand to look at him for another second, anyway."

"Of course."

Marion rushed over to Snow and pulled her to her feet, "Come on now, Lana, we're going."

"He saw them. He saw them. He saw them—"

"Shush, now…We're going home."

"He saw them…"

"Shush, it's okay. Hold onto me… Quiet now!" With an arm around Lana's waist, Marion was virtually pulling the girl from the room, and Rosa stared after her. *Such an about turn.* The temptation to go with them was immense but she told herself she ought to hear what Caruthers had to say first. Besides, Vivien was still here. It was okay.

Night had descended almost without her noticing and shadows licked the walls. It was odd, Rosa thought, looking around, that they called this the library when there were no books, just the heads of dead animals and a cabinet full of guns.

"Right, as I was saying," the solicitor continued. "Mrs Vivien Whistler. Ms Rosa Danby. Your mother was aware of this in full at the time of her husband's most untimely death, for which you have my full commiserations."

Rosa sighed. *Oh, shut up and get on with it, you odious little creep.*

"I'm afraid it is my sorry duty to inform you that the house – Lake View Villa, that is – and all its land, some forty-six acres including the lake, was legally signed over prior to the time of Mr Aaron

Danby's death, to a Mr Sam Holland in 1912. However, it was agreed by Mr and Mrs Holland that Mrs Danby and her children could continue to reside in the house until the event of Mrs Danby's death, after which it must be vacated forthwith."

Rosa barely registered the information. "But my father owned the mine, Coronation Mill, a row of houses, land—"

Mr Caruthers shook his head. "No, I'm afraid you are incorrect. His father before him, Edward Danby, owned those particular assets, Ms Danby. But your father, Aaron, merely ran them while ever his father was alive. When he married your mother, you see, Edward's Will was changed. It seemed there was a particular issue with your mother's family. Not with your mother herself, which is why provision was made for her, but with her family and in this regard I must keep the late Mr Edward Danby's confidence. Aaron had, however, already been allocated the land on which to build the house, but the rest..." He shook his head. "Well, with your father being such a gambler it seems it was in the best interests of the Danby family that the mills, the mine, the farming land and the various other concerns, all be bequeathed to his nephew instead – a Mr Thomas Danby. Aaron had an older sister, you see. She died in childbirth but the baby, Thomas, survived."

"Yes, Thomas Danby died last year, didn't he? I saw it in The Chronicle, but I thought–"

"Indeed. And his daughter inherited."

Rosa frowned, trying to digest the information. "But my father wasn't a gambler... and how has my mother lived all these years? She had an income from somewhere, I know she did."

"As I said – provision was made..."

"And what do you mean, my father was a gambler? Surely not the house–"

Mr Caruthers sighed and took off his spectacles. "Mrs Holland has graciously allowed you and your sister twenty-eight days to stay in Lake View Villa in order to give you time to find alternative accommodation. You must understand that Mrs Agnes Holland has owned Lake View Villa for a very long time now."

Rosa shook her head. So her mother had known this? Yet there had been money for schooling and help in the house. They had never wanted for anything. Certainly they'd had to watch the pennies and there was nothing left over but...

As if reading her mind, Mr Caruthers added. "A small income was bestowed on your mother by your father shortly before he died. Edward and Clara agreed it and I should know because I drew up the papers."

"How shortly before?"

The solicitor hesitated. "Is it—"

"Relevant? Yes."

"Two months... about that."

"I see. How very fortuitous."

"In view of his gambling, indeed."

"He was not a gambler, Mr Caruthers. How many more times?"

"Actually the evidence is quite to the contrary, Ms Danby. Poker. He squandered everything his father ever gave him - the land, the house, the money - lost it all to Sam Holland, a miner who consistently beat him at Poker."

Agnes' husband.

The room swam around her. Pinpricks of light reflected in Vivien's horn-rimmed glasses. Her sister's mouth seemed slashed in a red-lipstick grimace, her head bobbing and nodding. The room was way too hot and airless. She stumbled out into the hall as if drugged, and lurched towards the front door.

Outside the night air was cool and damp. She hurried down the steps.

Marion, she had to find Marion.

***

Chapter Twenty-Nine
Lake View Villa
Rosa

Lake View Villa stood in darkness. Rosa stepped into the unlit hallway and closed the front door behind her. Already the house exuded an air of abandonment, clattering with hollow sadness, the bulky oak furniture and oil paintings cast into the gloom of a bygone age. She hurried from room to room, flinging open every door, but each was empty, the only occupants its whispering ghosts.

Marion was not here and neither was Snow.

The kitchen range stood cold, the grate choked with ash. All these years and her mother's presence had been so ethereal and fragile, but she had always been here... part of the landscape. And now that person, the living breathing soul who had loved her unconditionally, wrapped her arms around her when she'd been upset, gazed on her so fondly with those soft, honey-coloured eyes...breathed no more.

From the hallway the grandfather clock chimed solidly. Six o'clock, and as dark now as the dead of night.... Click-clock...click-clock....Soon the swing of the brass pendulum would slow until finally it stopped altogether. She looked around. All this heavy wooden furniture – the cumbersome sideboard, the high-backed chairs, formal dining table - where had it come from? And upstairs, the four poster beds and mahogany wardrobes? Better days, her mother had said.

Would Agnes and Vic be seizing all of her parents' possessions, too? Her own wrought-iron bed slept on since childhood? The rose silk covered chaise-longue in the south-facing lounge – a wedding present from Edward and Clara Danby? The Persian rugs? The bone china dinner service decorated with hand-painted roses – a gift for the birth of their first child? But what was she to think about any of this now? Was she really to believe her father, who her mother had described so many times and in such detail, had not been a loving, hard-working Methodist after all, but a reckless, drunken betting-man who'd sold them all down the river?

Who was to say what had really happened and what had not? Her mother, after all, had been on barbiturates, and Marion still was. Perhaps they had made up the whole thing about Aaron being a loving husband and father, a popular boss and a good man. And here she was, a fool to have believed it. Certainly something had made her father gamble away his fortune. Facts were facts, after all. Perhaps that was why he'd fallen from his horse? Had he, in fact, been drunk and on his way back from The Quarryman? How would she know when she'd been a toddler of less than two years old when he died?

Marion knew something, though. Something which had her volcanic with rage as if years of frustration and tamped-down knowledge were about to explode; Marion, who never spoke out, never confronted anyone and was never, ever rude. Other people's discomfort had her cringing with embarrassment, yet this afternoon she'd seemed to relish it, goading it to the brink of an out-and-out fight. They all knew something, didn't they? Something kept secret for a long, long time...the whole, damn lot of them...

Rosa gazed out of the kitchen window at the row of dark sentinels lining the forest edge. They'd be in there she supposed - Marion and Snow.

But who now, for the love of God, could she trust? Which sister?

Did she take Marion's word? Marion, who took sedatives, had but the briefest memory of her late father, and refused to acknowledge her daughter needed proper care? Marion, who was vague and evasive, who talked to dead people and roamed the moors and the woods with a paintbrush in her hand?

Or Vivien? Vivien was the sensible one who worked hard, had her ear to the ground and seemed convinced by the alternative view of her father. If the Danbys had so disapproved of Ellen's family then maybe they had left the bulk of the estate to Aaron's nephew, Thomas, as said? Perhaps Aaron did lose a poker game to Sam Holland and with it the house? And maybe Agnes had been kind enough not to claim what was hers until after her sister's death?

But would her father have staked the family home? Really? And was that why Vivien had been so harsh about this family all these years – because somehow she knew he'd left them all in poverty, and that's why she'd married when she had the chance even though it had undoubtedly made her life harder? Rosa's eyes widened. If Vivien had somehow known about that poker game, it would explain a lot. What if she was right?

She put her fingers to her temples, her thoughts stuck in a quagmire.

But if that was the case and Vivien was correct – how could she possibly approve so wholeheartedly of Vic inheriting everything? Vic who built Spite Hall a matter of yards in front of her parents' beautiful lake house, even going so far as to have the malicious house name engraved on the gateposts? Vic, who sat there, satisfied and smug, while Marion, her own sister, battled with a fury so great it had rendered her bone-rigid, the muscles in her face so taut her nerves twitched. Why? Why did Vivien approve of that, no matter what the history? She and Marion had done nothing wrong.

Oh, God, were they really left with nothing?

And what about Snow? What on earth would happen to the girl now?

Outside, the path to the fountain shone in a trail of pearly moonlight, the stone cherubs eerily blind in their bowl of ice. Marion would have taken Snow into the forest. It was their refuge, where they felt free and able to be themselves, but it was not a prospect she relished herself. In fact she hadn't planned on going back in there ever again. At least not at night.

But Marion had...

Although she'd given the impression of being every bit as terrified as Rosa when they found the burial ground and discovered those macabre dolls in the trees, she had still gone back in there tonight, hadn't she? But why? Why would it still feel like a place of refuge after what they'd seen? Hell's teeth, why did she even have to think about bat-crazy stuff like this now when there were more serious issues at stake like being homeless in less than a month? Marion should be here with her so they could discuss this....

Even so, there was a strong feeling of missing something. Everyone else was talking in riddles, possessing knowledge on other levels when she was cognisant of only one.

It had certainly been one hell of a difficult day. And it wasn't over yet. Placing her palm flat to her stomach and ignoring the empty churning, she closed her eyes. If she stuck to her own rationalisation about what had happened to them that night they got lost – that they had stumbled off the path because of the snow and the rest was Marion being a little off-the-wall – then she would never be any wiser. So what was an illusion and what was not? Marion said the dolls had been put there recently so perhaps the area, previously well concealed, was a place for those who indulged in the dark arts? Gossip rippled around this village from those reportedly having seen torches and fires in the forest, and those stories affected Marion pretty badly. Did she perhaps see them as encroaching on her territory? A blight on a forest she found beautiful and special? Did the very thought of it, the horror, the nastiness invoked, affect the state of her mind? And Snow's?

Ellen had refused to ever go into the woods again after their father had been killed, but that too was no doubt mired in confusion, with all the talk about Annie being a black witch and the knowledge that she'd hated Aaron and despised their marriage. Probably all good reasons why Ellen had stayed in the house and garden, except to help out at Chapel; kept away from her sister and her mother, from gossip and trouble, and subsequently refused to say boo to the proverbial goose lest something terrible should happen again. Rosa had always thought Marion was of the same ilk, or at least until this afternoon when she was confronted with Vic Holland. How angry she'd been, how very, very angry....even before they got there...And that was without knowing Agnes now owned this house and wanted them out. So then, there must be something else....

Oh, where was she? They really needed to talk.

She stared into the dark glass of her own reflection.

Rosa Danby, are you real or part of a dream?

A bloodless face faded in and out of focus in the moonlit window. She looked old - out of time and out of step - a sepia photograph caught in the flash of a pre-war camera. A wraith peering out of the window, with her hair scraped back under a cloche hat, a brown tweed suit and brooch. She looked down at her sensible lace-up shoes and all at once life's journey seemed to rush up and meet her head-on. This was the tipping point into old age, wasn't it? The same clothes all her adult life because they still had plenty of wear left in them. And what had she done with it? With her life? A single tear swelled and tipped over the brim of her eye. She swiped it away with a gloved finger.

"Come on, Rosa. Get a grip and less of this revolting self-pity."

Galvanising herself into action she flung on Ellen's old coat from the hook by the back door, shoved her feet into wellingtons and grabbed a torch. Something told her Marion and Snow needed her and that it was suddenly very urgent. Just a feeling. She couldn't say why.

***

With thoughts ricocheting around her mind and the sound of her own breath hard and fast in her ears, it wasn't until she'd tramped all the way up to the forest edge that she heard it: the sound of a baby crying. She stopped to listen. How strange. Hadn't

Marion said there was a baby crying on the night they got lost? She hadn't heard anything herself, though.

Her ears strained into the quiet darkness. No, nothing. Had it been a cat?

The night was chilly and absolutely still. A light frost glistened on the boughs of the trees and sparkled on the leaves. There wouldn't be any children out in this, so... For a few moments longer she stood and listened, but whatever she thought she'd heard had stopped. It was either her imagination then, or a small animal.

Cautiously she stepped from the moonlit lawn into the woods and instantly its dark cloak wrapped around her. Hopefully she would not have to go too far into its depths. The milky orb from the torch bobbed around the tree trunks and every few minutes she called out, "Marion! Marion! Are you here? It's Rosa."

Her voice echoed around the immediate vicinity, with the only other sound twigs snapping beneath her feet. "Marion, I'm on the main path about five minutes from the brook. Marion!"

No answer.

The further into the forest she ventured the more oppressive it became. Determined not to keep wheeling around to flash the torch behind her she plodded determinedly on. Not a sound. And yet there was a feeling she was not alone. A breath sighed on her neck. Eyes bored into her back.

Hurrying along she called out repeatedly, "Marion! Marion!"

Five minutes or more passed and still there was no sound of the brook. This was the main path and she should be level with it by now. In total darkness the torchlight was weak, highlighting only a cluster of the nearest tree trunks. Perhaps there was no point to this and it would be a good idea to retrace her steps and wait at home? Marion would be looking for Snow – yes, that was it, and she would be the one to find her. This was not a good idea. Not good at all. Fear tugged at her inside. Someone else was definitely here. Close by. Watching but not speaking out. She stopped walking. Stood still. Then circled around several times, shining the torch in staccato flashes of light, half-expecting to catch a face peering back at her.

Should she turn back?

Again she circled three hundred and sixty degrees. And her heart almost stopped. A slight flicker of movement had caught her eye. Bloody hell, someone was there! The torch slid from her fingers, thumping to the ground, and from out of the shadowy depths a dark shape began to emerge.

Without the torch her eyes had to adjust quickly. Her breath stuck in her throat as, backing into a tree trunk, she held her hands out in front ready to fend off whoever it was.

But no one came forth. Her eyes strained into the blackness. No one was there. No one at all.

Puzzled, she leapt to pick up the torch while keeping her head up, constantly vigilant. There had been a dark shape – the form of someone - there had! Shrouded in black and utterly faceless. Her heart pulsed in great, sickly waves. She had to turn for home but her bearings had gone. Which way was forwards and which was back? *Oh God, please help me.*

Then out of nowhere it came again. Much louder now – only a few feet away – the baby crying. And something else - rushing water. *Oh, thank God!* Now she knew where she was. Picking up speed she hurried in its direction. "Marion? Marion? I'm at the Well."

Even to herself her voice sounded tremulous and panicky, lost in the roar of water hurtling over rocks – thousands of gallons still pouring off the moors in torrents. The sight of it was like stumbling on an old friend and she almost ran toward it. As children they used to call this the magic pool, but it was in fact a natural spring around which had been built a stone encasement, locally known as the Holy Well. Five stepping stones led across the fast-flowing stream at the head of it, and for a split second she hesitated. If she crossed here the path would take her into the heart of the forest. Every instinct held her back. But the baby's crying was escalating and there was still no sign of her sister.

"Marion?"

Should she cross over? Where would they be if not here? How could she go home without them, though, to wait alone and indefinitely? And she couldn't leave a baby to die alone and abandoned....

When they were children walking home from school in the dark, Ellen instructed them to stick to the lane and to sing hymns loudly so she would hear them coming, and to protect them from the evil trolls lurking in the undergrowth. She had, Rosa thought, instilled in them just enough fear to put them on their guard. And it might not be a bad idea now.

The stones were slippery but she took them in five leaps and landed on the other side; the path now noticeably narrower and less well travelled. As she walked further into the core, the noise from the stream quickly became muffled and the canopy of trees more dense, obscuring both moon and stars. Fear prickled once again, but the spirit of her mother and the overriding need to find her sister infused her with a courage she didn't feel.

The hymn came to her without further thought, her voice wavering at first but gaining in strength. "Immortal, invisible... God only wise... in light inaccessible hid from our eyes..."

She stopped. The baby's crying! There it was.

"...Most blessed, Most glorious, the ancient of days..."

There...most definitely... so close now that if she reached out she'd touch it...

"...Almighty, Victorious..."

In fact, oh God, it was right next to her. Someone really had left a baby here, out in the woods to die... Holding out her arms either side in a star shape her gloved fingertips brushed against the pinpricks of holly. And happened on something soft and squelchy. Snatching at what she thought must be a stuffed toy she shone the torch onto its face, and instantly flung it aside. Someone close by gasped. Fresh blood was spreading through her gloves. She stared down at her hands in disbelief, already backing away, the torch light wobbling precariously in every direction.

"Who are you? Where are you?"

There was something in the path – the thing she'd thrown down. And the scream stuck in her throat as it caught in the sweep of light. A horrible malformed, waxen creature lay staring up from the mud, with long pins stuck through the spine, the legs and the neck.

"Rosa!"

She swung round with the torch on full beam.

"God, Marion. Oh, thank God."

"Rosa, I've found it–"

"And you've got Snow with you. Thank God. Hurry, we have to get out of here right now."

Marion pushed her aside to see what Rosa had been looking at. "This is it," she said. "This place - I know what it is. I knew this afternoon. I've been here before, Rosa."

"No, enough. We have to go. Is that the main path back? I can't remember."

"Yes, but I want to tell you—"

"Should we take this horrible thing back with us?"

"No, don't touch it."

"But it might be evidence of some sort."

"Not the sort that would do anybody any good," Marion said. "Rosa, listen to me – it came to me this afternoon and—"

"No, stop. We'll talk later. There's someone here watching us. Come on, hurry."

Rosa set off at a pace with Marion and Snow in tow.

Breathless with trying to keep up, Marion continued to tell her what she wanted to say. "I had a feeling I'd been there before but I couldn't be sure when or who with, but it came to me when I looked into his eyes this—"

"There's someone behind us, I can hear them—"

"Yes. Yes, I think you're right. I didn't realise. Okay, keep walking. We're right behind you. Focus on the path ahead. Can you see the stream yet?"

"No, it's pitch black."

"It does seem longer walking back, I have to say."

"It's a trick. We're going in circles again," said Rosa.

"You were singing. Let's sing again like Mum used to tell us to. She's here with us, I can feel her." She grabbed Snow and held onto her, dragging her along.

"He who would valiant be, 'gainst all disaster…"

Both sisters sang loudly just as they had when they were children, as if Ellen would be waiting for them at the kitchen window like old times. Both pictured the image powerfully and clearly in their minds, hastening towards it as they sang, jumping across the stones and racing now along the path back to the house.

"I can see the lawn," Marion panted, struggling with Snow who was constantly hanging back. "The fountain, all silvery. But I've got to tell you something, I've got to tell you now. Right now. Come on, Snow, you're a dead weight."

"Let's get out first. Almost there."

Bursting onto the lawn they still kept running, not daring to stop and turn round until they reached the fountain and collapsed against it.

"Rosa," Marion panted. "Are you sure someone was there?"

"Yes, positive. I saw them."

"But who?"

"I don't know but I swear they were watching me...us. I didn't see their face, just a black cloak or coat or hood. Oh God, I can't remember what they looked like, I'm shaking all over." Tearfully she rounded on her sister. "Why the hell did you go off like that and in there of all places? You knew I'd have to tell you what happened this afternoon and you knew I'd have to come and find you."

"Because I know the truth."

"What do you mean? What truth? Marion, I'm scared to death and I don't know what to believe anymore."

Marion was shaking her head. "No, listen. It was coming to me gradually anyway, but now I know as sure as I ever will. During the snowstorm, after we got back and I was lying there with the flu and you were trying to look after Mum and cook for all of us - Well, I ran out of barbs for the first time since I was fourteen, and then I got really ill–"

"Why didn't you—"

"Listen. I was delirious. I lay in cold sweats shivering and burning. I was wretchedly sick over and over, my stomach cramped day and night, and horrible, slithering things crawled out of the walls. The floor was covered in writhing cobras, and bird-eating spiders ran up the bedcovers. I had terrible nightmares. I stuffed rags into my mouth so no one could hear me scream. But the thing was, once I knew they were symptoms of withdrawal I decided to stay with it because a lot of the nightmares I realised weren't hallucinations at all but real. Some things were repeated you see - incantations, the things that were done–"

"What do you mean? Oh God, Marion…"

Marion was as mad as a March hare. She couldn't trust a word of this.

"I'm not mad, Rosa. Listen to me. I started to remember things. And since Mum wasn't around to make sure I kept taking the pills I took my chance and asked you to look after everyone and—"

"Suffered in silence?"

"Yes. I told you it was a fever. I'm sorry but I had to know. Mum said it was all for the best that I took the pills, you see, and that I never remembered what happened. She didn't want me to have the memories or the pain, I suppose. She meant well."

Rosa frowned and shook her head. "Mum said? What memories? What pain?"

"Yes, that's how I knew some of it was real – because I remember so well her telling me to take the pills and not to think about it again, to block it out. I'd been so scared all these years."

"I don't understand."

"They took me there, Rosa - to that place with the weeping willow and the hollowed out trees. And they were all there… including Victor. He was just a child when you think about it, but the whole thing was dreamy and sickly as if I was drugged. I do know there were chains around my ankles and my wrists and I was looking up at the stars because that's the image I see again and again. They were all there, Rosa, don't you see?"

Rosa had turned to look at the house. Through a mist of tears for her poor, sick sister she focused on the kitchen light. "What do you mean, all there?"

Marion squeezed Snow's hand and spoke in a whisper to Rosa. "Including the good Doctor. When he came to certify Mum's death I saw his signet ring and recognised it."

Rosa continued staring at the kitchen window. "It's freezing out here. We should go inside."

"Do you hear me, Rosa? They were all there – at the witches' burial site. Thirteen of them. Vic raped me, Rosa."

Rosa turned to face her sister. "Marion, he could only have been thirteen."

"Old enough. And I was only fourteen, just turned." She glanced at Snow, who was craning her neck back to look at the Milky Way. "And she's the daughter he wants rid of. I suppose he was abused just as much as I was."

"And Mum knew about this, you say?"

"She said it would get a whole lot worse if we spoke out. The thing is – I saw Victor today in a clear light, Caruthers, too. I felt this uncontrollable rage when I got into the house and then all at once it made sense. I thought if I can get to the centre of the maze again I will unblock that horrible memory and see their faces. And I will know what they did. I had a full awareness and a clear intent, you see, so they showed me—"

"Bloody riddles–"

"We see what our minds are open to, Rosa. I told you, it's a place imbued with energy but you either tune into it or you don't. I'm so angry it was used for such a wicked purpose. Someone really knows what they're doing."

"And that's why you suddenly changed your mind this afternoon and took Snow out – so the answers would come to you?"

"Yes."

"So - the doctor and the solicitor, and who else was present?"

"I can name them all apart from four. Four are shadows with no faces."

"Marion," Rosa said. "I'm scared."

"I'm not mad and I'm not making this up."

"No, not that. It's…you know I said someone was watching us?"

"What do you mean?"

"I didn't leave the kitchen light on."

"You must have."

"No. The generator isn't working and I definitely didn't light a lamp or leave a candle burning."

Marion's eyes widened.

"Come on, let's go and see who's waiting for us."

When they reached the back door it was, however, to find it locked. Rosa fumbled for her key and pushed it open.

The house, bizarrely, now lay in darkness.

"Hold this," Rosa whispered, passing Marion a broom. "You might need it. Wait here."

"Oh, do be careful."

Then suddenly Snow shoved past them both and ran forwards with her arms wide. "Hello, Grandma," she said, lumbering over to the kitchen table. "Thank you for bringing us home safely."

***

Chapter Thirty
Louise

It took three weeks all in all for the snow to thaw completely. And with Grandma Ellen's funeral and so many other things to think about we'd all stopped talking about the lady in the boot. The police had drawn a blank. The husband had been released without charge, and no one knew of any reason why she had been murdered. Hazel Quinn had been an ordinary housewife and although she had a womanising husband, he had witnesses who saw him miles away on the night in question, and who could vouch for the fact he'd been snowed-in for several days afterwards.

Grace Holland had also been questioned but again there were witnesses who saw her leaving The Plug and Feather peaceably with Hazel on the evening of the blizzard. Word had it the ladies were a little tipsy and had linked arms as they left. Grace also had an elderly mother to look after – one who confirmed her daughter was at Alders Farm on the night Hazel had gone 'driving out alone on th' moors without the sense 'ou was born with.' And like everyone else they'd been cut off for three weeks by snow. Grace had gone out that night in high heels and hadn't even had the car out.

"It must be the vampire axe-murderer on the moors," Iddy concluded.

"There's certainly somebody as is very dangerous about," said Dad. "I don't want any of you kids wandering about after dark 'til 'e's caught, do you 'ear me?"

"Do you think as she got lost up there after taking our Grace back to Alders farm?" Mum said. "Took a left instead of a right? Then 'ou couldna turn that big car round and ended up 'aving t' walk?"

"And that's when she bumped into the vampire axe-murderer on the moors?" said Iddy.

Dad nodded. "Aye, I reckon something like that, duck."

Mum was nodding. "It's a rum affair, that's all as I know. Makes you frightened to walk 'ome on your own."

"I'll come up to th' mill and walk back with you 'til th' lighter nights kick in," said Dad.

"Dunna be so daft you silly bugger. There'll be a group on us any road."

"Right, well as long as none of you go wandering about on th' moors then, do you 'ear me? Not until they've caught the bugger."

We all nodded. Our imaginations were already in overdrive and soon it was all round the village how a giant axe-man was roaming the moors. How he had a beard dripping with blood; mad, bulbous red eyes, and loomed out of the fog when you were least expecting it. We practically ran home from school convinced he was breathing down our necks, pounding after us.

But the day after my grandma's funeral there was news. It came just as Valentine Dyal was about to begin *Saturday Night Theatre* on the wireless. We were all sitting round it waiting for him to start.

"This is your storyteller," he said in the somewhat sinister voice that sent us all tingly, "The Man in Black."

My mother was knitting, her head tilted towards it, so we knew she wanted to listen to every word and were not to interrupt. The fire was a red-hot furnace; I was doing crochet feeling a bit sleepy, and the boys were doing fretwork.

Dad must have been working late because I remember the back door latch clicking and him shouting he was home. "We're going to have a television set," he said, still taking off his hat and coat. "I've just had this family as want the whole house clearing and the old woman, well, she 'ad a lovely—"

"Shush!" Mum said.

By then we'd run over to him, though. Something exciting and nice was happening and we were jumping up and down. The only person we knew who had their own television set was Auntie Flo. We'd been to watch it a few times but to get our own! "When are we getting it? What's it like? Can we go and fetch it now?"

"I said shush," Mum snapped. "Pipe down the lot of you. Shush a minute. News has come on… summat about that woman."

She whizzed it up to full volume. The man with the clipped voice was talking urgently. "…with breaking news. A witness has come forward in the Danby murder case."

Mum's mouth formed a big, 'O' shape and we all held our breath.

Dad still had his scarf on, had only just hung his hat.

It seemed a sheep farmer had been up on the moors near Castle Draus on the night in question, and seen what police now believe could have been the murderer.

Dad shot over to the wireless and knelt down so his ear was a matter of inches away from the speaker.

"A Mr William Bailey," the clipped voice said, "who had been residing in his hut near Kites Ridge, had been out rescuing his flock on the night of the blizzard, when he spotted a small figure he thought to be a woman, walking away in the direction of Ludsmoor village. Interviewed earlier today by the local police, Mr Bailey said he had only come forth now having put two and two together.

'It could be something' Mr Bailey had said. 'Or it could be nothing' But he swore on his life that at around midnight on that dreadful night he had in fact seen a woman dressed in a long fur coat and high heels picking her way across the snow-logged moors in what was by all accounts a howling snowstorm. Quickly swallowed by thick cloud and driving snow, however, he couldn't say for sure who it was, and in light of the sheer improbability had dismissed it from his mind. The local police are not taking this seriously at the present time, apparently accusing Mr Bailey of being on his own for far too long and having drunk too many tots of brandy. Sergeant Judd alleges that on the night in question it would have been physically impossible for anyone – even a hardy soldier – to have walked across those moors in such conditions, least of all a slip of a lady like Ms Holland.

We laughed. We all did. How ridiculous. You could barely have stood upright that night even holding onto each other on the lane, let alone up there. And she was supposed to have walked over three miles in the black dark up to her knees in snow... in high heels? And what about the bogs and the rocks, and the gullies and crevices – lethal enough on a normal day? Many had become lost and disorientated up there over the years, when sudden belts of fog had rolled in. The place was a notorious death trap. Crocker Bill was the only person alive who could work and live up there in that weather. It was preposterous. Absolutely. Why on earth would he come out with an accusation as far-fetched as that?

"Well she had a motive, I suppose," said Dad.

"That's as maybe," Mum agreed. "If she wanted 'im but 'ou didna."

"And she told you that, did she?"

"As good as."

"You discussed 'er fancy man with 'er? Someone else's husband? I didn't know you were 'er confidante, Viv."

"Not in front of the children, thank you, Harry."

"Even so—"

"I said! Not in front of the children. And anyway, you know as I visit Annie and sometimes our Grace is there. Annie's is Grace's grandma too, you know?"

"Aye, I suppose."

"Yes, well, think on and then!"

But next day, a few hours after we'd got back from Chapel when Mum was making lobby and suet dumplings, or stew as most people would know it, Auntie Flo turned up all of-a-lather. She stood in the scullery red-faced and out of breath, hand on her chest, wheezing and gulping for air.

"Steady on, duck," said Dad, putting down the boots he'd been polishing.

It seemed a detective from outside Danby, not Puffer Judd, had been to question Auntie Grace again yesterday morning, only this time with a team of other policemen. Apparently, (and here Auntie Flo had lowered her voice, but my mother hadn't got her wits about her being so keen to get the news, so we children heard it loud and clear) they had searched the premises but finding nothing untoward had been about to leave when the detective, who was halfway down the front steps, suddenly noticed something.

"We'd 'ad the thaw, you see," said Auntie Flo, "since Puffer were there a week ago. Anyhow like I said, this fella were 'alf way down th' front steps saying sorry to have troubled our Grace and all that, when he saw summat as were 'anging off th' branches, just glinting in the light. Tiny droplets with specks of blood inside. They'd been preserved all that time in the snow…just thawing."

My mother gasped. "So she murdered her outside on th' steps?"

"Aye, with a ruddy, great big axe."

All the life bled from my mother's face, her complexion the colour of putty.

And Dad… he was just staring at her. Silent and staring. I'd never seen him look at her like that before. Never.

***

Chapter Thirty-One
Louise – continued...

You know when they say all hell broke loose? Oh, it really did. And it was so bad and my heart was thumping that hard it made me feel sick. Iddy was crying and we were both begging them to stop fighting, but no one took any notice; they were going at each other like demons, with teeth bared and spit flying. I've never seen or heard anything like it either before or since and I wouldn't want to.

We'd just had the shock of finding out it was Grace who'd murdered the woman from Danby when my two aunties arrived. Nobody ever knocked in those days – they walked straight in through the back door and that's exactly how I remembered it. Suddenly there they were.

Both Marion and Rosa were taller than my mother, and fair-haired with grey eyes. I had never thought of them as poor before that day because they were always so much better dressed than everyone else. While my mother, Flo and Connie lived in aprons and curlers, Marion wore floral dresses that wafted around her ankles and Rosa usually wore a tweed suit with a string of pearls. They always wore hats and gloves when out and smelled nice too, of soap and scent as opposed to borax and boiled vegetables.

That day they loomed into our tiny front room like a pair of ghosts – pale, grim and so, very, very angry. You could tell even before a word was spoken. Primed, I'd call it now – pumped-up and ready.

Flo was busy bringing Connie up to date with the news on Grace; and Mum and Dad were still staring at each other.

"Well, well, look who's here," said Marion when she spotted Flo and Connie. "Not that I'm surprised."

This was a new voice. A new person. Everyone jumped. Normally Auntie Marion glided around saying very little and when she did you couldn't make head or tail of it. But that day her face could have stopped a clock and every word fired out like a bullet.

"What's that supposed to mean?" said Mum.

"Oh, don't come the innocent with me, Vivien. I don't suppose you've lost any sleep either, have you? Because you knew this was coming, didn't you? And what's worse is you couldn't even wait for poor Mum to be cold in the ground before you frogmarched us over there to find out."

"I beg your pardon?"

She indicated my dad. "Have you told him? Have you told him yet what you've done?"

"How dare you come in here and—"

"You knew me and Rosa had been stitched up good and proper all these years. You knew Agnes had the title deeds to our house and we'd have to be out the minute Mum died; and you knew how Victor had been able to buy up all the land and build that monstrosity right in front of our house, even though you swore blind you didn't. You knew about the gambling debt. I saw it in your face yesterday. None of it was a shock to you, was it?"

"Of course it was. How the hell would I know what 'appened forty odd years ago? I was younger than you were."

"What's going on? What was it as 'appened forty odd years ago?" said Dad.

"Why don't you tell him?" said Rosa. "Tell him why we're all as poor as church mice when Dad was one of the wealthiest men in the county. Tell him who's inherited it all and why."

My mother's eyes shot to flint. "I only know what you do. I heard it Friday afternoon same as you."

"Heard what, Viv?" Dad insisted.

Still glaring at Marion, my mother snapped, "That Dad gambled away the house. That it was signed over to Sam Holland after a poker game in 1912. How was I to know what 'appened way back when, any road? Like it's my fault? It seems to me, though, that Agnes was good enough to let her sister live there all her life—"

"Good enough? When Agnes told her son to build a house right in front of ours so her sister had no view? Why would she do that if she was being 'good enough'? And you know darn well from everything Mum told us over the years and from how everyone in the village spoke of him that our Dad was no gambler and he loved us. It was a set-up and you bloody well know it."

"Hang on a minute, let me get this straight," said Dad. "So since 1912 Agnes has owned Lake View and all the land around it? What about the rest? And how have you girls lived?"

With Marion and my mother inches away from each other and taking no notice of Dad at all, Rosa spoke up. "The Danbys arranged a small allowance for Mum out of the estate, Harry. Enough to pay for some help and put us through school. Everything else went to Dad's nephew, Thomas. And of course there's been my teacher's salary. But now Mum's gone, Agnes wants us out of the house."

"And she and Victor own the lot? Apart from this nephew—"

"Who's dead," said Rosa. "Hazel Quinn was his only daughter."

Dad turned ashen. "Also now dead."

"Yes."

"And you say Aaron gambled away his estate?"

"He only had the house and the land it stood up on. We didn't know that. We didn't know the Danbys disinherited him from the businesses, the farms, the investments."

"Why?"

Rosa shrugged. "Because of the family he married into. We think—"

"Not good enough?"

Again Rosa Shrugged. "I really don't know. Probably. It seems likely."

"So he staked his only asset on a game of poker with a rough-arsed miner? His home with the woman he loved and gave everything up for? I don't get it. Wasn't he a Methodist – dead set against drink and gambling?"

Marion, still staring at Vivien, said, "Precisely. Odd, isn't it?"

Dad shook his head. "Hang on, let me think about this. So Hazel's widow, Max – he was the one carrying on with Grace?"

My mother rounded on him. "That's a totally separate issue."

"Is it though, Vivien?" said Marion, who had still not taken her eyes off my mother, not for one second. "Is it? Because the result's the same the way I see it. Victor gets the lot and if Grace had married Max Quinn then they'd have, between them, the entire Danby inheritance – Aaron and Thomas Danby's - would they not?"

My mother shook her head.

"I mean… did they promise you a cut or something? Were you fed up of getting your hands dirty, is that what it was, because here's what I don't get. What's in it for you to go siding with them against your own sisters?"

The mercury of my mother's temper shot all the way up the gauge and over the top. "You bloody, little madam! You come in here shouting the odds and blaming innocent people when it's you who's done alright for yourself all these years, Marion Danby. You and Rosa and that backward idiot you spawned, have swanned around living in comfort your whole lives. It won't do you any harm to get off your backsides and work like the rest of us have to do."

"Oh, so that's what it is. The nastiest, most dangerous sin of all – a cesspit of swilling, putrid, jealous hatred," said Marion. "You spiteful cow!"

"Come on now, ladies—" My dad ventured.

"Shut up, Harry! I'll sort this out," my mother said, stepping close up to Marion with her finger pointing in her face. "You've done sod all with your life, Marion. You got yourself knocked up at fourteen and ever since then you've floated around with a paintbrush like some dopy, fairy half-wit. You didn't earn a single penny or pull your weight through the war, and you've refused to get that retard put into a home where she can't hurt anyone. You should be grateful you've had a wake-up call. Now's your chance to actually do something."

"So *it is* jealousy then," said Rosa from the sidelines. "Good grief. You made your own life choices, Vivien."

"Right, well you tell me why she couldn't do a stroke of work all her life? Tell me why she shouldn't be kicked out of our parents' house?"

"And you tell me why she *should* be," said Rosa. "Marion's not well. She has nightmares and anxiety problems—"

"Aww—"

"She's on prescription medication as you well know; and while I was at work she had to look after Lana, keep the house clean and do the cooking because Mum was increasingly forgetful and it's a long time since we could afford any help. Meanwhile I've paid the bills and kept it all together. We've done nothing to deserve this and neither of us believe that our father would have left us in jeopardy, either. Your husband's right – he was not a drinker and he was not a gambler. He was a staunch Methodist and how dare you bloody hags tarnish his good name!"

"Hags? Who the hell do you think you're calling—?"

"You. We know you and Agnes and Annie, not to mention Vic and Grace, have secret meetings and we also know about the witchcraft. Don't deny it. We've known about that for a long time, Vivien. We just didn't understand why you'd want a part of it but now we do, don't we? So come on then, convince us you didn't know what was going to happen to us after Mum died?"

My dad was staring so hard at my mother I thought a hole would burn in the side of her cheek.

Flo and Connie had their mouths agape, cigarettes toppling with long tubes of ash.

"Witchcraft?" My mother snorted. "Now I know you've lost your marbles, the pair of you!"

Marion laughed then – a strangled sound in her throat. "Only you can't play the innocent with me, Vivien, can you? Agnes wanted to rope me in too, you see – years ago – because she knows I'm a medium, a gift only Annie had. You don't have it and neither does Agnes. I was the only one who inherited that one. And Agnes knew that for any black magic to happen you need an energy channel. Anyway, Agnes came calling one day. I was fourteen. Work it out!"

"What the bloody hell are you talking about?"

"Alright then, I'll spell it out. And I bet Connie and Flo can remember this too? So cast your minds back, ladies. I was invited to Wish Lane Cottage for tea and a game of cards. Only the cards weren't playing cards, were they? And the tea wasn't tea. I didn't know why you were all watching me so intensely but I saw all sorts of things I wish I hadn't. I'd liken it to a gate opening, and after that I couldn't shut it again; and what I thought were dreams turned out to be anything but. The thing is, when I woke up I was in the strangest place imaginable, lying on some kind of stone plinth in the black dark. Bonfire smoke stung my eyes and I could hear weird animalistic screeching like vixens or owls. I remember trying to get up but I couldn't because I was chained. Strapped down and gagged—"

"You're a mental case," my mother said. "You and that thing you gave birth to."

"That's enough, Vivien," said my dad.

But my mother went on, pushing home for the kill. "Have you heard yourself? You're just a slut who got knocked up as a teenager in the woods—"

Marion flew at my mother then. First she smacked her face so hard her head rocked to one side, then backhanded her and knocked it right over the other way.

My mother grabbed Marion's wrist before she could do it again and slammed her against the kitchen cupboard. "Do that again and you're bloody dead."

Dad tried to grab Mum, and Rosa tried to pull Marion away, but the two sisters had each other by the hair by then and were screeching like banshees. Chairs grated across the floor as they fell under the table, scattering the aunties and pummelling each other's faces with drawn-back fists.

Dad and Rosa were desperately trying to stop the fight but they couldn't. Auntie Flo and Auntie Connie were telling us children to go upstairs. None of us moved.

Eventually, Dad managed to drag my mother off by the waist while she yelled obscenities I didn't recognise and am therefore unable to repeat, but I know enough now to say that a lot of it was some kind of terrible curse.

Spitting out blood having lost a tooth in the fight, Marion let Rosa help her to her feet. "That won't work, Vivien," she said. "I'm the only one with any power. The truth is you backed the wrong horse."

"Wait a minute," Dad said, still with a straightjacket hold on my mother. "Before you go... Have I really got this right? Annie and Agnes fixed things so their own half of the family would eventually inherit everything the Danbys ever owned – the land, the houses, the businesses, the lot. Not to mention cursing Ellen for marrying one of them. So much hate it beggars belief. Why, though? I can't understand it. Just tell me why!"

"Dad built the chapel on pagan ground, Harry," Rosa said. "That's one reason, I suppose."

"Pagan ground, my arse. Odin's Tree was used for hanging."

"Annie did a lot of folk favours round here and then they stamped her out of existence—"

"No, I still don't buy it. There's summat else... Must be."

"Why don't you ask your wife?"

My mother was still panting. Her glasses had skated across the kitchen floor and there were scratches gouged into her face and neck. "Ask her what?"

"Tell him, Vivien," said Rosa. "Annie had her sights set on the Danbys right from the off, didn't she? Admit it - it's been a systematic attack using witchcraft—"

"What a load of bloody, old tosh. Just get out now, the pair of you, before I—"

"Really? So how do you account for this?" Rosa pulled from her pocket a bandage fuzzy with reddish-brown writing. And dropped it on the sink.

My mother stared. "What's that horrible thing?"

"Evidence," said Auntie Rosa. "Dried blood and dirt on a bandage of the type used decades ago. It's lint. The words aren't particularly clear but Marion and I have had a go. To be honest with being ill and then Mum's funeral, I forgot I'd got it until recently, but it's what we found in Grytton Forest on the night we got lost. We ended up at some kind of witches burial site littered with poppets and effigies…" She looked over at my mother's dresser, then at the window sill, at all the dead-eyed dolls. "They were hanging in the trees – dolls - everywhere we looked." Here she glanced over at us children and lowered her voice, although we still heard. "Evidence of the black arts – take a closer look at this. It came from a hideous poppet of a man distorted with wax and stuck with pins. The inscription, we think, says, 'Donec meam libidinosam compleveris voluntatem.' You did Latin at school like we did."

"Until you have fulfilled my erotic purpose…" Dad said, his voice trailing off.

"Yes."

My mother shook her head.

"That was for our father," Rosa said. "Wasn't it?"

My mother laughed. "And how did it last forty years if that's the case? Still hanging in the trees for all and sundry to see?"

Marion was glaring so hard at my mother I don't know how she withstood it. The air was electric. But still my mother was shaking her head, looking at her sisters as if they were certified lunatics.

"The bandage is lint – of the sort used by doctors pre-World War One."

"This is such a load of disgusting rubbish. Some people in this village hold grudges. They go into the woods and light fires, probably wish ill will on others, I don't know. How you can possibly lay this at our door? It's unbelievable. If Annie were alive today she'd have your guts for garters—"

"Annie died?" said Dad. "When did that happen?"

The silence hissed. It went on and on and on.

Everyone was staring at my mother.

The clock's ticking was deafening.

I felt like I was dreaming because the atmosphere was as if we were all caught in the still-frame of a camera. No one moved and no one spoke.

And then it was as if my mother couldn't help it. I know that now. This sly smile just slid over her face like oil oozing across the surface of a well.

I was watching my dad, though. A strange understanding seemed to lighten his expression. His jaw slackened and when he spoke his voice was slurred and syrupy as if he'd had a stroke. "When? When did she die exactly, Vivien, because Agnes said she was looking after her when I called just a few weeks ago?"

"About then…"

"Where's the body?"

"Wish Lane."

"Embalmed?"

She laughed. "Well you taught me."

Then my dad got his coat and walked out.

***

Chapter Thirty-Two
Hazel Quinn. On the night of the blizzard

After replacing the receiver, Hazel Quinn hurried back upstairs, swished shut the curtains and switched on a bedside lamp. Inside her custom-made wardrobes, row upon row of well-made dresses and coats hung categorised by colour. All bought from department stores in nearby Hanley or designed to order, they were mostly tweed suits or the new, fashionable swing skirts with netted petticoats underneath, along with twin-sets and court shoes. Christ, go out like that and she'd look like Sandra Dee...

It would be a painfully, unflattering comparison were she forced to stand next to Grace Holland in a demure full-skirted gown. No doubt the other woman would be wearing a tight wiggle-dress with a plunging neckline, complete with starlet red lipstick and winged, black-eyed liner.

She yanked from the hanger a classic forties dress her mother had once worn – a Dior pencil style in silver-grey wool she'd bought in Paris after the war, along with a fox fur coat. She didn't either agree with or care for real fur but it had been bought now and the night was freezing; she may as well wear it. Grace would certainly be wearing hers.

The sound of snow smattering on the window keened her sense of urgency. Soon the roads would be impassable. Still, she was only going to Danby and back on what were flat roads; and not for long – purely to hear what this dreadful tartar of a woman had to say.

The first pair of stockings she pulled on ripped straight through. Rifling through the bottom drawer for a spare pair, she took care not to repeat the disaster because annoyingly it seemed there were no more. What about underwear? No, there wasn't time to change or fuss about that and besides it was unlikely she'd take off the coat. A petticoat then, at least…and which shoes?

Once dressed, she regarded herself in the cheval mirror. And almost cried. Her eyes, still red-rimmed and puffy seemed to have sunk into the sockets, and her hair badly needed washing and setting, not to mention the roots touching-up. Frantically she set about back-combing it into a chignon, clipped and sprayed it into place then applied the brightest red lipstick she had, followed by face powder and a slick of eye-liner. Max didn't like her wearing make-up but then he wasn't here, was he? She smiled slightly at the thought and applied a little more; then pressed the lipstick in place with a tissue. Finally, she spritzed on some Chanel No. 5 and reached for her handbag. Better. There, yes, that looked more sophisticated, more in control.

Right, well it was now or never.

***

The Plug and Feather Hotel, or The Feathers as it was known locally, was on the High Street in the centre of Danby, its bar open to patrons of the hotel and diners in the restaurant. On a night like this however, there would be few customers, which was probably for the best since wherever Grace Holland went there was gossip - and two women having a drink on their own in a bar would definitely be noticed.

The prospect of being talked about was not one to be relished. It churned her up inside – all those people she barely knew referring to her as, 'that poor woman.' It played on her mind as she drove along the snow-covered road with the windscreen wipers on full. The tyres were skidding and she gripped the steering wheel, snow coming down thick and fast. She must be crazy to have come out in this. Why had she anyway? Because bloody Grace Holland told her to? Because anything was preferable to sitting home alone? Because there may be information that would help her divorce?

Something felt wrong, though. Should she turn around? Was this a huge mistake?

The high street was pretty deserted as well it might be, and after parking she sat for a few minutes outside the hotel in the tomb of the Jaguar, snowflakes flying onto the windscreen. Her hand hovered over the key to the ignition, the walnut dashboard gleaming under the streetlamp. If she turned the key she could be home again in twenty minutes, locking herself inside and Max out. A divorce would be in her favour. Her father's businesses had been left to her and despite Max selling it on, the money was legally hers. She could start again. She didn't have to be ridiculed in this way and made a fool of. Tears sprung into her eyes and she blinked rapidly to clear them. *Come on now, Hazel, get out of the car and get this done. Then it will all be over. You're a Danby and you are worth more than this – more than the pair of them put together. You can do this and you will do this.*

Decision made.

Inside the hotel, Grace was already in the bar, cloistered in one of the booths by the fire.

She sat cradling a glass of brandy, swilling it round and round as if mesmerised. The draft from the door made her look up sharply and the two women locked stares, each taking in the other's appearance. After several seconds too long for comfort, Grace indicated she should sit down opposite her in the booth.

Hazel turned instead towards the proprietor. "Would you mind awfully, bringing over a port and lemon, George?"

George, a portly gentleman of middling years who sported a girth befitting one well fed by the hotel kitchen and partial to a glass of ale, nodded amiably enough. "Right you are, duck."

Her shoes resounded conspicuously on the floorboards as she walked, openly and fully observed by the other woman. A good thing, she thought to herself, that she hadn't dashed out dressed sensibly for the weather after all, as the Parisian elegance of her mother's outfit had given her some much-needed confidence. And besides, Grace Holland was in full evening dress as expected, clearly fresh from the performance she'd just given in Ludsmoor. An emerald gown flowed from beneath a fur coat similar to her own, and her black hair was coiffed into an elaborate mass of loops and coils on top of her head. With the lamp behind her, however, she had the advantage over Hazel, who would have the light dazzling in her face.

She pulled the chair around a little so that her back was both to the room and to the door. Fortunately, the lounge was devoid of any other clientele and with luck would stay that way. As far as she was concerned, the fewer people who saw them together, the better.

"Oh, thanks awfully," she said to George, who set the port on the table in front of her, his pudgy hands trembling. He was not looking at herself though, Hazel realised, but gawping at Grace's copious cleavage.

"Will that be all, ladies?"

"Yes thank you, George," Hazel said, wishing he'd go away.

After taking a reviving sip, she pulled off her gloves and unclipped her handbag. "So," she said, trying hard to keep her voice steady. "You called."

"Well, I won't beat about the bush, duck," said Grace. Opening a packet of cigarettes she put one between her lips and offered one to Hazel. "Smoke?"

Hazel's mouth dropped open. That night in Bakewell she'd barely heard the woman speak – the men had done all the talking; Vivien's children had been playing up, and because she was so full of flu and so miserable, the all-consuming focus had been on Max and how entranced he was with this woman... this... She struggled to slot Grace into some kind of mould, to rationalise how she felt right here and now in this moment... and then it clicked in a heartbeat and she almost laughed. Grace Holland was, as her mother would have said, as common as muck – a trollop! Oh, it was nothing to do with her accent or how much money she did or didn't have. Rather it was entirely to do with her manners.

She took a cigarette and allowed Grace to light it for her. She rarely smoked, but now and again it was a little pleasure and besides, it would give her something to do with her hands, keep the nerves at bay. "I ought not to stay long. Max might be home soon. He's probably delayed with this frightful weather."

Grace leaned forwards in a conspiratorial manner, blew smoke to one side, then stared at her long and hard.

In her mid to late thirties, Hazel thought, and close up she's starting to look it. The ruby lipstick from her upper lip had bled vertically in spidery lines; and underneath her eyes the skin had caved into the orbit a little, giving the haunted look of an insomniac. Rings glittered on every finger of both hands; a gold locket shone around her throat, diamanté twinkled in her hair, more gold jangling at her wrists. Like a gypsy, Hazel thought – a beautiful, wild exotic gypsy. She'd still be the same in twenty years, thirty... or more...but wizened and weathered - someone who wouldn't be playing by any rules.

"He won't be back tonight, duck," Grace said, watching her every thought.

She fought to keep self-control, picked up the port to stop herself from shaking and took a deep drink, letting it course heat down the funnel of her throat. "And how would you know that, Ms Holland?"

There was no answer and she took another drink. Put down the glass.

"Look, why have you asked me here? Is there something you wish to tell me?"

"You surely can't be immune to the gossip, Hazel? About me and Max?"

Again she fought with her self-control. She took another drag of the cigarette and stubbed it out.

"Look here, since you've asked me come out on this dreadful night I think the least you can do is tell me what it is you want. Is it to ask me to divorce Max? If it is you can jolly well have him, you really can—"

Grace shook her head. "No. I knew you'd be thinking that and that's what I said to 'im, as like—"

"Oh, you've discussed it, then, the pair of you?" Glancing over her shoulder she noticed George hovering nearby, polishing the next table to a high sheen. She glared at him until he took the hint then lowered her voice to a whisper. "Like I said, you can have him. Just don't expect a wealthy man because he's stony broke without me. He's a jobbing salesman and nothing more. You do know that, of course?"

The flicker of a ghost passed behind Grace's eyes. "I won't deny as he's asked me, and I won't deny I were tempted – yes, he does want to leave you for me - but I dunna want 'im, duck. A man like that – I don't know as 'ow you put up with it. I feel sorry for you."

Despite her palms itching to slap the other woman's face, Hazel swallowed the rest of her port in one and prepared to stand up. "Now look here, it seems to me we've nothing more to say to each other. Like I said, darling, I intend to divorce him so you can have him."

"And like I said, I dunna bloody want 'im."

"Well, that's rather up to you, isn't it? I'm going home now. I really don't know why you asked me here. Why did you, Grace? Just to say you could have my husband if you wanted him but you don't? To try and humiliate me even more than you have already?"

"No. I wanted to tell you where he is and who he's with tonight, so you know as who to put on th' divorce papers."

"Oh, I see. You want me to do your dirty work. You get Max but you don't get named on the divorce petition? And while I'm here you can make sure I'll go ahead with it by painting him as even more of a heel. How dim do you think I am?"

Grace stubbed out her cigarette. "You've got it wrong, duck. I've told you – I don't want him. But I do think he should be taught a lesson, a man like that – ruining th' reputations of women miles around, including mine. I thought you and I might, you know, be the ones to do it?"

With her gloves half on, Hazel paused. "How do you mean, taught a lesson? What have you got in mind?"

Grace smiled, leaned over and pressed her hand.

Hazel snatched it away.

"Alright, 'ave it your own way. But don't tell me it wouldn't give you a nice warm feeling to make sure he doesn't get a penny? And to have evidence of what 'e's doing and how 'e's cheating on you? It's about self-respect, really, isn't it, Hazel? I'll not deny it would give me a bit o' satisfaction an 'all."

George was hovering again. "More drinks ladies?" he asked Grace's chest.

"If they're on the house, duck," said Grace, smiling up at him.

Hazel covered her glass. "No, I'm driving home in a minute and it's treacherous out there."

George came back with a bottle of brandy and filled both glasses to the brim. "That'll warm you up nicely, ladies."

Grace wriggled a little more and smiled from under her eyelashes. "It's doing just the job is that, George."

The moment he returned to the bar, however, Grace's smile vanished in an eclipse. She leaned close. "I'm going to come clean with you now, duck. I said as I felt sorry for you but that's not the 'alf of it. It's because he's done th' same to me. I know as you're 'is wife and I shouldn't 'ave got involved with a married man but I did. I fell for the bugger and now 'e's with someone else so I know as 'ow you feel, I really do. I can tell you who, and I can tell you where. And then there's also that young lass he knocked up in Leek who—"

"What?"

"Oh aye, duck, and thems just th' ones as I know about."

A dull, sickly thud slammed into her chest. *He had a child somewhere!*

"I'll tell you something else, an' all." Grace finished the brandy and beckoned George over for a refill, indicating Hazel should do the same.

"Drink it up, duck, it'll help with th' shock. Anyhow, the way I see it we've both been well and truly shafted. We've been hurt, both of us. But I've thought of a way t' give him a taste of his own medicine and I think as you should 'ear it."

Still reeling, Hazel downed the brandy, accepted the next one and downed that. Grace's face blurred and a fire in her head ignited. It seemed her husband had been courting other women not just over the last few months but the last few years. With every word the stab of realisation bore deeper. Everyone in town must know. He had come home to her with the stain of other women's sweat still on his skin.

Another brandy swilled before her and the ceiling started to spin. God, her face was hot. Who was it laughing so loudly? Herself?

A bell rang. An arm under her elbow. A blast of icy air in her face. Stumbling drunkenly into the oddly phosphorescent light of the snowy street, she found herself linking arms with Grace, the ground slipping underneath her heels.

"I feel awfully squiffy."

Grace took her Chanel handbag and rooted through it for the keys. "Don't worry, duck, I'll drive. I need a lift 'ome anyway."

Hazel leaned against the car. "Don't you live up at Ludsmoor? I'd have to get back."

"Stay th' night with us, duck. You're too drunk to drive and besides, you'll not want to be on your own tonight."

"I expect that's not too bad an idea, actually. If you're sure your mother won't mind?"

"And I've those photos t' show you. That 'usband of yours inna goin' t' get a penny by th' time you've finished with 'im."

It was funny, she thought, as Grace started up the car, how swimmy her mind felt, at the same time as something scalpel sharp jabbed in her guts: a feeling – for the second time that evening – that this was all wrong.

***

The journey up to Ludsmoor was perilous, with the Jaguar swerving from side to side, its back end sliding. Through far more of a stupor than Hazel thought the three drinks had merited – or was it four? – apprehension goosed all over her skin. There was a look on Grace Holland's face as she clutched the steering wheel that seemed to her to be unnaturally calm; a steely determination quite at odds with the conspiratorial, tipsy friend from earlier in the evening. With the windscreen wipers flipping rapidly back and forth and visibility down to a matter of inches, the car whirred and skidded, skating horizontally across the lane.

"We'll not make it," said Hazel. God, the heat in her face was insufferable. She was going to be sick.

"Yes we will. Did you put a spade in th' boot?"

"Yes."

"Then we'll make it."

"How did you get down from Ludsmoor Chapel, by the way? Weren't you singing there tonight?"

"Yes, I 'ad a lift from a friend. We were going out for a drink after my performance only th' weather turned and he 'ad a long way to get 'ome, so well, then I had the idea I'd see you."

Unformed questions dissolved like a disturbed dream every time she tried to focus on things that didn't seem to add up. "So where is Max tonight then, Grace? You said you knew."

The car appeared to be on the verge of stalling and Grace changed down to first gear, revving it too much. They held their breath…then slowly it picked up a little speed and miraculously the T-junction loomed into view. Neither spoke as they rounded the corner onto Hilltop Road, the force of the wind at that point so great it almost lifted the car.

"Bloody 'ell, it's rough up 'ere."

The storm was raging off the moors, pelting the windows with snow, the horizon a white-out.

"Please God, don't let us break down up here," Hazel whispered to herself.

"We're fine now, duck, we're on a level. It's just a matter of keeping going," said Grace. "Then it's downhill."

"Well, I certainly think I'll be staying the night if that's alright," said Hazel. "I don't want to get stuck out here on my own, and it's only going to get worse."

"Aye, and it'll be different in th' morning. Always better in daylight."

"I expect you're right."

Oh, God, the wisdom of this now she was sobering up. Grace should have got a room at the hotel in Danby. They both should. That would by far have been the most sensible option yet she'd gone merrily along with this hare-brained, dangerous - yes downright dangerous idea. God, why couldn't she ever stand up for herself – ever, ever? Why?

She cast a sidelong glance at the woman who'd persuaded her into this and her sense of unease grew. What had seemed plausible in the warmth of the hotel bar, with the fire crackling and the hot liquor in her veins, now seemed like utter lunacy. What did Grace have to show her that was so important it had to be tonight? In fact, why tonight at all? And if she had incriminating photos or letters then why hadn't she brought them with her to the meeting? And how come she knew Max wasn't home tonight and wasn't likely to be, either?

All at once nothing added up. She shot another look at Grace's profile and the thought occurred that she hadn't been honest, that there was another agenda here. Perhaps it was a case of hell hath no fury if Max wouldn't leave his wife for her – this woman who got every man she wanted but hadn't managed to marry any of them? This woman who would soon be turning forty, yet found herself stuck out here in the back of beyond with only her elderly mother for company? Perhaps she was getting desperate and needed to make sure Max would definitely divorce? Perhaps she thought if she worked on his wife she'd get him that way instead, if he, for example, was reluctant to divorce on account of losing the money? Even if the money wasn't his, she would at least have a man to keep her?

Hazel's head began to bang, petrol fumes stoking the nausea that swelled repeatedly into her throat. She'd never been as bad as this before with drink.

"Almost there," said Grace, turning off Hilltop Road and down towards the east end of Ludsmoor. They passed the chapel on the left. And soon after that there was a right turn onto a narrow lane. Hazel frowned. It looked as though this was taking them out of the village again onto a vast stretch of open moorland. She didn't realise Grace lived so far out. Wish Cottage, where she and Max had visited the family before, could be seen from the road, but this... Oh God, she really was going to be sick in a minute. The track was unmade and the Jaguar bounced in and out of potholes. All the animated conversation the two women had enjoyed back in the hotel, had now dwindled to that of strangers, the atmosphere loaded and unreadable. Again that needling in her stomach, the creeping feeling up her arms and across her back.

Finally an old farmhouse emerged from out of the swirling, grey clouds.

"Is this it?" Hazel asked. "Where you live?"

"Yes, duck. Alders Farm." Grace let the Jag glide to a halt, pulled on the handbrake and switched off the engine level with the front door.

Hazel looked out of the passenger window, past the spectre of her own face, to the house, which stood in total darkness.

"Is your mother not at home?"

"She'll be in bed by this time, duck. Or she'll have gone up to my nan's, to see as if she's alright in th' storm."

The full brunt of the cutting wind hit them as they got out of the car and both women gasped.

Grace indicated the front steps and shouted over the noise of the wind. "Go on in, duck, th' door's open."

Hazel hurried up the steps but the door was locked. She shook it, rattling at the handle. Then at the sound of Grace's voice turned around, squinting into the snow. "What did you–?"

But rather than the other woman's face, she saw instead the glint of a silver blade, sharp and fire cold.

***

Chapter Thirty-Three
1885
Danby Grange
Edward Danby

Edward Danby's eyes snapped open. The carriage clock on the mantelpiece in his bedroom tinkled sweetly: *one-two-three...*

Three in the bloody morning and something had woken him.

From the adjoining room came the rhythmic snores of his wife, Clara; and in his basket the black retriever snoozed undisturbed. It must have been a dream. For a few moments he strained his ears into the quiet gloom... No, nothing. No creaking of the floorboards, no shuffling around downstairs; not an intruder then, or the dog would have heard it.

It was a drowsy night in late October. A full moon lit the room in a pearlescent haze, and the leaded window latticed across the eiderdown. Dreams and shadows... Grumbling, he rolled over and closed his eyes, preparing to slumber once more. A bad dream was all, undoubtedly due to a heavy dinner and a few too many whiskies. These were his thoughts before his conscious mind suddenly caught up with what he'd just seen.

He sat shock upright and stared in palpitating horror at the apparition in the corner of the room. Cloaked in shadows, a figure was standing behind the door – statue-still – its skin the blue-white sheen of bone, staring directly at him with eyes as ink black as that of the devil himself.

His heart lumped into his chest, the hot swell of it banging hard into his arteries, and for a good few seconds his mind blanked. Still he continued to stare, staring and staring until his eyes ached in the sockets. Desperately he tried to make sense of it. A waking nightmare, perhaps? And he was really still asleep? But the more he looked, the more the realisation solidified that this was no dream. And he was very much wide awake. The creature had a face. He could hear it breathing.

"Who are you?" he whispered. "What do you want?"

Materialising out of the shadows, a woman stepped forwards, now clearly visible in the moonlight. Dressed in a long, black tiered skirt in the Victorian style of the day, with a fitted jacket and an elaborate hat, she had a small, pinched face, the mouth sour beneath a hawkish nose. But it was the eyes which arrested attention – deep-set and ebony black they pierced his soul with a loathing so full of malevolence as to invoke a rush of primeval terror.

He leapt back against the headboard. Helpless. As she flew across the room in staccato pulses…one…two…three…and vaulted onto his chest. Astride him the extreme weight of her came as a shock – more like that of a burly farmworker twice her size – crushing his ribs one by one with cracking, popping noises, forcing his breath to extinguish with each splintering, painful burst.

He could neither speak nor move, as into his increasingly reddening, bulbous face a foul, sulphurous breath assailed his nostrils. "Don't you remember me, Lord Danby?"

The breath squeaked out of his rapidly macerating lungs.

"Let me show you."

Into his head came the picture of a swaggering, drinking night. His own front room, several of his friends, shirts open, faces shiny with sweat and alcohol; a serving girl stripped and dumped on the floor between them. They were laughing, joking she wasn't even worth pissing on.

"I see you remember the incident?" said the crone, leaning in closely, her words slithering into his ears, silky as worms.

"They made me swallow it, rubbed their urine into my hair. One of them raped me, some of them kicked me like a rabid dog before throwing me back into the servants' quarters with a warning not to say a word or find myself six feet under in the woods, with no one to come looking."

Every image seared onto his mind as if it had happened to himself.

"Knew I was without family, didn't you? And at five next day I'd to get up as if nothing had happened and clean out your wife's bedroom grate. Early mind, so as not to be seen by *decent* folk?"

He tried to move his head away to stop the crawling feeling wriggling down his ears; to close his eyes against the hatred streaming into him, but found he could do nothing. It would be preferable to die. Every nerve screamed in pain.

Who was she?

"Still not remember? No, of course you don't. I was the faceless slave who didn't matter – not even human. But the slave you should not have crossed, Sir."

A vague memory of an ugly, young servant came to mind... a girl he'd not even realised had been dismissed... Until maybe now.

"Perhaps you don't recall the first night she came here? You had her brought to your room to look her over. This room. Her name was Annie Bailey."

He was unable to so much as blink. The blood vessels in his eyes were exploding. He would be blinded. Fire engulfed his brain. His heart was going to give out.

"And now, before this night is through, whatever you have done to me will come right back to you."

A witch.

A bloody witch...

She read his mind with ease, and her voice oozed like an oil-laced poisonous tincture. "And so I am. Carrying your child, too. A girl, a daughter - one who will, as surely as yours will soon die, inherit everything you own and more—"

In one last desperate bid for life he sought to call out. But the weight on his chest grew heavier than a ton of earth layered upon layer upon layer, crushing every bone, air sac and blood vessel all the way down to his spinal cord.

Why could no one hear him? Why did the dog not wake? Why could he not be released from this torment?

"No one will come, Lord Danby."

A groan gurgling in blood was his reply.

"And now I think you have the full picture, we can begin."

Momentarily he blacked out, only to be roused by a deep, guttural voice roaring from the doll-sized body he should have been able to overthrow with one hand.

This wasn't real...couldn't be...

"I call to the mighty bringer of light, Lucifer... Spirits of the abyss, hear my call most powerful one and all!"

Heaven help me! Heaven save me...

There seemed to be more than one of her...one-two-three-four...dancing, chanting, whirling round and round, speeding up, working into a frenzy. A bonfire sparked and crackled. Overhead a full moon flickered through the trees, everything spiralling around like the most sickly opium trip he'd ever had.

Still he could not move. Forced to experience every last second in full salacious detail.

"No one is coming, Lord Danby. And this is going to go on...and on...and on..."

At the point where he could endure no more and he silently pleaded with God to release him from this mortal coil, a searing agony daggered into the core of his chest and he arched his back, screaming for mercy.

Still there was no respite from the unbearable pain. Even as hands plundered the cavity of his chest where his heart should be; ripping and burning, prickling and stinging...on and on and on...just like she said...

"Hell hath no fury like a witch who's been scorned

So send the hell's devils with pointiest of horns.

Tear at his flesh with all of your might.

Take off him his business, his money, his life.

When all has been taken, when all is stripped away,

I shall rip off him his soul for the devil wants his pay.

This is my Will. So Mote it Be."

***

When he woke, it was to the half-light of dawn.

He looked down at his night shirt to find it intact – no signs of blood, no cracked ribs, no bruising. The dog was whimpering at the door waiting to be let out for his early morning walk and the maids could be heard scurrying around in the corridor outside. He sat up, surprised to find he had absolutely no pain and his vision was perfect. Nothing was untoward. The dream had unnerved him badly, however, and it was with trembling hand that he reached for a glass of water. Which was when he saw it. The doll. Or poppet. Propped on a cushion on the rocking chair by the fireplace.

He did a double-take. Then cautiously walked towards it. In the dawn light its face shone white and shiny, as if made of china. But as he drew closer, the revulsion of what it truly was stopped him short. The thing was made of wax, its features partially melted into the macabre distortion of a man. Its chest had been hollowed out and stuffed until it bulged, then sealed over and pierced with what appeared to be a crow's foot.

He snapped his fingers for the dog. "Fetch!"

The dog whined.

Edward pointed at the poppet and commanded the dog once more. "Fetch!"

Again the dog whined and backed away.

"Oh for Christ's sake." Well he couldn't let anyone else see it, least of all the servants. Which was why he picked it up. And buried it in his own garden.

***

Epilogue
Present Day: 2017
Spite Hall
Louise – now an elderly lady

"So was there an entire house behind this once?" said Gillian

"Oh, yes. I can't remember much about it, though. I must have been about your age at the time, about six. Yes, your age. Good grief, how the years slip by. I only stayed the night once but it was very dark and spooky. I do remember that."

"Did it have ghosts? Was it haunted?"

"There are no such things, Gillian, dear."

"Yes, there are. I can see them."

Louise put down her knitting and stared at the child. Her granddaughter had a most unnerving way of watching you, almost as if she could read your thoughts. "I do hope not. I used to think I could see ghosts too, when I was a child, but I can assure you it's just our imaginations and we grow out of it. If you've been reading story books, fairy tales and the like, well, when we're asleep our mind can play tricks on us. That'll be all it is." She resumed knitting.

Gillian was frowning. "So what happened to the house then, Granny Lou? The one that was behind here?"

Louise sighed. This child never gave up. "It burned down."

"How come?"

She put down her knitting once more. Her daughter and son-in-law should have been back from town ages ago. It was the first time they'd ever left Gillian behind.

"Well dear, it was an accident. No one really knows, you see? My aunties – your great grandma's sisters, Rosa and Marion – lived there at the time, but they were asleep in bed when it happened. Hopefully, well I pray to God, they never knew a thing about it. Anyway, it was one of the villagers who saw smoke billowing over the top of the forest and raised the alarm. But by the time the fire brigade and local farmers got there the whole house was ablaze and they couldn't put it out."

Gillian had her mouth open. "But how did it happen?"

"I don't know, Gilly. The house had a lot of wood panelling, though, and we all had real fires back then, and there'd been power failures due to the weather so everyone used candles. Perhaps they forgot to blow one out? Anyway, it was a very long time ago."

"I like playing in the ruins."

"Well, now, there's no harm in that."

"So have you always lived here, Granny Lou?"

"No, duck. I grew up in a little house on Moody Street. And then my father – your great grandad Harry – moved into a room over the funeral parlour in Ludsmoor when he and my mother split up; so sometimes my brothers and I would live there too."

"Why did they split up?"

"Oh, you do ask a lot of questions, Gilly. I don't know where you get that from, I must say. Still, it shows an intelligent, enquiring mind, I suppose."

"Did you like living in Moody Street?"

"Yes, for a while. But I prefer living here."

"When did you come here?"

"After I married. Your grandad and I wanted to start a family and by that time his brothers had both left home and so we moved in with your great grandmother, Nell. Look, why don't you go outside for a bit and play? There's a lovely tree swing out there and your old gran's getting tired. She needs a nap."

Gillian seemed to consider this carefully, before standing up, walking around the room picking things up and putting them down again, then thankfully skipping out onto the sunlit lawn.

Louise smiled, watching the child swing back and forth on the old tyre beneath the copper beech, with the glinting lake behind her. Fair haired like Ellen, she'd be the image of her if it wasn't for the filaments of copper winding through those ringlets. You could see it catching in the sunshine. She'd be a beauty, would Gillian, with those flashing emerald eyes and that golden hair. One day though… one day she'd ask about that fire again; and she'd ask who the spirit girl was – the one who sat on the stone by the magic pool hitting a ball with a piece of string, rocking and humming to herself. And why her great grandparents had really split up and gone to live in separate houses just yards from each other. It had been a huge scandal at the time. But the villagers, even Auntie Flo and Auntie Connie – long dead now – never knew the real reason. No one did.

Perhaps Vivien thought the only one still alive who knew the truth was herself. And at six years old she was hardly a threat. Children weren't back then – their voices didn't count. And besides, she hadn't understood much of anything except there had been a terrible fight and Dad had walked out and never come back. The horrible truth had only surfaced many years later.

She'd been out walking in Grytton Forest not long after marrying Victor's oldest son, Jonathan, in the summer of 1961. The fire hadn't reached the woods due to the time of year it happened, with everything sopping wet and dripping with thaw. Thankfully the lovely old oaks, silver birches and copper beeches had survived; and despite all the stories of black arts and evil deeds, she loved walking alone there. Quiet and still it calmed the mind; the brook ran fresh and clear, spraying the rocks with crystals, and the white-haired girl with the tinkling laugh who kept her company was a happy spirit.

On that particular day it was a God-given Autumnal afternoon. Bees buzzed drowsily around wild foxgloves and fat blackberries swelled on the brambles. She had lain down by the pool, heady with sleep, the sun on her face, idly pulling stems of grass through her fingers and thinking about nothing in particular, when without warning a vision shot into her mind's eye with such clarity she sat up gagging with sickness. The ground beneath her bucked and rolled and she almost blacked out with the shock.

A second was all. One flash. One image. Playing with Great Grandma Annie's kittens at Wish Lane Cottage. And looking up from the old sofa at the ring of adults around the table. Her mother, Auntie Flo, Auntie Connie, Violet, Old Annie, Agnes, Grace, Vic... and a very handsome man with a quiff of blond hair. There were two or maybe three men there too – but with their backs to her – and Snow. Snow had her head on the table and seemed to be asleep. It was dark but the glow of sunshine could be seen through the closed curtains. Candles flickered. There was something on the table in the middle. And a low hum vibrated in her ears. Then suddenly they all stood up, things flew off the table and Old Annie cried out.

A man was standing in the doorway.

The vision had dimmed just as quickly as it had appeared, leaving her sitting there holding onto the ground by the fingernails to stop the tide swell, swallowing saliva repeatedly to prevent herself from vomiting. For a few moments the colours in the forest appeared brighter - more vivid - and the birds' singing ricocheted inside her head. She covered her ears… The insects were screeching like chainsaws. Until finally it stopped. And when she looked up again the sun had gone down and it was dusk.

The vision haunted her for the rest of her days and still did. But now, the only people who knew about that circle who were not in it were either long dead or long gone. Except herself.

Grace Holland had been charged with a crime of passion and served just fifteen years before emigrating to Australia. Max had also emigrated to Australia – as a wealthy man.

Had it been a crime of passion, though? Had it?

Even after all these years it seemed safer not to question it, even in her own mind, for fear of what came in the night – every night like an omen – and would surely visit Gillian one day too if she was ever to possess the knowledge. The centre of the maze – now with a fifth stone – existed. Whether she walked in the woods on a summer's evening or lay in her bed chamber in the dark with her eyes wide. And then of course, there was the night terror… the one where Marion and Rosa were banging on the windows of Lake View Villa, surrounded by flames, engulfed with smoke, as the roof, the girders and the walls collapsed around them.

Only she knew why Annie was not buried in consecrated ground; and why Vivien had kept her mother's death a secret, even from her own husband. The time had to be exactly right so Annie could be laid to rest alongside The Four in the core of Grytton Forest. Perhaps she was the only one alive who still possessed that knowledge...who knew about the old ways, the crossing of the songlines, and the phases of the moon? But with that knowledge came danger because when the Dark Side knew you were looking it looked right back.

Best then... best she took the family's legacy to the grave, lest it follow her beyond it.

***

References

1. *A History of the Pendle Witches and Their Magic* by Joyce Froome.
2. *The Legend of the Gods* by Freddy Silva

***

More Books by S. E. England

Father of Lies
A Darkly Disturbing Occult Horror Trilogy:
Book 1

Ruby is the most violently disturbed patient ever admitted to Drummersgate Asylum, high on the bleak moors of northern England. With no improvement after two years, Dr. Jack McGowan finally decides to take a risk and hypnotises her. With terrifying consequences.

A horrific dark force is now unleashed on the entire medical team, as each in turn attempts to unlock Ruby's shocking and sinister past. Who is this girl? And how did she manage to survive such unimaginable evil? Set in a desolate ex-mining village, where secrets are tightly kept and intruders hounded out, their questions soon lead to a haunted mill, the heart of darkness...and The Father of Lies.

***

Tanners Dell – Book 2

Now only one of the original team remains – Ward Sister, Becky. However, despite her fiancé, Callum, being unconscious and many of her colleagues either dead or critically ill, she is determined to rescue Ruby's twelve year old daughter from a similar fate to her mother.

But no one asking questions in the desolate ex-mining village Ruby hails from ever comes to a good end. And as the diabolical history of the area is gradually revealed, it seems the evil invoked is both real and contagious.

Don't turn the lights out yet!

***

Magda – Book 3

The dark and twisted community of Woodsend harbours a terrible secret – one tracing back to the age of the Elizabethan witch hunts, when many innocent women were persecuted and hanged.

But there is a far deeper vein of horror running through this village; an evil that once invoked has no intention of relinquishing its grip on the modern world. Rather it watches and waits with focused intelligence, leaving Ward Sister, Becky, and CID Officer, Toby, constantly checking over their shoulders and jumping at shadows.

Just who invited in this malevolent presence? And is the demonic woman who possessed Magda back in the sixteenth century, the same one now gazing at Becky whenever she looks in the mirror?

Are you ready to meet Magda in this final instalment of the trilogy? Are you sure?

***

The Owlmen
If They See You They Will Come For You

Ellie Blake is recovering from a nervous breakdown.

Deciding to move back to her northern roots, she and her psychiatrist husband buy Tanners Dell at auction - an old water mill in the moorland village of Bridesmoor.

However, there is disquiet in the village. Tanners Dell has a terrible secret, one so well guarded no one speaks its name. But in her search for meaning and very much alone, Ellie is drawn to traditional witchcraft and determined to pursue it. All her life she has been cowed. All her life she has apologised for her very existence. And witchcraft has opened a door she could never have imagined. Imbued with power and overawed with its magick, for the first time she feels she has come home, truly knows who she is.

Tanners Dell though, with its centuries old demonic history...well, it's a dangerous place for a novice...

***

Hidden Company
A dark psychological thriller set in a Victorian asylum in the heart of Wales.

1893, and nineteen-year-old Flora George is admitted to a remote asylum with no idea why she is there, what happened to her child, or how her wealthy family could have abandoned her to such a fate. However, within a short space of time, it becomes apparent she must save herself from something far worse than that of a harsh regime.

2018, and forty-one-year-old Isobel Lee moves into the gatehouse of what was once the old asylum. A reluctant medium, it is with dismay she realises there is a terrible secret here – one desperate to be heard. Angry and upset, Isobel baulks at what she must now face. But with the help of local dark arts practitioner Branwen, face it she must.

This is a dark story of human cruelty, folklore and superstition. But the human spirit can and will prevail… unless of course, the wrath of the fae is incited…

***

Monkspike
A Medieval Occult Horror

1149 was a violent year in the Forest of Dean.

Today, nearly 900 years later, the forest village of Monkspike sits brooding. There is a sickness here passed down through ancient lines, one noted and deeply felt by Sylvia Massey, the new psychologist. What is wrong with nurse, Belinda Sully's, son? Why did her husband take his own life? Why are the old people in Temple Lake Nursing Home so terrified? And what are the lawless inhabitants of nearby Wolfs Cross hiding?

It is a dark village indeed, but one which has kept its secrets well. That is until local girl, Kezia Elwyn, returns home as a practising Satanist, and resurrects a hellish wrath no longer containable. Burdo, the white monk, will infest your dreams....This is pure occult horror and definitely not for the faint of heart...

Baba Lenka
Pure Occult Horror

1970, and Baba Lenka begins in an icy Bavarian village with a highly unorthodox funeral. The deceased is Baba Lenka, great-grandmother to Eva Hart. But a terrible thing happens at the funeral, and from that moment on everything changes for seven year old Eva. The family flies back to Yorkshire but it seems the cold Alpine winds have followed them home...and the ghost of Baba Lenka has followed Eva. This is a story of demonic sorcery and occult practices during the World Wars, the horrors of which are drip-fed into young Eva's mind to devastating effect. Once again, this is absolutely not for the faint of heart. Nightmares pretty much guaranteed...

***

Masquerade
A Beth Harper Supernatural Thriller
Book 1

The first in a series of Beth Harper books, Masquerade is a supernatural thriller set in a remote North Yorkshire village. Following a whirlwind re-location for a live-in job at the local inn, Beth quickly realises the whole village is thoroughly haunted, the people here fearful and cowed. As a spiritual medium, her attention is drawn to Scarsdale Hall nearby, the enormous stately home dominating what is undoubtedly a wild and beautiful landscape. Built of black stone with majestic turrets, it seems to drain the energy from the land. There is, she feels, something malevolent about it, as if time has stopped...

***

Caduceus
Book Two in the Beth Harper Supernatural Thriller Series.

'Beth Harper is a highly gifted spiritual medium and clairvoyant. Having fled Scarsdale Hall, she's drawn to the remote coastal town of Crewby in North West England, and it soon becomes apparent she has a job to do. The congeniality here is but a thin veneer masking decades of deeply embedded secrets, madness and fear. Although she has help from her spirit guides and many clues are shown in visions, it isn't until the senseless and ritualistic murders happen on Mailing Street, however, that the truth is finally unearthed. And Joe Sully, the investigating officer, is about to have the spiritual awakening of his life.

What's buried beneath these houses though, is far more horrific and widespread than anything either of them could have imagined. Who is the man in black? What is the black goo crawling all over the rooftops? What exactly is The Gatehouse? And as for the local hospital, one night is more than enough for Beth...let alone three...'

***

Groom Lake
A Dark Novella

Lauren Stafford, a traumatised divorcee, decides to rent a cottage on the edge of a beautiful ancestral estate in the Welsh Marches. But from the very first day of arrival, she instinctively knows there's something terribly wrong here – something malevolent and ancient – a feeling the whole place is trapped in a time warp. She really ought to leave. But the pull of the lake is too strong, its dark magic so powerful that it crosses over into dreams... turning them into nightmares. What lies beneath its still black surface? And why can't Lauren drag herself away? Why her? And why now?

***

The Droll Teller
A Ghostly Novella

1962, and on Christmas Day at precisely 6pm, a mysterious old man by the name of Silas Finn, calls on the new owners of an ancestral home in Devon and asks which they'd prefer to hear – a story or a song. Ten-year old Enys Quiller is adamant they must have a story, just as Cousin Beatrice instructed.

'You'll be sure to tell me dreckly, won't you?' says Beatrice. 'What the droll teller says?' But the strange and macabre tale of Victorian poisoning and madness that follows, has far-reaching repercussions for Enys and her family, and after the droll teller has finished, any notion of staying there, or even together, is shattered.

***

Creech Cross
A paranormal mystery thriller
'Thirteen in number... It is my belief my daughter danced with the devil...'

As soon as Lyddie crosses the old stone bridge into Creech Cross, there's a strong feeling of stepping, not so much back in time, as out of it. Ancient magic overlaid with dark witchcraft and superstition bleeds into the present day, events and people as woven into the fabric of history as the age-old tracks traversing the land itself. Local people barely acknowledge her, and the incomers are that bit too friendly, until gradually it becomes clear she and her husband are in danger.

Who to trust? Who not to trust? Before the situation becomes alarmingly, inexplicably... unsafe.'

***

The Witching Hour
A Collection of thrillers, chillers and mysteries

The title story, 'The Witching Hour' inspired the prologue for 'Father of Lies'. Other stories include, 'Someone out There,' a three part crime thriller set on the Yorkshire moorlands; 'The Witchfinders', a spooky 17th century witch hunt; and 'Cold Melon Tart,' where the waitress discovers there are some things she simply cannot do. In, 'A Second Opinion,' a consultant surgeon is haunted by his late mistress; and 'Sixty Seconds' sees a nursing home manager driven to murder. Whatever you choose, hopefully you'll enjoy the ride.

***

www.sarahenglandauthor.co.uk